I reckon
you'll like this

. Di + Carl

23

You'll like this
reckon.

Jit Con.

13

THE IRON TRAIL

THE IRON TRAIL

MAX BRAND

Thorndike Press • Thorndike, Maine

Library of Congress Cataloging in Publication Data:

Brand, Max, 1892-1944.
   The iron trail / Max Brand.
      p. cm.
   ISBN 1-56054-105-9 (alk. paper : lg. print)
   1. Large type books. I. Title.
[PS3511.A87I7 1991]   90-21278
813'.52—dc20   CIP

All the characters and events portrayed in this work are
fictitious. The material in this work does not reflect the
views or policy of Thorndike Press.

Thorndike Press Large Print edition published in 1991
by arrangement with G. P. Putnam's Sons.

Cover design by James B. Murray.

The tree indicium is a trademark of Thorndike Press.

This book is printed on acid-free, high opacity paper. ∞

CONTENTS

CHAPTER ONE

The Sheriff Lays a Bet

You could not call Sheriff Cliff Matthews a natural detective, but you might say that he was an antitype of the true "law-hound," with a sense of humor added. He knew a joke when he saw one, and by dint of not taking himself too seriously he was continued in office as sheriff of Burnside County. However, he occasionally made an arrest, and at the very moment when we see him first such a rare event was about to take place. But he stood for a time at the door of the office, his hand upon the knob, and listened to his victim discoursing cheerfully within. On the clouded white glass of that office door was written "P. D. Burke, Junior," because the original P. D. Burke still clung to life in his eighty-eighth year and kept his son, by a sense of shame, from retiring also and handing over the law practice to *his* son — because it would seem rather odd for two generations to be retired while one did the work.

7

It was not the voice of P. D. Burke, Junior, to which the sheriff listened so attentively, but another, brisker, younger man, who at this moment was pouring forth his heart in the following manner:

"Well, Mr. Burke, when I saw this sample of ore and when I listened to the old prospector's story, I looked out from the door of the shack and into the valley; and the first thing that I saw in the floor of the valley was the gleam of the dome of the courthouse in Burnside! Like a light on shore, sir, when your ship is laboring through a storm at sea! It occurred to me, at that moment, that the best thing I could do was to strike for Burnside; because, sir, why should a magnificent prospect like this mine be turned over to Eastern capital, to be exploited? Why shouldn't our own West have the pleasure and the credit?"

"Why, indeed?" said P. D. Burke heartily, and the sheriff could hear the lawyer clap his hands vigorously together.

"So I left the prospector as comfortable as I could make him, with plenty of food at hand and bandages for his wounded leg, and I made straight for Burnside. The moment I came here, I stepped up the main street looking for a name that I might have heard about, because, naturally, I didn't want to associate some unknown man with us in this proposition. And when I looked up at your window and saw P. D. Burke written there, I knew at once that this was the place where I should try first! Because, of course, I had heard a good deal about you as the leading citizen of — "

"Oh, I wouldn't say that!" protested Mr. Burke coyly.

"Well, Mr. Burke, I suppose the best men are always the most modest ones, also. However, that brings us down to the first step in the business. Fifteen hundred dollars is not a great deal, but I think that if I take a flying trip straight back to the mine, and show the old prospector that much hard cash, he'll be glad enough to sell out his share. Not that we want to rob him — "

"Oh, of course not!" protested Mr. Burke.

"But an old-fashioned man of that sort would be a frightful drag to any progressive work — "

"Exactly so! Wait till I get my check book! We'll go down to the bank and cash it at once and — "

The sheriff had heard enough. He tapped on the door and presently it was opened by Mr. Burke, wearing an impatient frown at this interruption.

"Hello, hello, Matthews," said he. "You catch me at my busy time, but what can I do for you?"

9

"Not a thing, Burke," said the sheriff, "unless you'll give me thirty seconds' talk with that young — mining promoter in there."

Mr. Burke looked at him, amazed.

"Where in the world can you have heard — " he began.

"You'd better let me come in," said Matthews, and he looked so grave that Mr. Burke changed color a little and stepped back.

"I want to introduce you," said he as the sheriff entered, "to a new, young friend of mine, name Charlton L. Legrange of — "

"Hello, Legrange," said the sheriff, "but as a matter of fact, I was looking for you under one of your other names, or I might have been here sooner!"

Mr. Legrange, a young man with a noble forehead and a slender, intellectual face, looked earnestly at the sheriff and then flicked a glance toward the window.

"You'd better stand fast," said Matthews, resting the muzzle of his revolver on the edge of the desk. "Excuse me for showing the shooting iron, Burke, but I hear that this young one is slippery and quick."

"Matthews, Matthews!" cried P. D. Burke, Junior. "What on earth are you talking about? This is a man in whom I have every confidence and — "

10

"Look here, Burke," said the man of the law, "just as I got to the door I heard you say that you had about fifteen hundred dollars worth of confidence in him. I can tell you that other folks have given him even more confidence than that, and it's never come back to them again. Particularly from Eddie Clewes, which is his most usual name!"

Mr. Burke turned a wild eye upon his young visitor, and still he found the eye of Legrange-Clewes so steady that he could hardly face him. He looked past him over the lower roofs of Burnside and on to the brown hills over which grazed the cattle which gave the town its prosperity, and beyond the hills to the tall blue mountains where his soul had just been delving in glittering tons of gold.

Such dreams fade unwillingly.

"Are you sure, Sheriff?" he asked.

"Nothing is sure till the judge says 'yes,' " remarked the sheriff with the philosophy of one who has made mistakes in his day. "But the best thing is to let Clewes rest in jail for a day or two while some of the evidence that's coming by train ripens against him!"

He said to Legrange-Clewes, "Will you put your hands up, young fellow!"

"Certainly," said Clewes, and obediently raised his hands above his head while the sheriff went through his clothes, but no sign

11

of a mortal weapon did he find upon his prisoner save a little penknife, hardly two inches long!

"You're wrong," said Mr. Burke. "You're wrong, Matthews. That isn't the way a criminal goes equipped!"

But the sheriff only smiled, and something in his smile made the lawyer wince. "As a matter of fact, Matthews, this doesn't need to get out — I mean — it would do me no good to pass for a buyer of green goods — "

"You would have seen through him before the finish," said the merciful sheriff. "And besides, he's done nothing to you. We won't send him to the pen for this trick, but for some that he's worked through to the limit!"

After his monosyllabic reply to the sheriff's order, Mr. Legrange-Clewes did not speak until he was marching out of the office in front of Matthews. Then it was simply to say: "I like your faith in me, Mr. Burke. You'll see that this rubs out as clear as crystal. In the meantime, we know our business."

He extended his arm and shook the limp, clammy hand of the lawyer.

"If there's anything that I can do — " began Mr. Burke very feebly.

"Not a thing," said the cheerful Mr. Legrange-Clewes. "I'll be out of this before morning."

And he went out on the street with the sheriff.

The jail was only around the corner, and they walked to it more like friend and friend than like sheriff and prisoner.

"We have you cold, Clewes," said Cliff Matthews, when his man was safely locked into a neatly barred cell. "And of course, as I said before, whatever you say will be held for testimony. You know that. But, at the same time, a confession that clears the way for us will get you a very light sentence."

"The way needs clearing, then?" the other inquired.

"Aw, Clewes," sighed the sheriff, "I'm not playing smart with you. I'm just telling you the easiest way out. Because, as a matter of fact, I'm sort of sorry for you!"

"Thanks," said Clewes. "Do I smoke here?"

"Never been in a jail before, I suppose?"

"Never, so I'm glad of the experience."

"What business will it help you in?"

"The job of getting out the second time they get me."

"Get you for what?"

"The confidence game, Sheriff; the confidence game, of course!"

"Look here, son, that might be enough to convict you — just that!"

13

"Is it?" grinned the other. "However, I don't know that I'll wait to see the judge, much as I'd like to. I hear that he's a fatherly old chap."

"You won't wait to see him?" said the sheriff.

"I don't think so," remarked Clewes, looking steadily about him. "I must start on, sometime tonight. I almost promised Burke that I'd go, you know."

The sheriff frowned a little, and then decided to smile.

"That'll do as a sort of one-legged joke," he said. He tapped the bars. "Tool-proof steel, partner."

"Good," said Mr. Clewes. "I would hate to melt my way through butter. And nobody to watch me at work, either? That'll be lonely!"

He looked gayly up and down the empty ranks of cells.

"You never let your business rush you, Matthews, I see."

"I'll tell you what," said the sheriff. "I have a thousand in the bank that isn't doing anything. I'd like to know if you have as much."

"Here is a pet of mine," replied Mr. Clewes, "that's worth more than a thousand."

He showed a ring with a broad-faced ruby set into it.

"All right," said the sheriff. "My thousand

against the ruby, that you don't get out."

"Taken," said Mr. Clewes. "You'll have no trouble collecting, if I lose!"

The sheriff nodded. But he was still, in spite of the bet, inclined to take his prisoner in a jovial mood.

"Look here, Clewes," said he, "how did you ever happen to take up this business?"

"And why not this business?" asked Mr. Clewes. "Do you know of a better, or a cleaner, or a harder business than that of a confidence man?"

CHAPTER TWO

A Bit of Plated Steel

The sheriff blinked a little. Even if he had heard this related in apologue or fairy tale it would have been somewhat of a shock, but this smooth-faced youngster chatted on with perfect ease.

"By confidence game," said he, "I don't mean the ordinary run of the workers along this line. They're a dirty crew. They won't keep their hands clean!"

"Explain," said the sheriff. "Explain, son. Though I can't help saying that the judge will have to hear all of this."

"You let the judge hear it," retorted Clewes, "and he'll have you examined to see if you're not simple-minded, letting a prisoner pull your leg with a line of talk like this. Do you think that anybody but me can believe the truth about myself?"

"Go on," the sheriff urged. "You tickle me, kid!"

"Thanks," said Clewes. "I'm lighting this cigarette, then?"

"All right. It won't break the rules, so long as I stay here and smoke with you. You were saying how clean you keep your hands in your business."

"I mean that I don't work the women, for instance. They're too easy, and that work is dirty. It's queer how easy you can get a woman started weeping over you. And then her purse is yours. Or you can pick them for long shots of a gambling nature. A woman will always take a thousand-to-one shot — for a few dollars!"

"You don't know any of this at first hand?" asked the sheriff.

"Yes, I trimmed a few when I was young. That was before I grew a soul and found out how a man should work. But I'm glad to say that I paid back every penny that I'd ever taken from them in the past."

"Humph!" grunted the sheriff.

"Come, come," said Mr. Clewes, lifting an imperious hand. "The minute you start doubting, I stop telling the truth. I feel like talking about myself, just now, but if you make it hard for me, I'll have to string you along. And no lie can be as entertaining as the truth about myself."

He said this so blandly and smilingly that the sheriff leaned back on the stool which he had propped against the bars and chuckled a little.

"Go on, Clewes," he said. "By the way, how old are you?"

"Twenty-three," replied Clewes. "Don't interrupt. I'm talking to a priest, not a sheriff! I was telling you about the fine points of the code of the confidence man — the perfect worker, like myself!"

"Right! You were explaining that it is a business that's as clean, as good, and as hard as any other!"

"About it being hard, sheriff, you won't fight with me."

"Not a bit."

"About the goodness of it — what does a lawyer do to make a living?"

"He wins cases, of course."

"In other words, he beats the other man?"

"I suppose so."

"What does the grocery keeper do?"

"Runs a store; well?"

"Runs such a good store that he puts out of business every other store in the town, if he can?"

"I suppose that he does."

"When you run for office, Sheriff, you and your friends go up and down the streets telling what a fine fellow the other candidate is, don't you?"

"Not exactly that!"

"No, not exactly. You make him out a thug

and a crook — you laugh at the idea of the job being put into his hands. And you try to wreck that fellow who runs against you!"

"You make a black case of it."

"Confess, Matthews, that every man gets on by beating out some other man. Even the poor devil who repairs shoes tries to cut out the other fellow who repairs shoes across the street, eh?"

"Inside of limits, yes," the sheriff acknowledged.

"Inside of limits, of course. That is to say, he doesn't burn the other man's house down at night, and he doesn't put a gun to his head. He tries to beat him simply by the use of his wits, eh?"

"Exactly."

"There you are, Matthews! By the use of his wits a good confidence man tries to talk dollars out of the purses of other men and into his own pocket. What could be fairer than that? What could be a cleaner business? It's hard to outtalk and outthink the other fellow. And the real workers, like myself, tackle nothing but the biggest game. We don't rap at back doors. We go up to the fellows in the finest offices. And we introduce ourselves, and at the end of a quarter of an hour, without a gun or a can opener, we painlessly extract fifteen hundred dollars! Now, Sheriff, can you beat that, honestly, for a good clean business?"

"Good for you," nodded the sheriff. "But how is it good for the rest of the world?"

"You're an idealist, I see," grinned Eddie Clewes. "I'll tell you what it does for the rest of the world. Keeps their brains from being covered with fat. Keeps them awake. Keeps them working hard. Keeps them from getting too contented with themselves. As a matter of fact, Sheriff, it brings tears to my eyes, when I think of all the good that a hard-working confidence man can do in the world, or a salesman of green goods. So, from the ideal side of it, there you are, Matthews."

"You almost believe it yourself, don't you?" murmured the sheriff.

"Why not?" asked Eddie Clewes. "I believe anything, until somebody talks me down!"

"Well," said Matthews, "I'm a simple man, and I dunno that I could ever aspire any higher than toward the job of a sheriff. But in this here argument, Clewes, I aim to have the last word."

With that, he left Mr. Clewes and, going to the jailkeeper, left instructions that Clewes should be turned out of his clothes, searched to the skin, his very shoes probed. Then, after he had been permitted to dress again, he was to be loaded with all the irons that the jail-

20

keeper had at his disposal.

It was done to the letter. The jailkeeper was a fellow even gloomier than his profession warranted, and he took the keenest pleasure in performing the orders of Matthews. Young Mr. Clewes was searched to the skin, and then, when nothing was found on him, he was covered with ponderous irons. The keeper, when he had finished, stood back sweating, but he was amazed to see that the prisoner was smiling broadly.

"It proves that the sheriff is an honest man," said he. "He doesn't want to have to pay his bet."

"What in hell are you talking about?" asked the jailer.

"You tell the sheriff," answered Eddie Clewes, "that a late search is worse than no search at all."

The jailer considered this remark for a moment, but he merely remarked, at last, "You're a fresh kid." And he marched from the cell room and sat basking in the warm sun of the late afternoon. Presently a shrill, piercing whistling began from the inside of the jail. The keeper endured it as long as he could. Then he opened a door and roared, "Stop that damned noise!"

"I've got to do something," said the prisoner cheerfully, "got to do something to make a noise. Otherwise you'd hear the file screeching on the steel. This tool-proof stuff is hard work, jailer!"

The jailer, thrilling with alarm in spite of himself, went hurriedly to the farther corner, and there he found Eddie Clewes, as usual, lying on his bunk, with an almost indistinguishable mass of irons hanging from him.

"You watch your step, kid," he warned.

"I'm sleepy," said Eddie. "Fetch me some supper, and then leave me alone. I want to think."

The jailer departed. There was no amusement to be had from this confidence man. For the pleasure of that particular jailer was gained by bearing down as hard as the law allowed on those in his charge, and seeing them cringe under the pressure.

Supper came early, in that jail, so that the keeper could turn over his cares to the night watchman. And before dusk had well settled over the town, the jailkeeper was saying to his night assistant: "You got an easy job tonight. The sheriff has a grudge against a kid he picked up today, and I've got him blanketed down with irons. Fresh young sap. You'll hear him whistling to keep himself company. There he goes now!"

"Let him go," said the night man. "Noise in the jail don't bother me on the outside!"

"Take a look at him by midnight," ordered the jailer, "and if he's all right then, there ain't any reason why you shouldn't take a nap."

Eddie Clewes waited until the darkness was complete, for darkness made no difference to him. During the afternoon, he had mapped in his mind every detail of that cell and that jail, so far as his eyes had been able to probe it, while he was coming in and while he lay in his bunk.

But when the darkness had utterly screened him, he sat up and began to work.

There was a gold band, or what seemed a gold band, on the inside of Eddie's upper front teeth. He managed to work a forefinger up to that band, and behold, it came freely away. It was a very tiny bit of plated steel; the plate was thinnest gold, on one side, the steel of the beautiful kind which only watchmakers can secure for their most expensive springs.

With this tiny film of steel, Eddie Clewes attacked his locks. It was as though he had the proper key for each one! And if he delayed over some, it was hardly longer than one might well have paused working the key among such rust!

But, one by one, the lock opened, and the chains were laid aside softly.

Then, free of hand and foot, he reached under the mattress and found there certain necessities which he had extracted from his clothes while the sheriff was talking to him in his cell. Three or four fine files came out in the hands of Mr. Clewes. Then there was a plain automatic pencil — or so it seemed. But when a certain cap was unscrewed, it was found that the barrel of the pencil was filled with the very finest lubricating oil!

CHAPTER THREE
"Prisoner Away! Help!"

Sitting crosslegged on the floor, with the screech of his whistle never silent on his lips, except when he changed off for a raucous song, Eddie Clewes worked his files. At the second long, swift, biting stroke, he knew that it was not the tool-proof steel with which the sheriff had threatened him. It was very ordinary stuff, and Eddie's set of files ate through it, assisted now and then with a slight moistening of oil. He cut two bars completely through. Then he cut them until they were hanging above by mere shreds. Then he bent them out.

It was a bit of work in steel-cutting that might have taken whole weary days. But the files of Eddie Clewes were no ordinary ones. The tips of his fingers were chafe but not sore when he methodically put away pencil and files and brushed the steel dust from his hands. Then he stepped out into the corridor.

There were two massive doors between him

and the rear exit from the jail. Those doors were in fact lined with tool-proof steel. But Eddie Clewes had no intention of attempting to force his way through. A narrow bit of steel, and a moment spent leaning at each lock, and he was through them.

In the back yard of the jail, he crushed down his hair with his hand, remembering with a sigh that his hat had been taken from him. But that was soon remedied. The very first window that he passed showed a narrow little lighted hallway, and in it a rack covered with the hats and caps of a prosperous family.

So he jumped up to the sill of the window, reached in, helped himself to a hat that luckily fitted well enough, and dropped down again to the path below.

To the next house beyond he also gained access, but this time by a window in the second story, which he gained by climbing cat-like up the drain pipe from the roof gutter. He passed softly from room to room until he found what he wanted, which was a wallet in a locked drawer. Because, as a matter of fact, it was only the locked drawers that interested Mr. Clewes.

From the wallet he extracted a thick roll of bills, and counted out no less than fourteen hundred and sixty-eight dollars. Of that sum, he took exactly eighty-six dollars. In his own pockets, when he was taken to the jail, there had been found eighty-six dollars and seventy-five cents!

So, with a sigh, he restored the rest of the money to the wallet and retreated through the window, murmuring to himself, "Society owes you seventy-five cents."

"But society gave me a free meal," he argued with himself.

And at that point in his reflections he heard a voice saying gently beneath him: "All right, Clewes. Just come down and talk it over, will you?"

He kept his grip tight on the drain pipe and glanced down. It was the voice and the too-familiar figure of Sheriff Matthews, and the predicament of Mr. Clewes was clumsy, to say the least. If he attempted to flee, he could only move in one of two directions. If he clambered up, he could not hope to go half so fast as a shower of bullets from the revolver of Mr. Matthews. And if he clambered down, he was giving himself straight into the hands of the sheriff.

"Well, well, Matthews," he said, "you see that I've been taking my little constitutional after dinner."

"Sure you have, and a fairly brisk one, too. But talking is better than walking. Come down and talk to me, kid!"

27

"Certainly!" said Eddie Clewes, and began to clamber briskly and yet noiselessly down the drain pipe. Gay voices floated out to him from the interior of the house. But somehow those cheerful voices represented to him, as he worked his way down, all the pleasures of a free existence, most miserably contrasting with the dark of a prison life. And suddenly it seemed to Eddie Clewes that life without freedom was worthless indeed!

One side glance showed him his mark. He had still a dozen feet to clamber down, and with an outthrust of arms and legs he cast himself down at the sheriff, whirling about. The gun exploded almost in his face, he thought. Then with elbows and bunched knees he struck Matthews and crushed him to the ground.

Voices sounded here and there. A window was yanked up just above him, and a long shaft of dim lamplight wandered across the vacant lot and glistened in the sleepy eyes of a cow which was pasturing there.

"I thought it was right outside, Henry."

"It was just a tire blowing out — or a back-fire. You can't tell a back-fire from a gun going off, hardly. Not unless you really know!"

The window closed, the shade was drawn. Just a narrow pencil of light fell through the night and, by this meager illumination, Mr.

28

Clewes examined the purse which he had just taken from the breast pocket of the sheriff.

At the same time, the sheriff himself stirred and groaned.

The cold mouth of his own Colt, pressed beneath his chin, brought him more swiftly to a sense of where he was.

"It's you again, kid!" sighed Matthews.

"It's I again," nodded Eddie Clewes. "I find that you have twelve hundred dollars in this wallet."

"County's money, kid," said the sheriff. "But I suppose that you'll take it, just the same?"

"A thousand of it is mine by rights," said Eddie. "You haven't forgotten the bet?"

"It's true," gasped Matthews. "That damned bet! But you win — fair and square."

"I'll tell you," said Eddie Clewes. "I'm a bit shorter of change than I usually like to be when I'm working so far into the field, so I'm taking two hundred and fifty dollars. However, I'm not taking them for keeps. One of these days you'll get an envelope with that money tucked away inside. I hope you believe it."

"You're a queer mess of a kid," said the sheriff. "Damned if I know *what* to think about you!"

"Think nothing, Matthews," replied Eddie

29

Clewes, "because the easiest way through this vale of tears — this path of sorrows — this coil of weariness — "

"Oh, hell," exclaimed the sheriff. "Get off my chest."

Eddie Clewes stood up.

"Very well," said he. "It's plain that you've never learned patience in a church — but I *have*."

He stepped back.

"I'm putting both your guns on the edge of this fence. But why two of them, Matthews?"

"And why not?" asked Matthews, sitting up, vaguely wondering how it was that he was left at liberty in this rash fashion by an escaped criminal. "Why not two?" he continued, "when I have to tackle slippery ones like yourself, Eddie?"

"You'll never need two for me," said Eddie calmly, "because I've never packed a gat and I never shall. I don't treat myself to the luxury of being dangerous."

"It ain't the way that you see yourself, but the way that others see you that counts, y'understand?" said the sheriff. "Just you get down to hard cases, m'son, and lemme tell you that the next time I go on your trail I'm going to pack along a *machine* gun, and that is that!"

"Thank you," said Eddie Clewes. "But, re-

30

turning to the guns — they're so heavy, Matthews, that they must be a weight on your mind. And now I tell you what I can do. I can throw those two guns away into the brush — and then some stray kid will find the revolvers of the sheriff, in the next week or two. Or else, I can leave the guns lying here on the ledge of the fence, and when I get to the edge of the trees, yonder, you're free to come here and take them. And in that way, Matthews, there'll be no talk raised about the mysterious way in which those blackberry bushes have raised a crop of the sheriff's guns — you understand?"

"I understand," sighed the sheriff gloomily. "But will you please tell me why it is that you want to be so easy with me, kid?"

"I'll tell you why," said Mr. Clewes. "I have one great weakness. Otherwise, I'm almost the perfect confidence man. But my weakness is that I'm sentimental, and sentimental about a damned ridiculous thing — honesty! I like simple, honest people, Matthews. And that's why I'm willing to take your word that these two guns of yours on the fence ledge will not be used by you until I've reached those trees."

"It's a go," said Matthews. "But the moment you're across that border of the tree shadows, I'm after you!"

"That's fair. So good night, old-timer."

"Good night, kid. I hope that you have luck

31

— but none from me!"

Scrupulously, the sheriff waited until his ex-prisoner was at the edge of the trees, and then he fired twice, as accurately as the shadows permitted. He almost knew that he was missing with each shot, but also he could guess that those bullets had traveled close enough for Eddie Clewes to hear the hiss of them as they went by, and that was all that the sheriff actually asked. He wanted to be respected by this young man. It was ridiculous how keenly he desired the esteem of Eddie Clewes!

He fired, and then he raced ahead as fast as his rather short, fat legs would carry him, shouting: "Prisoner away! Help!"

Men came tumbling out of houses. They swept with Mr. Matthews through that wood. They rushed into the streets beyond. They poured the current of their noise and their enthusiasm down every far alley, and swarmed into every house with questions. Had such and such a man been seen?

He had not been seen. For, after the torrent of the searchers had at last flooded itself dry and passed beyond the trees, Mr. Clewes dropped down from the branches of a pine and strolled back across the other part of the town, taking no care to hide himself, and even pausing under the light of a street lamp while he touched a match to a cigarette.

He marched through the town. The velvet fields of the night lay before him. In his pocket reposed something over three hundred dollars. The lights of Burnside were gathering behind him into narrower focus. They hung in the blackness like lanterns, red and yellow and blue. They dwindled to a cluster of fireflies, gleaming close to the ground. And then a dip of the road blotted them out altogether.

A sweet, resinous wind blew into the nostrils of Clewes, and he sang gently to himself, in rhythm with his marching.

CHAPTER FOUR
The Jungle Trail

He heard the train before he saw it — a moan
of labor out of the darkness. Then he came on
the tracks, curving up the grade and gliding
dimly out of sight in the starlight. The headlight swung through the trees, after a time,
like a moving fire; the engine went by, glowing and shuddering with its own might. And
Eddie Clewes hooked onto the platform of the
caboose as the long freight went by.

He hung on the ladder, for a moment, letting his coattail flap in the wind and feeling the
gale curl down inside his collar and run skeleton fingers down his spine. And no dexterous
rider, swinging into the saddle, ever settled
himself into the stirrups with more satisfaction than did Clewes. For these were the horses
with which he had been familiar from child-
hood. Fast passenger or lumbering freight, he
knew their dangerous details by heart, and all
the wiles and ways of conductors and brake-
men who herded them thundering back and

forth across the continent.

He watched a few miles of the forest spin behind him. Then he stepped onto the platform and tried the floor. It opened at once, and he found himself in the caboose, where a brakeman was hunched over, balancing a great hunk of bread and cheese on one knee and a mug of coffee in his other hand.

"Hello," said Eddie Clewes. "I'm just in time, I see!"

The brakie reached a hand for the lantern which sat on the floor beside him, one of those stout, iron-bound affairs which, as Clewes well knew, made an excellent impromptu club.

"Hello," growled the brakie, glowering darkly. "A tramp royal, by God!"

"Thanks," said Clewes. "Where's the rest of the bread and cheese?"

The brakie balanced the lantern in his hand and a thought in his mind.

"Where did you eat last?" he asked.

"In jail," smiled Clewes.

And suddenly the brakeman grinned with cavernous mirth, like a dog when one scratches the right place.

"Are you charity?" he asked.

"Me? Not at all! What's your rate?"

"Two bucks for my division."

"Here's three."

The brakeman took the money, glanced at it in keen scrutiny, and then pocketed it with a grunt.

"I'm through," said he, and handed over the remainder of his lunch. And Clewes, without undue pride, sat down on his heels to eat and chat.

And the miles rumbled swiftly away beneath the car, and Sheriff Cliff Matthews and his jail dropped farther and farther until they were hull down on the horizon of Clewes' memory.

He reached the end of that division in the gray of the dawn. Big mountains towered about him toward the sky. A river flashed down the valley, its voice drowned by the thunder of the train. And the wind was thick and rich with the fragrance of the pines. As for the town, there was not much to it. It lay on the flattened shore of the stream, around a single bend, but it seemed to Clewes that he would doubt his luck and his presiding Goddess of Fortune if he did not take his chance here. So, before the train reached the station, he dropped from the rear platform, raced like a deer until he could master his equilibrium, and then saw the freight snatched away from him and drawing toward the station with a fluttering apron of dust behind it.

He delayed just long enough to enjoy the

gleam of the snow on the upper peaks. Then he went down to the riverside, following his nose, for he made a habit of letting instinct lead him. He, like Napoleon, trusted his destiny.

He had not walked a quarter of a mile beside the brawling of the river when he saw a rising ghost of smoke beyond the trees and made for it. He reached, presently, a little clearing, high overtopped by great trees, and at one side of the open space a fire smoked. There was a litter of tin cans of all sizes, here and there, and one of these, of big dimensions, had been propped on three little fire-blackened stones, with the fire working beneath it. The pleasant odor of boiling chicken came forth to the nose of Eddie Clewes. He leaned closer and saw the fragment stirred slowly by the currents of boiling water.

"Make yourself at home, youngster," said a gruff voice behind him.

"Thanks," replied Clewes, looking slowly around, and seeing a big man in the garb of a cowpuncher, with a hand resting on the butt of a holstered revolver, "we've met before, haven't we?"

For there was something familiar in the dark, stern features of the other.

"We ain't," said the big man with decision. "What are you doing here?"

"I just stepped off the freight to look around for breakfast, and I seem to be in luck."

The other approached slowly until he towered above Eddie Clewes.

"Young and fresh," said the big man. "But if you stay around this part of the country long enough, you'll get salted down, well enough. Step back from that can, will you? No, just keep facing me. Hold on! I'll see how many guns you wear, first."

He reached a hand toward Eddie Clewes, but the latter backed up a trifle more.

"Steady, steady, McKenzie!" said he.

That name seemed to make the gun of McKenzie jump into his hand.

"By God," said he, "you *do* know me!"

"You've had your face in enough papers," answered Eddie Clewes, wisely disregarding the Colt, which was leveled waist high on the region of his stomach. "But don't worry. I'm on your side of the fence."

Murdoch McKenzie regarded him dourly.

"You ain't on a pleasure trip, then," he suggested at last.

"No," said Clewes, "you might say that I'm seeing the country by accident. Sit down and watch the stew, while I get some more wood."

He did not offer to slip away among the

trees, for he knew that those biting eyes were fastened upon him all the time, with a wolfish intentness. But from the edge of the clearing he picked up what he wanted and brought it back. He removed his coat, folded it neatly, rolled back his sleeves to save his cuffs from dirt, and then began to feed the fire adroitly with little dried twigs. McKenzie all the while studied him with much interest.

"Green, but cool," he said at last. "I dunno but that you'll do, kid. Only — did you think that you bluffed me out a minute ago?"

"Not at all," Clewes assured him, and he looked up with his cheerful smile, "but you decided that the pickings might not be worth the trouble. Wasn't that it?"

The gloomy, sneering face of McKenzie relaxed a little, at this tribute. He allowed himself to nod indulgently.

"More wood, kid," he commanded, "and keep the fire broad, but not so's the smoke'll curl over into the soup, y'understand?"

"Certainly," said Eddie Clewes, and was instantly obedient.

"A kid that ain't too old to take lessons; he ain't too old to learn how to be a man," said McKenzie judicially. "Reach me that stick. I want to give the slum-gullion a stir."

Eddie Clewes, obeying again, considered the big man from profile, and from that angle he could see more clearly the crushed bridge of the Scotchman's nose, disfiguring him for life, and making his nostrils flare out brutishly, perforce.

Another giant had inflicted that hurt upon McKenzie, so rumor had it, in the midst of a terrible hand-to-hand battle in which McKenzie was the ultimate victor. It was said that McKenzie, after the struggle, took his victim's body by night into the nearest town and laid it on the steps of the courthouse, and wrote with blood from one his many wounds:

I done this fair and square.
                                        MCKENZIE.

It had made a great sensation at the time.

But that was only one of the chapters which kept fleeting through the memory of Clewes as he watched his host. Strong as a bull and swift and treacherous as a snake, legend reported McKenzie to be. And all that legend had reported, Eddie Clewes believed. The three hundred dollars in his pocket became a load upon his mind, for McKenzie had committed murder many times for a smaller prize than that.

"And now," began McKenzie. Then his ear caught another sound, and, heaving up his dark head, he listened intently for an instant.

"Somebody else," said the giant. "Damn me if I ever come to this jungle again. Used to be a peaceable place, but the West ain't what it once was. It's crowded all the time. Crowded with damned tenderfeet, and whatnot!"

He motioned Clewes before him, and the two slipped into the circle of brush.

Presently they could hear a horse approaching from the farther side. Then all noise ceased.

"He's investigating," said McKenzie, "but, by God, I'm gunna finish that breakfast if I have to do a killing for it! Keep low and quiet, kid, and remember, if you chance to feel frisky, that I got two eyes in my head and two *guns!*"

But Eddie Clewes needed no such reminder. He already knew enough and too much about his host.

"Hello!" called a bold voice from the farther side of the clearing. "What's the game, partner?"

"What's yours?" answered McKenzie after an instant of hesitation.

"Aces high and draw when you please," said the stranger.

"It's Delehanty," muttered McKenzie to himself. "What brought that devil on my trail agin?"

He called aloud, "Step out, Delehanty."

"Hey, McKenzie, is it you, you —— "

"It's me," said McKenzie. "Are we friends?"

"Friends? Why not?"

"Then show yourself."

"Sure. I'll take my chance with you, Mack."

And into the clearing stepped a man big enough and powerful enough in outline to have stood as the very twin brother of McKenzie.

CHAPTER FIVE

Stew For Three

"You first," said McKenzie to Clewes, adding softly in his throat, "Why not drill the skunk clean, while I got the chance?"

But he did not "drill the skunk." As Eddie stepped from his hiding place, he felt the big shadow of McKenzie striding out softly behind him.

"And how are you, Mack?" asked Delehanty, a grin on his broad, ugly face.

"Tolerable," said McKenzie, "but I ain't forgetful!"

"You mean that day in Phoenix? It was a joke, Mack. Nothin' to stand between the likes of us! Gimme your hand, old boy."

"Humph!" grunted McKenzie. "Well, here's my hand!"

Their right hands closed and remained for a moment gripped. It was no casual salute, for Clewes could see their shoulders lower a trifle, and a tremor as of wind shaking their sleeves, so he knew that every ounce of power in their bodies was being used to crush the hand of the other man. Their jaws were set. Their eyes were flashing.

But suddenly each seemed to realize that he had met his equal, and their fingers parted.

"And him?" said Delehanty, flirting a thumb in the direction of Clewes.

"Him? Oh, he's nothing!" remarked McKenzie with a shrug of the shoulders. "But he'll do to tend the fire, y'understand? Fetch up some more wood, kid!"

There was no trace of an unnecessary pride in Clewes; besides, he felt that he was witnessing moments big with possibilities and he would not have changed his position with another, no matter what danger might be here.

So, gathering the wood and bringing it back, he smiled as he watched the two big men sidling toward the fire, each mortally afraid that he might be forced for a single instant to put himself out of position for quick and accurate gunplay, each with muscles tensed and eyes alert.

"Chicken, eh?" said Delehanty, inhaling the flavor of the pot.

"Chicken, old-timer! I just lifted a rooster while I was coming up the valley. But I'm short on bread and stuff to sop up the gravy."

"Send the kid to fetch in my horse. I got plenty of stuff in my pack."

"Ay, and suppose that the kid takes the horse and don't come back?"

"I'll fix that. Come here, kid!"

Clewes stood obediently before this new taskmaster, and he was met by a beetling scowl.

"D'you know me, Skinny?" asked the big man.

"I heard McKenzie call you Delehanty."

"And what does that mean to you?"

"Nothing," said Clewes, covering a little yawn.

But he missed nothing, no matter how careless he might seem. He saw the glitter of satisfaction and the quickly swallowed smile of McKenzie. He saw the darkening of the face of Delehanty.

"I'll tell you what I am," said Delehanty. "I'm a kind of concentrated poison for skunks. You remember that, y'understand? And if you was to try tricks with that mare of mine — why, I'd get you, kid, if it took me a million years. Have you got that?"

"How about it, McKenzie?" asked Clewes. "Is this fellow windjamming or talking sense?"

It brought a snarl from Delehanty, but McKenzie could not help chuckling.

"Leave him be, Delehanty," said he. "The kid will do. Green, but cool, I'd call him. You fetch in the mare, son!"

So Eddie Clewes went to bring Delehanty's mare. He found a magnificent creature, a bit heavy and "coachy" in type, but none too strong to bear the massive bulk of such a man as its rider. The mare was covered with sweat, and still she stood with her head hanging a little, not yet blown out.

The active hands of Clewes dipped quick as light into the saddlebags as he led her in.

A rifle in the boot, a pair of revolvers in the saddle holsters, some pounds of extra ammunition — and then, under the flap of the saddle, a flat compartment which seemed to be filled with solid strips of something like stacks of paper —

The heart of Eddie Clewes rose into his throat, steady though his nerves usually were.

But then he turned and led the mare on toward the clearing.

He found Delehanty already half risen from his place, in a towering fit of excitement.

"What you been doing? What you been doing?" he bellowed. "Asking her her name?"

"She's so winded that she would hardly come along for me," said Clewes quietly. "Now what do you want from the pack?"

"Don't ride the kid. He ain't a bad kid," said McKenzie.

"Aw, damn him," shouted Delehanty. "He's got too much lip to suit me. I say, bring the whole saddle over here, and bring it quick, and turn the mare loose. She won't run away. She knows me!"

While Clewes executed these orders without complaint, McKenzie was remarking, "You didn't miss any time up the valley, Delehanty."

"How d'you know that I came up the valley?" asked Delehanty, peering at the stew.

"I only guess," said McKenzie. "Because I know that you didn't come *down* it. But you've rode her pretty hard, old-timer! You're gunna rub her as thin as nothing at all, if you keep up this lick!"

"What's a horse for?" asked Delehanty, taking the saddle which Eddie Clewes brought to him. "Is it for a mantel ornament, maybe? No, it's something to be used. And when one is rubbed thin, as you call it, there is plenty more. Besides, that's a high-headed fool of a mare that ain't got any sense in her feet! All she wants to do is to run herself to death for you, and if anything comes into her way, she'll fall over it! I'll be glad to be done with her! Hey — gimme!"

He snatched the saddle from the hands of Clewes without thanks, and presently he produced from the capacious pack bread and jam and other delicacies and necessaries for the feast.

In another moment they were eating. Clewes, according to instructions, had scoured out two tins for the big men, but while he was cleaning out his own, the vast throat of Delehanty had finished his own share and he still hungered for more.

"Hey, but the kid has a share coming," suggested McKenzie, softly.

"Damn the kid," said the broad-minded Delehanty! "It don't take more than a couple of crumbs of bread to fill up a splinter like him. But you and me, we're man-sized, and we got work ahead of us, maybe!"

"Ay, maybe we have," growled McKenzie, and he willingly accepted his half of the remaining share.

Now, this conversation had reached the ear of Eddie Clewes, for his hearing was just a little sharper than the ear of a fox. And yet he came and stood as one surprised over the empty pot.

"Well, well," chuckled Clewes, as one greatly amused, "this is a very neat one on me! There's bread left, though, and coffee — and that's enough for me."

And he sat down, apparently as contented as could be.

Eating had been going on at a rate that made talk impossible for the last few moments, and now it was Clewes that picked up the ball and started it rolling once more.

He said: "What's your line, Delehanty? Road work? Or what?"

Delehanty moved his head a trifle and flashed his little black eye at his questioner.

"You ought to teach the kid manners, Mack," said he.

"Leave him be," grinned McKenzie. "He's making no trouble, and you can't keep a tongue from clacking a little, now and then!"

"You can't," agreed Delehanty, "and that's the trouble of it. The wife, she and me never hit it off for that reason!"

"Hey, Delehanty! Married?"

"Me? Sure. A long time ago."

"I never heard that."

"No! She got sick and up and died on me," said Delehanty and he fixed his glance so gloomily and so steadily on the other that there was no more talk on this subject.

Vague suggestions of the possible truth rose into the mind of Eddie Clewes. But what he chiefly wondered at was the blatant brutality of this man, who threw out a hint of wife murder as carelessly as he might have spoken of kicking a mad dog.

"Or," went on Clewes, pursuing his talk where it had been interrupted, "are you heavier on safe-blowing?"

"He still talks," complained Delehanty,

looking at McKenzie as if asking for a suggestion.

"Let him yap," said McKenzie comfortably. "Words, they ain't poison."

"I've heard some that was," said Delehanty. "And this kid, he's too smart. I ain't a booster for smartness, old-timer. Hand me a chunk of that bread. Well, kid, are you gunna hand me some advice about my work?"

"Advice? Oh, no," said Clewes. "Of course, you'll be getting your instruction from headquarters, now."

"What headquarters?" asked Delehanty, turning his head so sharply that the great cords of his neck were thrown out into a bold relief.

"I mean, the big man — I mean the boss," said Clewes.

"Boss?" echoed Mr. Delehanty. "Since I was fifteen I never worked for no boss. What are you driving at?"

"All right! All right!" said Clewes. "I don't want to hurt your feelings. I only supposed that you would be *proud* to take lessons from McKenzie."

Delehanty fixed a grim regard upon the youth. But the face of Eddie Clewes was as smiling and open as day itself.

"Me proud to take lessons?" he asked.

"Yes."

"Now, kid," said Delehanty, leaning an elbow upon one knee, and glaring alternately at McKenzie and Clewes, "what has McKenzie been telling you that he has give me lessons in?"

CHAPTER SIX

Fire Fight Fire

The center of interest had lain half way between McKenzie and Delehanty ever since the two had met in the clearing. And as for Clewes, he had disturbed the revolutions of the others hardly more than a tiny comet, flashing across the solar system, disturbs the course of the sun through the universe. But now matters were altered. Eddie Clewes had become someone of a little importance and, in fixing the new center of interest, it would have to be a place in the triangle of which Eddie was one of the points.

It would be foolish to say that he did not enjoy the new situation. He leaned back a little and brushed away the hair which had fallen over that magnificent forehead of his, which had surely not been given to him in order that he might waste his time in mischief. He brushed back his hair, then, and he smiled on Delehanty. And he nodded and winked at McKenzie.

It was a very subtle wink, as though calculated to escape the observance of Delehanty. But it did not escape him. And, of course, it was intended not to do so!

"McKenzie hasn't been telling me that he taught you everything that you know," confessed Eddie Clewes.

It was the truth, but it was so large a way of stating the truth that it allowed just the proper suspicion to lodge in the mind of Delehanty, and he swung his great mastiff's head back toward McKenzie.

"Look here, Mack!"

"Well?"

"Have you been stringin' the kid about me?"

"I dunno that I have."

"Because," said Delehanty deliberately, "I won't stand it!"

"Hello! Hello!" broke in Eddie Clewes.

"What're you yapping about?" snapped Delehanty over his shoulder.

"I only wanted to warn you, Delehanty."

"You? You wanted to *warn* me?"

"Delehanty," explained Eddie Clewes with apparent earnestness, "I simply wanted to tell you to mind the way you speak! I mean, of course, to McKenzie."

"Wait!" snarled the Irishman. "You're warning me! Wait! I want to get all of this.

You're warning me about how I should talk to Mack, eh?"

"You may have known him longer than I have," said Eddie Clewes, "but, as a matter of fact, he isn't so patient as he seems, and you're apt to find yourself in hot water pretty soon!"

"Ha!" gasped Delehanty.

The idea seemed to choke him.

"Did you hear that, Mack?"

"Well?" queried McKenzie, without sympathy.

"I got to learn from him how I can talk to you!"

"Humph!" said McKenzie, but he scowled at Delehanty, not at the youth.

"As a matter of fact, kid," Delehanty went on, "I want you to get this straight!"

"I'm listening." Eddie Clewes nodded.

"Then you hear me talk! I never had no lessons that amounted to a damn from nobody at all! Y'understand that?"

"I hear you," said Eddie Clewes, without conviction.

"Nope. When you talk to me, you talk to a self-made man!"

"Very interesting!" said Clewes, and yawned a little.

He saw Delehanty grow black instantly, while just a yellow spark of fire glowed in the eyes of McKenzie.

Black smoke and red fire — and Eddie Clewes working to fan up the flame! Surely a conflagration was promised before long, if he could have his way with it.

And yet it was not safe. Twice Delehanty had made slight but significant motions toward his revolver. And surely playing with these two giants was like juggling flame in one hand and nitroglycerine in the other.

"You damn rat!" said Delehanty with a heavy emphasis. "I got a mind, damned if I ain't, to teach you manners and to start in right now!"

"Thanks," chuckled Eddie Clewes. "I'll pattern my manners after McKenzie. He's good enough for me!"

McKenzie laughed a little — a very little — not so much as would unsteady the nerves of his gun hand, say!

"You would think," went on Delehanty, "that this here McKenzie wasn't no roughneck at all. You would think that he was the second son of some damn lord or something. You got your education in Oxford, didn't you, McKenzie?"

"Hey! What?" cried McKenzie, rousing himself a little. "What are you talking about now? Eddication? Hell, Delehanty, don't you go talking over your head, y'understand?"

"How come I'm talking over my head? How *could* I be talking over my head when I'm talking to you?"

"Ah!" said McKenzie, drawing in a deep breath, "do ye mind what ye're a-sayin', man?"

"Why should I mind it?"

"Are you *asking* for trouble, Delehanty, ye ignerant pig of an Irish swine, ye?"

"Good!" shouted Delehanty. "I can see how it is! You and the kid, you're gunna corner me — oh, hell, don't I see it clear as day? You've heard of what I hauled in last night, and you're after it, now, one on each side of me — "

"You lie!" put in Eddie Clewes calmly.

"Listen!" breathed Delehanty, his teeth set. "He calls me a liar. That skinny runt calls *me* a liar! And would he dare to if you ain't sittin' here putting him up to it?"

"Why, Delehanty, you thick-headed fool," said Clewes, "do you imagine for an instant that McKenzie would ask the help of anybody in the world, as long as he had only one man to fight against, and that one man the Dumb Delehanty?"

"Dumb Dele— " began the maddened Irishman. "I'll send you to hell to tell the devil that Mack is comin'!"

As he spoke, he flicked a gun from his holster at the right hip and it spat a bullet straight at Eddie Clewes.

It should have cleft straight through his body and his heart, but Eddie Clewes was not the sort of a man to juggle fire without expecting momently to be burned. He had been waiting for the explosion to come! He had been making his count upon that very score.

As a result, he was dropping for the ground as the gun was drawn, and as he fell, he heard the bullet hiss briefly just above his head.

He was watching while he dropped, however. There was no chance for a second bullet to come his way, for big McKenzie, with a shout of rage and excitement, even forgetting his gun, for the moment, had flung himself at Delehanty and, in so charging home, had received the second bullet through his body.

But the impact of his rush knocked Delehanty headlong backward, so that he crashed into the midst of the broad fire, which Eddie Clewes had so carefully nursed for the cookery of McKenzie.

The red-hot coals bit instantly into the flesh of the prostrate man, and, with a scream of pain and surprise, he rolled to his feet — and came up standing, with smoke rising from his hair and his eyes staring.

He was thinking of water to cool himself, at that moment, rather than the fight which had been so oddly interrupted. And Eddie Clewes, resting quietly on one elbow, watched the fallen hulk of McKenzie twist slowly over on one side at the same instant that Delehanty sprang up from the fire, and saw the Colt leveled in the death-weakened hand of the Scotchman.

Delehanty himself saw, almost in time. He had dropped his first gun. Now he ripped out the second and fired at the same instant that McKenzie planted his shot.

Both struck, and both had aimed with fatal accuracy.

When Eddie Clewes rose to his feet there were only two living creatures in the clearing. He was one, and the mare was the other, standing at a little distance, with her ears pricked curiously and her eyes shining mildly toward this mysterious spectacle.

His first care was to brush away a spark of the fire which was smoldering in the hair of Delehanty.

And then he composed the pair, straightening them upon their backs, and closed their eyes almost tenderly.

Yet there was no tenderness in this strange young man.

He sat down upon the saddle of Delehanty, lighted a cigarette, and regarded the dead men with a sort of philosophical interest.

But his only spoken comment was, a little later: "Well, you really can't expect two aces of spades to stay in one deck!"

After that, he stood up. Then he bent down over Delehanty's saddle and opened the flat pocket under the saddle flap.

There was far more in it than he could have expected. He took out one little packet after another, not wrapped in so much as a single film of paper, and secured only by one or two narrow bands of rubber. As he removed them, he counted each stack of greenbacks — forty twenty-dollar bills, then fifty slips that called for fifty dollars apiece, from the government of the United States and the treasurer of the same, in gold coin! And still packet after packet came forth — of all denominations — up to one thin but precious sheaf of five-hundred-dollar bills!

Even the steady nerves of Eddie Clewes fluttered a little as he passed his fingers over these delightful bits of paper. And still he took out more and more — until he almost began to feel that it was a miraculous saddle pocket, like the ever-flowing pitcher in the fable.

Five thousand dollars he passed, and he could see the brigand entering some prosperous store and looting the cash register.

He reached ten thousand and revised his

opinion. No, it was the payroll of some great mine, all the hundreds of workers to get their monthly envelopes —

He went past twenty thousand and changed his opinion again. And still it seemed that he was only starting! Fifty thousand dollars — and he saw Delehanty blowing by night the safe of some small bank —

Eighty thousand dollars!

No, such a man as Delehanty could never have taken as much money as this without shedding blood.

"I shall give back," said Eddie Clewes thoughtfully, "enough to make things easy for the widow of the night watchman."

But still the count went on. A hundred thousand! A hundred and fifty thousand. At a hundred and eighty-two thousand and five hundred dollars the count stopped.

"My dear boy," said Eddie Clewes, "I congratulate you! You are almost rich enough to become honest!"

CHAPTER SEVEN

Just Steel

Someone has said, or should have said, that a good deed brings a good appetite; and, when Eddie Clewes had finished counting the spoils of war, he remembered that he had not had a share of that same chicken stew. But there were other things to replace it, particularly some bacon from the pack of Delehanty. With the long, keen-edged bowie knife of McKenzie, he cut himself some liberal slices and laid them on a grill made of crossed ramrods and a few twigs. Then he washed the coffee pot and went down to the brink of the river to take a measure of water fresh from the snows.

Never had the eye of Mr. Clewes looked upon Mother Nature's face with such kindliness. A bird sat on a rock behind him and sang with such violent delight that all the feathers stood out in a ruff around its neck. And it seemed to Clewes that that song was for him.

Then he went back to the clearing and sat

down to the cooking of his breakfast and the further examination of the plunder. He sliced several pieces of the bread of Delehanty, and set it up on edge around the fire. Presently the different aromas of toasting bread and bacon and the delicate perfume of simmering coffee were adrift beneath the trees. And while the fire worked for him, Eddie Clewes ransacked the pockets of the two men of crime.

He put the contents all in a little pile, upon a horse blanket — Bull Durham sacks, and bandanas, and cartridge belts, and knives, and pouches, and Colts, and rifles, and matches, and plug tobacco, and even a handful of chicken feed in the shape of nickels, dimes, and quarters.

It made a goodly pile, and, seeing it stacked up, he could not resist the temptation to take the sheafs of greenbacks and arrange them in a neat little cord-wood stack to crown the lot.

Then he settled down to his breakfast.

You would say that this was a most unfeeling young man, but when the rising sun cast a slant ray of brilliance on the dead face of McKenzie, he stood up and put that gentleman's hat across his chest and head.

After that, the breakfast proceeded merrily until the same little brown bird which had sung to him on the edge of the river came fluttering into the clearing as though it knew that plenty of crumbs and an overflowing heart of kindness could be found there.

While Eddie Clewes sipped from a tin of coffee in his right hand, in his left he extended a crust, and presently the little brown songster had perched with amazing boldness on his thumb and was picking vigorously at the bread, while Clewes smiled with pleasure.

That hearty meal ended, the bird lighted on a stump not two yards away and broke into song once more, as though in gratitude.

"Everybody loves the winner," said Eddie Clewes. "Even a bird, I think! My dear," he said at last, pouring himself another modicum of steaming coffee, "you're not the only artist in this wood. Listen to this!"

And tilting back his head, he sent a fine tenor voice floating across the clearing in a song which declared that he was going back to "Alabammy" to his "mammy," and sit in the shade the rest of his days, watching the cotton whiten the fields —

The bird, with a critical head held on one side, listened and occasionally flirted out its wings and ruffled its throat feathers as though bursting with impatience to crush this rival singer.

The last note had not died on the lips of Eddie Clewes when the brown bird was at it again in gay response, with trill, and whistle, and bubbling cadence, as though it had caught the melody of the river and were singing to bring all the brightness and the joy of the stream here among the shadows.

Vague prickings of the mind disturbed Eddie Clewes. He felt that he should replace the saddle upon the tall mare and start straightway up the valley. But he could not take himself away from this tiny enchanter. So, with his coffee finished, he hugged his knees and dandled one of the great Colts which he had taken from Delehanty, and let the moments slide guiltily behind him.

He was on the very verge of rising, however, when he heard something behind him which turned his blood cold — the sharp crackling of a twig, broken under a weight, an unmistakable and crunching sound!

He had been hearing other such sounds from the trees beyond the open space, but he had taken it for granted that they were made by the wanderings of Delehanty's mare and the horse of big McKenzie. However, there was no horse behind him.

And then, peering through the woods before him, almost too startled to turn his head to the rear, he saw one, two, three forms of men gliding toward him through the last veil of underbrush!

He was trapped! He was unmistakably trapped in the very moment of his rejoicing.

And yet, certainly, he had never accredited Cliff Matthews with brains enough to follow such a trail as he had left — and travel it so swiftly!

He turned about now, and, to make surety doubly sure, he saw two dusty men standing on the edge of the woods with guns trained upon him!

He laid the Colt on the ground. He stood up and faced them.

"Very well, my friends," said Eddie Clewes; "after the long ride that you've had, I haven't the heart to disappoint you!"

At that moment, the wind blew the hat from the face of McKenzie.

"By the Eternal," said the more grizzled of the pair who confronted him, gun in hand, "he's killed Delehanty — and he's killed Mc-Kenzie, too! Hey, fellows, come on in! The job is finished for us!"

There was a rushing through the woods all around. A score of men were pouring into the clearing, and Eddie Clewes waited, amazed. There were no orders to him to hold up his hands. Instead these armed men rushed from all directions to gaze on the two who lay dead upon the ground.

And a veritable Babel of astonished comment rose.

So great was their excitement that it seemed

to Eddie Clewes just possible that he might be able to slip away unnoticed. So he stole back toward the verge of the trees, little by little, and at last he was in the act of turning away into the woods and then sprinting for safety when a rough voice shouted, "Hey, there, come back!"

Eddie Clewes stopped as though shot. He had seen too much shooting this morning to take any further chances with guns. And, at the most, they could not give him a a very long sentence for the crimes which he had committed. Only — it was very strange that Cliff Matthews was not on hand with his posse!

A huge fellow, his face aflame with excitement, swooped down upon him and caught him by the arm with a terrible grip.

"Gunna sneak off, was you?" he asked savagely. "Gunna slide right away and leave us, was you? Oh, no, son, you're gunna stay right here and let us have a look at you, because, by God, we ain't never seen the likes of you before, and I dunno that we'll ever see the likes of you agin! Jerry, gimme a hand, or he'll be busting me in two and getting away. Hey, Charlie, give us a mite of help, will you? Damned if he ain't too modest to listen to the music, after he's started up the band!"

Willing hands assisted that first giant, and

they rushed Eddie Clewes roughly to the center of the circle.

He was rarely confused, but he was confused now! There had seemed to him a delicious sarcasm in the remark of the iron-handed giant who had asked for help lest he be "busted in two!" by his slender captive. And yet no one seemed to regard it as sarcasm in the slightest degree.

They surrounded him now with sun-browned, happy faces, smiling at him, nodding at him; eager to reach out and clap him on the shoulder!

"Hey, Sheriff! Come here and talk to him for us! He's getting a mite mad, being man-handled this way, and damn me if I want the gent that killed Delehanty *and* McKenzie to be an enemy of mine!"

It brought a roar of sympathetic laughter from the rest, and while that crash of noise beat into the ears of Eddie, he thought it the sweetest organ of music that he had ever heard! The first great light had darted across his brain, and more explanation was coming.

An elderly gentleman came through the mêlée, a tall, thin-faced, white-haired man of fifty, perhaps, supple as a youth, and tougher than rawhide.

"I'm Askew," he said, "the sheriff from Culloden County, yonder. And since none of the boys seems to know you, I'd be mighty glad to hear your name, stranger, because, of all the fine bits of work that ever I seen, there was never one half so clean, or so fine, or so honest as this here play of yours, and the stuff that they stole piled up on the top of their luggage, ready and waiting for the law!"

Let it be said in behalf of Eddie Clewes that at least he had the grace to lower his eyes and to sigh, before he answered: "My name is Eddie Larned. And I'm strange to this section of the country, Sheriff. I'm very glad to know you."

"You ain't one half so glad as we are to know you, Larned. I want you to meet some friends of mine that are friends of yours, too, from this here minute! Here's Jud Grainger, and Sammy Harris, and Oliver Maples, and Chris Loring, and Duds Malone, and Bill Orange, and Doc White, and — "

Those names came with a sort of cheerful solemnity off the tongue of the sheriff, and, with each name, a pair of brawny shoulders heaved into the view of Eddie Clewes and a mighty hand reached for his and crushed it, while he heard some gruff, brief message.

"*I* had something in the Culloden Bank, old man, so the lead you pumped into them was partly for me!"

"Remember me, Larned, when you need

68

me! Loring, that's my name."

"Damned if it ain't a *pleasure* to shake with you, Larned!"

"Would of killed my old man if the bank had gone bust — "

So some twenty men crowded before Eddie Clewes alias that brand new gentleman, E. C. Larned.

And then a new sensation. For someone had discovered that the back and the hair of Delehanty were deeply scorched.

"My God, boys, he not only killed 'em, but before the finish, he must of fought hand to hand with big Delehanty. How did he do it?"

"Shut up, Jack. He ain't big, but he's just steel, you can see that!"

CHAPTER EIGHT

Five Minutes to Spare

They wanted to know details. Ah, how they hungered to learn them! And when Eddie Clewes most earnestly besought them to let him go on his way, they simply roared him down.

He was to return with them with all due haste to the town of Culloden, because that was his town, from this moment. It belonged to him, as a matter of fact!

But, first and foremost, there was the story of exactly what had happened — would he please tell them?

The sheriff intervened, at this moment: "Boys," said he with much disgust, "where and how was you raised, to think that a gent like my friend Larned, here, would be spouting about how grand he fought, and how he done the trick! Why, gents, blasted if I ain't almost ashamed that I come from the same town with you! Come along and ride with me, Larned, will you? And forget the rest of them.

They don't mean no harm. But there's a considerable gap between intentions and facts, a lot of the time! Ride up here — and I can't help saying, Larned, that this is about the grandest morning of my life, and that it'll mean more to the colonel than it does to me, even!"

"The colonel?"said Eddie politely.

"I mean Colonel William Exeter. Sometimes we forget that the whole dog-gone world doesn't know about the colonel the same as we do in Culloden Valley. You never heard about him, eh?"

"I never have, I believe," said Eddie Clewes.

"It's this way," said Sheriff Askew: "The colonel ain't Culloden, but he's about half of it, and the best half, by a long shot. He's our George Washington and he's our Abraham Lincoln. He's our Statue of Liberty, our post office, and our town hall! And every acre in Culloden Valley is worth five dollars more because we've got a Colonel Exeter with us. Y'understand?"

"I understand," said Eddie Clewes, and the soul of the confidence man began to expand.

"Of course." said the sheriff, "he owns the best part of the bank!"

"It's quite a bank, then?" said Eddie Clewes.

71

"Quite a bank? Now, I'll tell a man that it's quite a bank! Matter of fact, we don't need no orphan asylum nor old-folks home so long as the colonel runs that bank. He turns the profits into doing good, you might say. When you step into that bank and ask for a loan, he don't ask you how many acres you got, but how many children you have. He don't look at your bank account but at your heart, you understand?"

But Eddie Clewes was seized with an unpleasant fit of coughing, at this moment, and could not answer.

"Now the colonel," went on the sheriff, "will, of course, be glad to see the gent that brought back to the bank the money that would have busted him and it — "

"He's not rich, then?" said Clewes, some of the light departing from his eyes.

"Rich? Oh, rich enough. But money ain't what the colonel puts a value on. On his house, and on his family, first of all. He had a pair — a boy named Tom, and a girl named Dolly. Now, Tom was a fine fellow, though he needed a little bridling down, I suppose, and five or six years ago, he got into a mix-up with that same McKenzie, back there — and McKenzie left him dead, of course. We thought that it would of killed the poor colonel. And it *did* turn him white, but he

72

kept on living for the sake of Dolly. So you can see, Larned, that it will be a great day for Exeter when he meets the gent that brings back the stolen coin and that put McKenzie under the sod in one grand fight!"

"I think that it might be a good idea if I were first — " began Eddie Clewes.

"Not to meet him, eh? I know that you're modest, Larned. But don't you be a fool and turn your back on a twelve-thousand-dollar reward."

"Twelve thousand!" cried Eddie Clewes.

"Seven for Delehanty, and five for McKenzie, though McKenzie was the real snake, and done ten times as much damage as Delehanty would ever have had the wits to do. But I would like to know about the way you came across the pair of them — "

But of the manner in which Eddie Clewes told of the things which he did and which he did *not* do, it is perhaps better to discuss in the words of the sheriff, as "Boots" Askew related these events a little later in the day to the colonel.

For, leaving the bodies of the dead men and the loot, and most of all, "Mr. Larned" himself, the sheriff galloped eagerly ahead because he could fairly well guess that, by this time, a savage run must have been started against the colonel's bank. Mile after mile, Askew pushed his sweating, tired horse down the valley. Frightened depositors might run the bank dry, as he well knew, and five minutes might make the difference between safety and ruin to William Exeter.

For all of those reasons, Sheriff Askew rushed his horse at a perilous speed down that winding valley road, and brought it staggering into Culloden.

He could see that he was a true prophet while he was still blocks away. For a little line of people stood in front of the doors of the bank, and across the street had gathered a crowd which waited and waited, and reminded the sheriff of a group of wolves, waiting until starvation has weakened the bull moose.

They were watching to see if that steady file of depositors, drawing out and closing their accounts, might not cause the sudden announcement that the bank had failed to meet payments and had closed its doors!

That the bank had failed!

Yes, that would be tidings worth hearing at first hand. And the sheriff swore with excitement as his failing horse reeled over the last two hundred yards.

He was greeted with a wail of expectation the moment he was recognized. And they came thronging toward him. "What's the news, Askew? Hey, Boots, what's happened? Will you loosen up and say?"

"I got news for the colonel!" he told them roughly. "Lemme get through!"

And he thrust a channel through their midst and came presently to the doors of the bank. He glanced contemptuously up and down the anxious line of faces — not men only, but women, also.

"You got a lot of confidence in the colonel, ain't you?" said the sheriff coldly, throwing away a hundred votes at the next election by that very speech, but the sheriff hardly cared. On such a day as this, a man could afford to be himself and stop politics.

He strode through the doors.

"I ain't coming to draw my account out," he told the weary janitor, who was trying to keep the line straight. "But I want the colonel!"

He found the colonel himself behind the cashier's window.

And never had William Exeter been more magnificent than in this moment of apparent ruin. For he greeted each new face at the window with his readiest smile, and a cordial shake of the hand, and when they would have apologized, he silenced them with the utmost cheerfulness.

"Every man has a duty to the interests of

his family!" the colonel would say. "Don't apologize, but take your money and keep it safe!"

And so he paid them, one after another, as soon as the clerks, working with drawn faces at the last set of accounts which they were sure they would ever arrange in this bank, could check off the correct balance.

The coming of the sheriff, however, was somewhat of a shock for Exeter, steady as his nerves were. For he blenched as he saw the form of Boots Askew.

"Back so soon, Askew?" he said. "Did the trail fade out as soon as all this? However, you're welcome back. If you'll step into my office, Askew, I'll come in, in a moment, and give you your money."

"Money?" said the sheriff harshly. "What money, Colonel?"

"Your account, your account, of course," answered Exeter. "And what else would bring you back here?"

"Why, devil take it, Colonel," said the sheriff, "am I always a scarecrow to frighten away good times?"

Oh, he had built up enough expectation by this time! And he roused it to a still higher pitch as he paused a moment and glanced up and down at the gleaming eyes of those excited depositors.

Only the colonel did not speak. But he gripped the edge of the shelf inside the cashier's window and looked suddenly down to the floor.

"Because," said Boots Askew, "we're bringing back Delehanty dead!"

He let them gasp.

"And with Delehanty," he continued, raising his voice a little, "we're bringing back Murdoch McKenzie — dead also!"

A shout began from the little crowd, but in their expectancy of more news, the noise was instantly stifled. And leaning forward with blazing eyes, they waited for Sheriff Askew's next announcement.

"And with the dead men," went on the sheriff, "we're bringing back every penny that was stolen from the colonel's bank!"

Oh, what a cheer went up then! There was no question of drawing out their accounts, now. But they swept out of the bank to communicate the good word to the others who waited anxiously in the street, and to spread it on and on through Culloden Valley — that the peril was over, and that the colonel's bank was saved, and all the money which was deposited in it.

The sheriff watched them go. In an instant, that bank was empty, except for the glad, dazed faces of the clerks in it.

And then Boots Askew advanced through the door into the private office of President Exeter.

He found Exeter already there, sitting in his leather chair, behind the big, brown-faced, shining desk. A very serious man was the colonel, a little pale, but not shaken. He had gone through the battle; the first fruits of the victory had been tasted; and yet it was not wonderful that there was more than a little bitterness in his heart.

For when the sheriff said: "Hear them cheering, Colonel!"

"They're cheering you, Askew," said the colonel soberly. "They're not cheering me. They're cheering you and the wit and the courage that killed Delehanty and McKenzie. But as for me, man, they would have walked over my dead body gladly, if they could have been sure of getting to their money safely, in that way!

"However," he added suddenly, "this is a shabby way to treat you and to thank you, Askew. But I do thank you, with my whole heart! For my own sake, and for the sake of the poor, panic-stricken beggars who were crushing me in trying to save themselves. In another five minutes, Sheriff, the bank would have failed!"

CHAPTER NINE
As the Sheriff Told It

The sheriff, hearing this, had sat down in the opposite chair, wiping the sweat and the coagulated dust from forehead and neck, for it had been a wearying ride down the valley.

"You're thanking the wrong man, Colonel," said he.

"You'll dodge the praise," smiled Exeter, "because it wasn't your own hand that brought them down, perhaps, but the man who organized the posse and led them to — "

The sheriff raised his hand.

"One minute," said the colonel. "I'll hear you dodge glory after I've let Dolly know how things are. She wanted to come down here. I wouldn't let her. It might have looked as though I were trying to use her pretty face, Askew, to keep the depositors from crowding into the bank. Now she must know!"

He took his telephone off the hook, and in another moment he was saying: "We're safe, Dolly." He made a little pause, and the joyous

79

cry of the girl came thin and faint to the ears of the sheriff on the farther side of the room.

"We're safe! All that I know now is that your old friend, Uncle Boots Askew, has just brought the news that he's bringing in Delehanty dead — and all the stolen money!"

He paused again, and with a strange mixture of sadness and triumph he added; "And with Delehanty, they're bringing the dead body of Murdoch McKenzie down the valley. That's all I can tell you. Don't come downtown. They're whooping and yelling a good deal. Stay home. I'll be there as soon as I can get all the tale from the sheriff — but he's like a bashful boy. He won't talk, hardly. I need you to loosen his tongue. Good-by, dear."

He turned back to the sheriff.

"Now, Askew, out with it! Put modesty into your pocket, and let's hear just how you worked."

"I'll tell you my part of it in a nutshell," said the sheriff. "We waded out of town, riding hard. And in half an hour we had lost the trail! It was clean gone. A fox like Delehanty doesn't leave his sign scattered about when he's running away from trouble. At any rate, we aimed up the valley, blind. And as we worked along, above the upper town, we came on a wood with a curl of smoke over the top of it, and I told the boys to scatter, and fade into that bunch of trees from all sides.

"Not that I expected to catch anything, there. I *knew* that Delehanty would never make a breakfast camp last as long as we had taken crawl up there, figuring trail all the way. But I simply had to give those boys something to work on. And so they scattered, as I told them to do, and they worked their way very soft through the woods, until they came out in full sight of — "

He paused for a moment.

"Well?" said the banker.

"I'm trying to see it all again, to make sure that it wasn't a dream," said Boots Askew. "But as we came along, first I heard a gent singing in a tenor voice — a darned good voice to hear. And then his song stopped. Seemed to me that I could hear a bird piping up. And I laughed, when I thought of finding Delehanty in a place like that.

"But then I got to the edge of the woods — and there by a camp fire, finishing his breakfast, and listening to a little fool bird standing on a stump, was a young gent, built fine and slim, with a face like a thinker and a hand like a violinist — or a forger! There was he sitting, enjoying the song of that fool bird, as I should say — and a little distance from him there was a pile of junk — with stacks of greenbacks fluttering on the top of it. The money from the bank, which this gent had won back, and which he was so honest that he wouldn't put it into his own pocket, not even for a minute, y'understand?"

"That's a fine picture, Askew," said the colonel, his fine eyes half melted and half on fire with this sketch of human honesty. "A young man like that — why, gad, man, it would make me young again to know him!"

"Well, Colonel, that ain't all of it. Because, on the ground there beside this gent, I seen Delehanty lying dead, with his eyes closed for him, and his big hands folded on the top of his chest! And then the wind blowed the hat from the face of another gent, that had been laying there all the while that this youngster had been having his breakfast — and there I seen McKenzie!"

Mr. Exeter drew a deep breath.

"I don't want to feel a brutal satisfaction in the death of any man, Askew," he said, "but when I think that it was this McKenzie who murdered my lad — my Tom — but go on, Askew. Go on man. I don't dare to draw the inference that this youngster you speak of had actually met and killed both of these man-eaters?"

"Lemme tell you, Colonel," said Askew, "that when you see the body of Delehanty, you'll find that his back and his hair has been singed. And that youngster had not only killed the pair of them, but he had closed with Delehanty and fought him hand to hand — by gad, it ain't hardly noways possible to believe it!"

"No," murmured the banker, "it's not!"

And he added: "Were their wounds from in front?"

"Every one! I'll tell you that the name of this youngster is Eddie Larned. And that he was so dog-gone modest that he tried to slip away while we were examining the bodies of the two dead men. And that he wouldn't tell anything of what happened, and that I had to worm it out of him on the trail, as we fair *dragged* him down the valley. Why, Colonel, not even knowing that he was to get a twelve-thousand-dollar reward would budge that boy! Simply didn't want no notoriety!"

The colonel closed his eyes and smiled, as one who hears the sweetest music.

"You're painting over again," he said gently, "the picture of what my boy Tom would have been in the same situation!"

The sheriff looked down to the floor and cleared his throat.

"But," he went on, "the facts seem to be something like this: This Larned is a fellow who's alone in the world. Got tired of his work. Decided to leave the East and go West.

Had no money. Probably spent it all paying off his landlord, and his doctor bill — because he looks pale enough to of spent a lot of time sick — and then he hooked onto a freight and traveled that way — hard but cheap. Cheerful gent, though; smiled while he told me that he had come in a box car! And when he got to Culloden Valley, he liked the look of it, dropped off the train — and he started up the valley until he seen smoke coming up over that patch of trees."

"And the two of them were in it!" breathed the colonel, vastly excited.

"They was! I mean that I had to drag this stuff out of him, because he didn't want to talk about himself. He came through the woods and stepped into the clearing — and found two pairs of guns looking him in the eye. But in five minutes, he was sitting down talking to them — and all went smooth, until he got to guessing what they really was. And then — why, at that point his yarn was just a blur. He wouldn't talk. And I had to let the dead men talk for him! But the facts were there lying on the ground for us to see, and there ain't any reasonable doubt that he just lit into the pair of them. Most likely he dropped McKenzie first. Then he tackled Delehanty in close. You'll wonder at it when you see him. But he's all steel. Stronger than you'd ever guess!

"And, anyway, he killed Delehanty, after knocking him into the fire. And then he whirled around and put the finishing slug into the head of McKenzie. And after that, Colonel — and this is the beautiful part of it — he took all their personals, and piled them up in a heap, and put the stolen money on top of the stack; and then before he started to take the money back to where it belonged, he sat down and cooked himself a good breakfast and ate it, with the two dead men lying there and looking at him!"

The sheriff, having finished, sat back with a heavy thump in his chair and dropped his hands upon his hips.

"Those are the facts as far as I can make them out," said Askew, "and I never done harder thinking or looked over evidence more careful, because, of course, I knew that this here was a red-letter day for Culloden Valley, and that a good many folks would want to know all of the truth later on! And I say that this here is the strangest yarn that I ever been mixed up in! Colonel, did you ever hear it beat?"

The colonel did not answer for a moment, but he sat with his head thrown far back, and his eyes squinted almost closed, and a look as of pain on his face. It was the intense concentration of one lost in thought.

"I think, Askew," said he, "that you're very right! It's a great day for Culloden Valley — but I have an idea that it's apt to prove an even greater day for me!"

To this, the sheriff listened with the deepest attention. Just what the colonel meant, he could not tell, but he was well aware that no mere money matter could ever stir William Exeter to such deeps as this.

A clamor broke out far off, on the edge of the town up the valley.

"They've hit Culloden!" said the sheriff. "Listen to the mob howl!"

"Aye," said Exeter. "They're glad to see him."

"And though they may howl louder," said the sheriff, "they'll never again have a chance to look on a gent that's any finer, any cleaner, any stronger, or any braver, than young Larned, that is up there being brought in by the boys!"

"I believe it! I believe it!" said the colonel, almost trembling with his emotion. "And let's get out onto the street so that we can see them come!"

Standing in the middle of the street, they had sight of the moving procession presently. And, at the head of it, rode three men. He upon the right held the reins of the horse of the central man. He upon the left seemed to have hold upon the arm of that central rider. And the man in the midst was a comparatively slight young man, who rode with his head bent and his eyes upon the street just in front of him.

"It's him!" breathed the sheriff! "Now I ask you to look at him! I ask you to take a slant at him and to tell me, would he like to get away from that gang? Yes, pretty near rather get away from this fuss than to have a million dollars! That's him. That's his kind, and all this band-wagon stuff, he just hates it!"

Colonel Exeter leaned a hand upon the shoulder of his friend. And indeed, it seemed almost as though he needed some support in order to keep himself from wavering.

"It's like something that I've seen before!" he said. "It's like a dream that I had many, many years ago — a daydream, Askew — of my boy Tom, brave and gentle and modest, like that — loved by crowds — and I tell you, Askew, that as he comes closer, every step of that horse is bringing Larned deeper into my heart!"

CHAPTER TEN

An Honest Man

What crimes and virtues could be attributed to Eddie Clewes, surely modesty was the last of them all. And he believed that it was better to have asked and lost than never to have asked at all. On the other hand, he had always shunned deeds of violence. Because, no matter to what end he was heading, he assured himself that he would never step out of this "mortal coil" with a rope around his neck. He had never carried a revolver in all his days for that very reason, because he did not wish to be tempted.

But now he found himself thrust by odd circumstances into the rôle of the modest hero — and the gunfighting hero at that!

It amused Eddie Clewes, and he determined to play the part with all of the might that was in him. Because he began to see that, if all went well with him, he might have a chance here to make such cash profits as would make all the other deeds of his stirring life seem like child's play.

For it was a rich place, that Valley of Culloden. There was a fortune in tall lumber, alone, clothing the hills. And wherever the trees did not stand was fine pasture, with cattle grazing everywhere. Then, by the edge of the river, the occasional strips of bottom land were sure to be worked to their limits as farms. All that Eddie Clewes saw pleased his eye, and he was one who could judge of such matters, though his viewpoint was not exactly that of a banker!

So he stepped deeper and deeper into his rôle. And when he approached the edges of Culloden, he actually tried to break from the posse and escape with his horse among the trees. He almost succeeded better than his desire. But presently half a dozen cowpunchers on fast ponies swept around him and caught the reins of his horse.

"I hate a crowd, boys," he told them. "I don't want to parade through Culloden like a circus."

"You hate a crowd," they acknowledged, "but there's a crowd in that town that don't hate you. Come along, Larned. Why, man, if we was to let you go, could we ever look the sheriff in the eye again?"

So it was that when they appeared in Culloden streets, they were leading the "hero" along very much more as a captive than as one in triumph.

Instantly the idea was understood through Culloden. And with laughter and cheers and bright eyes they swarmed into the street. For here was a man after their own heart — one who would rather do the deeds of ten men than boast like one.

How it tickled Eddie Clewes to the very heart to be conducted in this fashion! And all the while, his active eyes saw everything while he seemed to be studying nothing but the pavement. Not a house, not a face, not a garden, not a tree, escaped him.

And it behooved him to study all with care, since he intended to make this town pay back to him the booty which it had snatched from his hands so inopportunely that same day. One hundred and eighty-two thousand dollars!

He felt, moreover, that he had really earned such a reward. For though his hand had had no share in the work, his wits had been the instrument that removed both Delehanty and McKenzie from the earth. He had stood in mighty peril while the destruction was going on. And it seemed to Eddie Clewes a sad trick of fate that he should have had this prize taken from him by the very people who now thronged so thick and so fast to cheer him for his valor. It was a joke, considered by a very distant eye, but Clewes could only smile at it from one side of his face.

They went rioting down the main street of Culloden, then, the "hero" and his guard first, and to the rear, the improvised horse litters in which lay the bodies of the two outlaws. They went straight to the bank, and there a halt was made for the purpose of conveying back into the bank the money which had been stolen from it only the night before.

And there Clewes met the colonel for the first time. They had the sheriff to introduce them, and Clewes was smiling, and the colonel was kindly and a little distant. The keen eye of Clewes was looking through him deep and deep.

"And the reward, Colonel?" said the sheriff. "If you could pay it in ready cash, then the State will fix things with you — "

Straightway they went into the little inner office of Exeter, and there Eddie Clewes had counted into his hand the largest sum of money that it had ever been his fortune to own — twelve thousand dollars in good coin of the realm! And that was not all.

"Just what the directors of the bank will wish to do for you, I don't know," said the colonel. "But in the meantime, Larned, I am adding three thousand to round off the reward, which will give you fifteen thousand for your morning's work."

Fire rose in the heart of Eddie Clewes.

And yet it was not enough! Even with two hundred thousand, there had hardly been enough to make it worth his while to be "honest." He felt that there was something more in this game, which he could play for.

"I can't take that much with me," said Eddie Clewes. "If you will keep it in the bank for me — "

He could feel the keen, kind eyes of the colonel probing him.

"I shall keep it for you gladly. And if you have nothing to do at once, come to my house. Stay with me there, Mr. Larned, until you have made up your mind how you wish to dispose of this little windfall of yours!"

Before they started, the sheriff drew the colonel to one side.

"I ain't gunna advise a man that's older and a lot wiser than me," he said. "Particular because I understand just about how you feel. I've lost a son of my own, Colonel! But I want to remind you that taking him into your house might be easier than taking him out again!"

At this, the colonel merely smiled.

He laid a hand upon the shoulder of the sheriff as he answered: "Let me tell you, Askew, that though you have to spend a good deal of your life in the study of criminals and criminal ways, still I don't think that you have to look on the shady side of life as much as I do. Every man who comes through the doors of my bank is my prospective enemy. I control a thing that he wants — money! And he'll get it away from me on the terms of a robber, if he can. I've learned enough about men to know that most of them are filled with shadows as well as high-lights, but now and then one meets a fellow who is absolutely honest. It shows upon his face like a mirror. And, the moment that I laid my eyes upon young Edward Larned, I knew that he was that sort of a man. Courage and modesty rarely go together in such a degree. And I tell you, man, that I am surer of his integrity than I am of my own, by a great deal. I thank you for your warning. But I have learned to take first impressions as the truest guide to character, in many cases, and this I know to be one of them!"

The sheriff said no more. For that matter, his heart yearned after that slender young man well nigh as much as did the heart of the banker.

He watched them drive up the street in the buckboard of the colonel. He saw them turn out of sight, and with that, a certain darkness fell across the mind of Sheriff Askew, and he went homeward with slow steps. Yet there had been so much glorious achievement on this day, that though it seemed the sheriff had had little to do with the work, yet an overflow of brightness, as it were, descended upon him and clung about his gray head. And as he went to his house he was greeted with more smiles and shouts and wavings of the hand than he could ever remember having received before.

But up the hill went young Eddie Clewes, leaning back and watching the backs of the horses as they swung out in a clipping trot that made nothing of the incline. They wound out from the town. They turned from the main road, and they passed through a tall, strong gate, whose iron leaves were drawn back. Then hard-rolled gravel took the hoofs of the horses, and they jumped away at a redoubled speed.

It seemed to Eddie Clewes that it was a very jolly, gay adventure, and where it might lead he could not guess. Certainly he did not dream that he was entering upon a new page of his life!

They came before the face of a house built long and low, after the cottage style, with wings rambling in disorder, here and there — a house with many dormer windows, and with promise of a thousand nooks and crannies of comfort and interest inside.

As they swung up before it, a girl ran out from the door to meet them. Eddie Clewes hardly glanced at her, more than to see that she was most simply dressed.

"I've brought home the man who sent down Delehanty and Murdoch McKenzie," said her father. "I've brought Larned home with me to rest for a few days and get acquainted with us. Larned, this is my daughter, Dorothy. Dolly, run and see that a room is ready for him, will you. Ah, one minute — you might put him in Tom's room, my dear!"

Eddie Clewes saw the girl wince a little.

But before he had finished, he felt it would be very odd if he did not make her wince still more. And he was almost glad that she received him with a smiling hostility. Indeed, it was the first time in the life of Clewes that he had had anything to do with the robbing of a friend, and it irked him to the core of his heart to have to reach a hand into the pocket of the colonel. Therefore, the more enemies in this house, the better. He made his glance as cold as ice as he repeated the name of his young hostess.

Besides, what were women to him?

"It's a great place here, Colonel Exeter," said he, "with the mountains at the back of you, I mean, and the river running under your face. And such a house, too!"

"Tush, my boy, tush!" said Colonel Exeter. "Do you talk about houses and scenery and such things five minutes after you've met my girl? Where's your eyes, my lad?"

"Why, sir," said young Eddie Clewes, "I've never had time to look at girls."

"Too busy with your business, eh?"

"Yes."

"By the way, what *is* your business?"

It did not ruffle the calm of Eddie Clewes!

"Well, sir," said he, "I've tried a good many things, but I suppose that you might call me a booster, or an exploiter. I mean, sir, that I have always tried to make the best of every situation that I was thrown into — even if I had to move on the next day!"

Which is another proof, in a way, that Eddie Clewes was something of an honest man.

CHAPTER ELEVEN
Enter Smoky Dick

Some idea of what it meant to be put into the room of the colonel's dead son was gained by Eddie Clewes when he was taken upstairs to his new quarters. They had had barely time to open the windows and let the air blow in; they could not change or take out the things which had been there. And the room seemed to him as completely furnished as though Tom Exeter had stepped out of it five minutes before — furnished, that is to say, with the whole aroma of the dead youngster's personality. In one closet stood his rack of guns in which he had evidently taken much pride — a pump gun, and two of the finest makes of double-barreled shotguns — four rifles, all of various makes and calibers, and a full dozen of revolvers. This was the armament which he discovered in the room; and in the same closet there was a fine group of fishing rods with which young Tom must have whipped the waters of the river that flowed down Culloden Valley.

And then there were the books of Tom ranged on shelves against the wall — stories and text books from "Robinson Crusoe" at one end of the rack to "Euclid" and the Bible at the other, with "The True History of Billy the Kid" more obviously worn and thumbed than any other of the volumes. And when Eddie Clewes took the book down, he found that the True History had been annotated with marginal drawings from the hand of Tom Exeter. Those drawings were, some of them, the scratchy outlines made by a youngster of ten; but some were well formed and executed with some talent. They generally showed Billy in the performance of some one of the thousand bloody deeds which were attributed to him by the True History. They showed Billy driving home a knife in a burly fellow's throat. They showed Billy charging through a group of fighting Mexicans, a revolver spouting smoke and death from either hand. They showed Billy the Kid killing his guard on the historic occasion of that killer's escape from the hand of justice. And all of the gory details were so faithfully rendered, that Eddie Clewes regarded the book with a grim little smile.

He closed it and turned it back and forth, still with the same mirthless smile. For he felt that he had been given a sudden glimpse into the soul of the dead boy. And he wondered if the fight between McKenzie and Tom Exeter had been all the making of the outlaw.

A knock came at the door, and there was the colonel himself.

"Are you comfortable here, my lad?" he asked.

"Comfortable as can be," said the gentle, cheerful voice of Clewes. "But I hope," he went on, "that my being in this room won't bring any unhappy memories into your mind, sir?"

The colonel shook his head slowly.

"There was a time," said he, "when I used to close my eyes against the past. It seemed that I had suffered such a useless loss, you see. It was bitter for years. But now that is changed. One must accept the past as well as the present. Closed eyes bring no real end to pain, you know! And as for having you here, it is an honest happiness to me to have another young fellow in this place. I tell you, Larned, that nothing would give me greater pleasure than to know that Tom's books and guns and fishing rods were being used by another youngster! Do you understand? There has been an empty place in this house too long. It would be pleasant to have it filled, for a time!"

And he said this with such a quiet touch of emotion that the other could not help understanding, and his heart leaped. But not, I am afraid, for any reason such as the colonel might have hoped.

"I came up particularly," said the colonel, "to tell you that there is a man at the door saying that he knows you. Do you wish to see him there, or up here? I'll send him up, if you wish?"

Clewes thanked him, and a moment later he heard a quick, strong step on the stairs, and then the door was opened upon a face long familiar to him, and never less welcome than now.

The newcomer closed the door gently behind him and, as though by instinct, listened for an instant with his ear close to the crack, while his keen eyes glanced up and down Eddie Clewes. Then he straightened and faced the younger man, his hands upon his hips, his athletic shoulders squared back, his feet set wide apart, and he broke into a hearty, soundless laughter.

Eddie Clewes did not wince under this assault. He took his seat in a chair beside the window, tilted the chair back against the wall, and lighted a cigarette, while his glance wandered forth across the tops of the orchard trees and past the garden lawns, and then down the swinging slopes of the valley to the bright waters of the Culloden River, beyond. They widened into a lake, at that point, and he

100

wondered how many times on hot summer days young Tom Exeter had swam in the waters of that pool.

The vibrating, silent laughter of the newcomer ceased. He posted himself suddenly before Clewes.

"You've forgot me, Eddie?" he asked.

Clewes looked him gravely up and down.

"You're the yegg and sneak thief, and gunfighter, and a good many other things that the police are looking for," announced Eddie Clewes, without emotion. "You're the Gumshoer; you're the Sand-bag Kid; you're Smoky Dick; and also, you're Dandy Dick Pritchard, I suppose. Is there anything more that you'd like to hear about yourself?"

"You ain't glad to see me, it seems," said Pritchard, settling himself comfortably in a chair opposite to that of Clewes. "What I've done for you ain't no account, maybe?"

"What you did to make me a crook?"

"You've left that line, I suppose," said Pritchard. "You've pulled out and now you're headed for a Bible class, somewheres?"

Eddie Clewes drew his eyes back from the vista beyond the window and looked at the other with a sigh.

"Don't be deep and ironical, Dick," said he. "Because it makes you seem even clumsier than you are! As a matter of fact, you appear best when you appear more like yourself."

"And how is that?" quickly asked the other.

Like an unvarnished brute."

"You little sneakin' rat!" burst from the lips of Dandy Dick.

And he stood over the other, trembling with rage.

"Sit down, or get out," said Eddie Clewes. "I'd rather that you got out, but I don't suppose that you will."

"Why don't I do it?" gasped Dick Pritchard. "Why don't I wring your neck? What keeps me from it? Ain't I got the strength to do it? And ain't I got the will to do it? And why do I stand here flappin' in the wind instead of smearing you, you — "

He paused, almost choking for lack of breath and the right word.

"You're afraid, Dick," said Eddie.

"Me — afraid?" snarled Pritchard.

"Horribly afraid of me!"

"You're crazy!" gasped Pritchard. "That's all — you're crazy. I tell you, if there was ten of you sitting there in a row, I'd tackle the whole lot of you without even thinking. Why, kid, do you think that you can bamboozle me, because you've made this jay town believe that you're a great gunfighter that could kill Delehanty and McKenzie in a fair scrap?"

"Who *did* kill them?" asked Clewes.

"How do I know?"

"Who killed them and took their stuff and put it in a pile?"

"And who got caught and brought into town before he could get away with the loot, and who got himself made a fool of by the whole valley?" echoed Pritchard.

"Very true," said Eddie Clewes. "But you were asking about the gunfight."

"Listen, kid, listen, will you?" demanded the other, sweating with exasperation. "*Please* don't talk that way to me, because it makes me peeved, y'understand? It chafes me! Lemme tell you, son, that I know you've never fooled with the guns. You're too *smart* to fool with them!"

Eddie Clewes leaned still farther back in his chair and smiled into the excited face of the other.

"Are you trying to prove that you're not a fool, Pritchard?" he asked.

"By God," said the yegg, "I've stood too much of it! I'm gunna finish you off, kid, and —"

His voice fell away a little uncertainly, for there was not even the ghost of a shadow of doubt in the eyes of Eddie Clewes. He seemed as certain of himself and of his companion as though Pritchard had been a mechanical toy, the strings of which he held in his hand.

"The point is, Dick," said he, "that I know all about you, and you know nothing about me."

"I don't, eh? I couldn't give you your record from — "

"You know what I've done, perhaps, but you've never known how I did it. That's where your brain stops. Whereas, I know all about you, Dick, from head to foot. I have studied your brains until I know every bit of 'em — the whole ounce of gray matter that's in your head. And therefore, don't be a fool and talk savage talk around me. Because I don't care to listen to you. And if you keep on — "

"And if I keep on — what then?"

"Why, I'll have you turned out of the house!"

"No, kid, you won't do that. And I'll tell you the reason why you won't. I happen to know that Cliff Matthews is after you, and I know *why* he's after you. You hear? And besides, you got fifteen thousand that, like a fool, you left in the colonel's bank! You would never have the face to show up for that money after I'd told what I could tell about you."

"Pritchard," said Clewes, "do you believe that would stop me?"

"I believe it. I know it, of course!"

"You have me in your hands, eh?"

"Absolutely, kid. *Abso*lutely!"

"I'll show you the difference," said Clewes, "between gunfighting courage and real nerve."

And slipping from his chair, he headed straight for the door.

As for Pritchard, he watched the other for an instant with gaping mouth. Then he leaped in pursuit and caught him by the shoulder.

"Hey, Eddie!" he whispered. "You don't mean it?"

"Why don't I mean it?"

"I take it back, Eddie. I won't blow on you — but are you gunna chuck this here whole deal —"

Eddie Clewes paused with a sigh.

"Do you plan on some dirty work with me?"

"I plan on making the pair of us rich!" said Pritchard. "Will you listen to me talk, kid?"

"I don't know," said Clewes. "I don't know whether the pleasure of turning you out of the house wouldn't be worth fifteen thousand dollars, and all the chances of easy money to come!"

CHAPTER TWELVE

The Price on His Honor

But it was plain that Eddie Clewes had relented from his first cold fierceness, and Pritchard began to breathe more easily.

"The devil in you, Eddie," he explained, "is so different from the devil in most other folks that I never know which way it is going to make you jump. But now I'm glad that we're through with the foolishness because you and me are gunna make a big thing and a good thing out of this here deal kid!"

"Take you on the whole, Dick," said the younger man, "I suppose that you have more brass than any other man in the world. Sometimes I have an idea that I myself have a good share of nerve. But I feel like a modest, little shrinking flower compared with you."

"Go on, kid," said Pritchard. "It's a pleasure to hear you. I never enjoyed anything so much as having you do me up in words! One of the first things that a stranger would guess would be that you didn't care much for me!"

"A *stranger* might guess that?" echoed Eddie Clewes. "Yes, I suppose that he might. In the meantime, Dick, how do you figure to horn in here? Who staked this job out? Who framed it and trimmed it down fine? Who opened the door and got himself inside?"

"You're talking about yourself, now," agreed Pritchard.

"And therefore, why should I consider you?"

"Partly," said Pritchard, "because I *want* to be considered. No matter how you may rave about it, the fact is that I have the drop on you just now and here. The gun I have on you is that I know who and what you are, and nobody else in this fool valley does, though you'd think that even in a jay town like this they'd know about a gent that has done as much as you, kid."

He made a pause, but Clewes did not answer.

"Then besides," went on Pritchard, "for running off a job of this size you'll need a bit of help."

"Of what size?" asked Clewes.

"All right," grinned Dandy Dick. "I ain't pressing you for inside information, because I don't need any teacher to tell me what you're after in the house of Exeter. Maybe you're here just to rest and hear the colonel praise

107

you. And maybe kid, you're here just to enjoy the scenery. It ain't likely that you'd be interested in the Exeter jewels! No, that ain't likely at all!"

He shook his head in mock deprecation.

"Go on," said Clewes, "because I really enjoy hearing your lingo. What about the jewels?"

"You don't know nothing about them, of course?" said Pritchard, deeply ironical. "You don't even know how long they've been in the family! No, I couldn't expect that you'd be interested in nothing like that!"

He leaned suddenly forward.

"Kid, tell me straight. Did you ever hear what this stuff is worth?"

Eddie Clewes shook his head frankly.

"I never heard," he admitted.

It made Pritchard draw his chair closer, and in a hoarse whisper, delivered from one side of his mouth, he said with the greatest secrecy and excitement:

"I've heard them say that there's more than half a million dollars' worth of stuff in the Exeter safe!"

There was enough in that to sting even Eddie Clewes to interest. He sat up slowly and fixed his keen eyes on the face of the other.

"I ain't stringing you, kid," breathed Pritchard. "It's gospel. And I come all the way to the Culloden Valley to have a look at things. How was I to guess that my old pal, Eddie Clewes, would be here to welcome me right into the house?"

"Thanks," said Clewes dryly. "But tell me this: How can that much stuff go with a fellow like the colonel? He has money! But half a million in jewels — "

He paused and shook his head.

"Don't you understand?" explained Pritchard, spreading both of his hands palm up in a desperate effort to explain. "It's this way: The old colonel is too high in the air — the stiff-backed old goat — to ever do a simple thing like getting the stuff priced. The reason for why he values the things is only because they're pretty, and they look well on his girl, and they been in the family a long time. Chiefly that! Why, did you see the pin at the neck of the girl today?"

"The one with the big red garnet?" asked Clewes.

"Garnet? You simp, you sap, you poor chucklehead, that's a pigeon's-blood ruby! The finest kind. It made me sort of giddy when I seen it! You could buy three diamonds of the same size for the price of that one ruby!"

Eddie Clewes folded his hands together. It was the surest sign of a most profound interest in him.

"You don't understand, still," said Pritchard. "Well, it *is* a bit hard to make out. You'd say that the old goat would sell off three or four hundred thousand dollars' worth of the stuff and stick it in a bank, eh? But as a matter of fact, kid, he don't have no idea of the price of what he's got in his safe. It's just something with a sentimental value to him. Maybe he's heard the price of some of the stones, but all that he knows is the *buying* price of them! And d'you know when most of them was bought? I'll tell you! It was something like two hundred years ago, before the Exeters ever come to this country out of England. And a thing that they paid a hundred dollars for in those old days is maybe worth five hundred or a thousand now! The buying power of coin has sunk a terrible lot, since those days, far as jewels are concerned. Why, if the old boy was to add up all the figures that he knows about his jewels, he would maybe write them down as seventy or eighty thousand dollars. A lot, sure! Enough to make him guard them pretty close; though that's more because he figures that family jewels are sort of like the family honor — something beyond the price of coin to buy! He's just an old sap, y'understand? And as a matter of fact, he keeps them so close that it's gunna be hard even for a couple of wise guys like you and

110

me, kid, to pry the stuff loose from him. He's never let anybody have the key except himself, and his son and — "

"You know the whole history of them?" asked Clewes. "And let me ask you where you learned the price of the stuff in the modern market?"

"I heard it from the Jew. He's to be the fence if we get the stuff. And when he said: Five hundred thousand dollars, he was meaning the price that he would pay *us* for them. After we get the stuff, we can maybe buck him up to six hundred thousand, because you can bet that he laid down a price that would still leave him plenty of leeway!"

"That's reasonable. I know the Jew! But what I'm asking is: How did *he* have a chance to price the stuff?"

"Why, you'll laugh when you hear that! You see, the old colonel had a son that he figured was about the closest to an angel that the world ever flashed an eye on. But this kid was a stepper. He liked guns, and he liked cards, and if he'd lived, he would of raised his share of hell. Even when he was getting started, he landed deep at poker, and he got scared. He thought that as long as he had the key to the jewels, he would be able to sell a part of them, if he got into a pinch. So he arranged things for himself to take the whole bunch of them to be priced, and the Jew come clear to the valley to get the job. He says that he near fainted when he looked over the lot. The kid didn't know the value of the stuff. Fifty thousand would have been big to him for the whole lot. But he wasn't naturally crooked — just sort of wild. And he was afraid to ask his old man for a gambling debt. And that was the way of it. The Jew had everything lined up for one of the best deals in his life, when Tom Exeter got into his fight with Murdoch McKenzie, and that was the end, and ever since that time, the Jew has been sitting back with his mouth watering, hankering after the stuff, and trying to hook up with some gent that would do the job. Now I've talked myself out, kid. I've showed you everything that I know about the deal, and I can tell you that I've held nothing back, facts or round numbers, or nothing. The coin is ours, kid. We'll have two hundred and fifty thousand apiece — and that's that!"

"I hold up the old boy?" said Eddie Clewes, frowning a little.

"Are you going to balk at that? Hey, Eddie, what *did* you plan on?"

"A little confidence game, perhaps. But to sneak-thief jewels out of his house when he trusts me — "

"Now, Eddie, you got sense! Think it over.

112

It's a quarter of a million, not pin money that you're playing for! You've always wanted to make such a stake that you could go straight. Will you ever have a sweeter chance than this?"

Eddie Clewes lay back in the chair and closed his eyes, while Dandy Dick looked down at him with a strange mingling of awe and contempt and disgust and fear.

"Most men have their price," said Eddie Clewes. "And this is mine. Except, Dick," he added, sitting erect, "that you need not think I'll be fool enough to split the thing even with you."

"Would you welch on me?" moaned Dandy Dick.

"You'd call it that, I suppose. But *I* call it business, plain and simple. If there's half a million in this, you get a hundred thousand and nothing more!"

Dandy Dick leaped up with a sort of silent scream.

"Hey, kid — are you crazy? Are you handing me a double cross like this? Hey — Eddie — don't you know me? Don't you know what I been to you?"

"Stand away from me, Dick," said Eddie Clewes. "A hundred thousand is enough for you! All you've done is to supply a little information. But all of the real work will be done by me. Besides — I wouldn't sell out the old colonel for a penny less than four hundred thousand. I have too much honor in me!"

And he laughed in an ugly, sneering way, as though even his own soul was a matter for scorn and mirth to Eddie Clewes.

"I'm beat," said Dandy Dick, white with rage and helpless self-pity. "I've put all the cards in your hands. If I'd knowed that you'd even think of a one-sided split like this — "

"Steady!" said Clewes. "You've never so much as played at a hundred thousand in your life. And now you're getting it handed to you on a tray. You work with the Jew. All I want is the four hundred thousand. If you can squeeze some extra margin out of the Jew, go ahead and do it! You say there may be an extra hundred thousand. Well, it's yours for the bargaining. I wouldn't pay that price for having to talk five minutes with that greasy devil! And now, get out, Dick. I've talked to you too long, already!"

CHAPTER THIRTEEN
The Five in the Crib

Only one instant did Dandy Dick Pritchard pause in the doorway when his host accompanied him to the front of the house.

"I don't need to give a smooth worker like you advice, kid," said he. "Only — be fast, be fast! You dunno when that Cliff Matthews will pick up your trail. He's slow, but nobody's fool. And if you can, think of some little grandstand play to get the old boy completely blindfolded — you want the key to that safe, old-timer!"

And Dandy Dick was gone.

They had dinner that night on the veranda, because the evening was very warm and still, and at dinner for the first time Clewes met a man he was to see much of, thereafter. It was big Oliver Portman, who had a cattle ranch somewhere in the hills, a quiet young man whose presence in the house was easily explained, for wherever Dolly Exeter went, the eyes of Portman drifted uneasily after her.

And as Clewes gathered, hardly two days passed that Portman was not calling on Dolly. He had a special reason for calling this evening, because, of course, he shared in the universal admiration and curiosity which burned up and down Culloden Valley concerning the new hero. But Eddie Clewes would not talk about the historic battle. He was as bland and calm as could be, but he parried every question with perfect adroitness. And then, after dinner, he was soon settled down to a game of cribbage with the colonel.

"I play cribbage partly out of spite," the smiling colonel had said as they took their places at a little card table. "Years ago I held three fives and a Jack, and the five turned. I've made a sort of resolve that I should play until I held that hand again. But luck never came my way!"

And presently they were playing without a sound except a murmur, now and then, for the colonel played cribbage according to a strict system that governed his pegging and his discards. And young Mr. Larned seemed equally absorbed in the game.

Yet, now and again, he let a swift glance fly beneath his lashes to the corner of the veranda where Dolly Exeter and big Oliver Portman sat, ostensibly watching the sunset color turn from rose to purple on the surface of the lake beneath them. What Eddie Clewes noted was that, no matter how often he glanced in that direction, he usually found the gaze of Dolly Exeter fixed upon him — or else her head was only then turning away. He had guessed at first that she did not like him. He could guess now that she was suspicious. But of what?

If he could have listened to her conversation with young Oliver he would soon have learned!

"I've watched him and tried to size him up," said Oliver Portman, "but he's one of those extraordinary fellows who can't be put into a category very easily. It would be easy to believe almost anything about him. If he were pointed out as a good, honest, faithful, steady clerk — you could believe that. If you had him noted to you as the son of an idle-rich family — why, he would fit that idea as neatly as a glove fits a hand! And on the other hand, it isn't a bit surprising that he should be what we know him — a hero and a fighting devil under that quiet exterior. No, as a matter of fact, he's unlike any other man I've ever seen. You can believe almost anything about him!"

"And how," said Dolly Exeter, "would he fit into the rôle of a professional gambler?"

Oliver turned his fine, strong head with a start.

"Come, come, Dolly," he said, "you were

always a doubter of everything."

"Well," she asked him quietly, "you believe that Mr. Larned could be almost anything; do you mean — almost anything good, and not bad?"

Mr. Portman revised is ideas a little. And then he colored a bit.

"I don't want to say ugly things about a fellow I've never seen before," said he. "And everything that's known about Larned is ace-high!"

"Hush!" said Dolly. "You are thinking my own thoughts, and you know it. Even when a wolf looks like dog — there's a difference!"

"Dolly, I mustn't listen to this sort of talk!"

"Oh, Oliver, you're so honest that it hurts. You won't have a bad thought about anyone, until you're willing to stand up and tell him about it face to face! But I say — watch his hands as he shuffles the cards! Don't you think that he does it almost too well?"

In fact, it was a pleasant thing to see how Eddie Clewes gathered the pack neatly together with the tips of his fingers, and then mixed them with no rattling and crushing, but with a fluid, little whispering sound — after which, they flowed rapidly out. It was all done so easily, so naturally, that one had to look twice to realize the art and the training behind it.

"That's the sort of a hand that may very well have killed men like McKenzie and Delehanty!" commented Oliver Portman.

"Aren't you dodging me, Oliver?"

"I don't know what to say! You do put ugly thoughts into my head, but — "

"Hello, hello!" burst out the colonel, at this point. "And now for the draw!"

He sat upon the edge of his chair, his fine face flushed, his eyes bright.

"What is up?" whispered Portman.

"He has three fives and a Jack and wants the other five," said Dolly, her voice low, but with a hard ring in it. "And I'll wager that he gets it. I tell you, Oliver, I *knew* that Mr. Larned would be able to give dad what he wanted out of that pack, sooner or later!"

"It can't be!" muttered Oliver Portman.

"Watch!"

The colonel had twice extended his hand to cut the pack, and twice he withdrew it again.

"Silly old dear!" breathed Dolly. "It doesn't matter where he cuts — he'll have the right card turned for him."

And then another shout from the colonel.

"By gad, Ned, I've got it again. After these years — I've got it again!"

He jumped up from his chair and laid down his cards.

"It's a twenty-niner. Come look at it, Dolly!

Come here, Portman, and feast your eyes on it! May go the rest of your life without seeing that again! Not another turn of the cards. It's not a money game, Ned, and you'll let me stop now, won't you? You don't mind a beating from an old man, eh? But cribbage is a science, my boy! Let's stretch our legs a little. I want to take you on a walk down to the lake where Tom and I used to go of an evening in the old days. Excuse us for a moment, Oliver. Come along, Ned. Have you something to smoke?"

And taking Eddie Clewes by the arm, he marched him off down the winding path toward the river, while the last words that Dolly and her suitor overheard were:

"You see, Ned, there are two things to watch — the pegging and the discard. Must watch those two things. They're the whole game. But I'll explain what you must do. Now, when you make your discard — "

They wound from view. Their voices became a blur. And Dolly Exeter started up from her chair and looked anxiously after them.

"Now, Dolly, don't let your imagination run away with you!" said Oliver Portman, most uneasy as he stood beside her.

"Ah, Oliver, Oliver, you great, big, trusting baby!" said Dolly. "I can't help worrying.

I feel just as though I had seen a clever young fox walk off with the oldest and best gander in the farmyard!"

"It isn't fair to the colonel," said Portman. "But men who do business with him know that he has a grand head on his shoulders. I never could understand how you talk down to him so!"

"Because I know him and love him, Oliver, and because he loves me, and because all his life he's been totally blind to the faults of those he's fond of. If I did a murder before his eyes, he wouldn't believe it. He *couldn't* believe it! Because loving me, I have to be perfect. Don't you see? And he's grown terribly worked up over this man. This — "

"Dolly, you actually hate this fellow!"

"I'm afraid of him. I'm mortally afraid of him. He's too cool and calm. They said that he was so modest that he tried to break away from the crowd before he was brought to Culloden. Look at him and think of him, Oliver! Is there *any* modesty in him? No, but everything that calm young man does is done for a proper effect. And it makes me half cry and half laugh when I think of my dear old father trying to teach that rascal how to play *any* game of cards!"

Oliver Portman was in a state of perplexity.

"I shouldn't listen to this sort of thing

any longer," he declared. "It's wrong of me. It's as though I were slandering him behind his back. You mustn't talk to me, Dolly."

"Come, come, Oliver! As a man — you know that it's *extremely* odd that the five should turn up, just as I said that it would!"

"It *is* odd," admitted Oliver heavily.

"And then, what am I to do to find out about this man?"

"I'll do what I can — "

"You'll take a month turning about to find the honorable way. But I'll tell you what *I'll* do: I'm going to make love to our hero!"

"Dolly — God bless me! — you don't mean that!"

"Oh, but I do! I'm going to make tremendous love to him. And if there's anything in hard work, I'm going to make him talk about himself. Also, I'm going to get a snapshot of him, if I can. And when I have that, I'll send it to you to take it about and see what people may recognize Mr. Ned Larned."

"It's like a conspiracy, Dolly. I feel uncomfortable."

"So do McKenzie and Delehanty," said the girl. "It's better to feel uncomfortable while finding out, than to feel uncomfortable after the truth about him has been shown to you!"

There was something so apt and so brisk in

this last remark that Oliver Portman became silent.

"There's no stopping you," he said at last. "I came over here with my courage worked up high enough to ask you to marry me, for the tenth time. But you've scared me out of it."

"Help me to trail him down," said the girl, "because I promise you that there's something worth knowing behind him. A woman's instinct is never all wrong!"

Oliver Portman did not answer. He had never known enough about women to be able to generalize about the sex. In fact, since his boyhood his attention had been solely devoted to the study of a single girl, and with every week, she became a greater and a greater mystery, quite insolvable to Oliver! But he decided now that she was so infinitely wiser than he that it would be best to put aside his scruples, and to obey her blindly.

CHAPTER FOURTEEN
The Scissors in His Hair

When Eddie Clewes went to bed that night he was reasonably sure that he had the colonel in a position where he could twist that kind and generous gentleman around his finger, and he was equally assured that Dolly was a suspicious foeman.

But when the morning came she was subtly changed.

He thought at first that the governor's telegram might have something to do with it. For the telegram came in due course, brought up by a breathless man on a breathless, sweating horse. The governor had heard a full report of the daring feat of Mr. Edward Larned and he congratulated Mr. Larned upon his amazing courage and fighting skill which had brushed away in a single encounter two criminals so dreaded by the entire State. He was writing Mr. Larned that same day to express his sentiments more fully.

So said the governor's telegram.

It began the day most happily. The colonel drove off to the bank, and Eddie Clewes was left with his thoughts — and Dolly. But before long there was too much Dolly for a great deal of thought about anything else.

He found himself walking with Dolly.

He found himself paddling Dolly in a canoe, along the lake, with the bright face of Dolly before him, and the bright shadow of Dolly floating beside the boat with only a rare ripple to dim her smile.

He found for the first time in his life that even the silences of a woman need not be dull; and when she spoke, sometimes her voice was brisk and cheerful, but more often it was soft and brooding as if something other than her spoken words possessed her mind. And gradually, very gradually, Eddie Clewes began to feel that that something was himself!

In his orderly mind, at the first meeting, certain items had been jotted down as:

Item: A pretty face.

Item: A great deal of self-control.

Item: A sharp set of wits, continually at work on things and people around her.

Item: A great deal of reliance placed in Dolly's own brains.

Out of these mental remarks, he had completed his picture of the girl and put it away in one of those crowded pigeonholes of his mind where he stored the intellectual pictures of all the people who had ever crossed the margin of his life.

But now he began to note down other things, very small details such as had rarely troubled him in the past — as, for instance, a dimpling softness across her knuckles, when her hand was held flat; or the roundness of her wrist, which the sun had shadowed to a pale bronze; bronze was her throat, also, fading to a delicately pure white about the base. And though it was pleasant to hear her speak, he was more glad when she was silent, because then he could watch from time to time how her face was modeled about the chin and the lips, and all suffused and blended with bright color and a sort of inward light of happiness.

There was a very great deal to see! And Mr. Clewes, who had been in the habit of noting half a dozen faces at one sweep of the eyes, now discovered that even during the time required for two strokes of the paddle he could not be quite sure of the singular daintiness with which a blue vein ran a tracery upon one of her temples, or of the quality of that dreaming look with which she stared at the shores that drifted past them, or why it was that she picked the water lily, and then let it trail from her hand in the water, while she thought of other things!

What other things?

Why, once or twice his glance met hers, fairly, and then a pleasant little shock went tingling through all the nerves of Mr. Clewes' body and ended with a crowd of startled messages, focused on his heart, and making it leap with a queer happiness and with a queer pain.

It was like homesickness, only it was not. For when had Eddie Clewes had a home?

But when those glances clashed, in this manner, he could not help observing that she always hastily looked away, and there was just an instant of confusion in her manner — she who had been so very sure of herself, the evening before, she who had watched him with such hostility from the corner of the veranda!

He was partly baffled; he was partly enchanted; and he was partly alarmed; for he could feel that he was slipping away from himself into an uncertain, uneasy region of dreams. Once and twice and again he began to paddle more briskly to break the spell, and once, twice, and again the waters of the quiet lake clung to the sliding keel and dissolved its speed, and the very shadows of the overhanging branches laid ghostly hands upon the canoe and stole away its momentum.

Oh, wicked Dolly Exeter! For who can be

so wicked as a good woman, strong and secure in the knowledge that she is above temptation?

"You are thinking of something unhappy," said Eddie Clewes.

"I am thinking of you," said she.

And this time, when she raised her eyes to his, her glance did not leap away again, but remained upon him, and dwelt on him, and in a mysterious way, drew him inside the dim horizon of her thoughts. The heart of Mr. Clewes, which had leaped before, now kept right on pounding, and refused to settle down. Exactly as if he had been afraid of something which was not to be feared!

"And what I am thinking is this," said she. "Suppose that a great eagle, Ned, were to drop out of the air — "

He almost lost the sense of what she was saying, it was such a delight to hear his name come so familiarly upon her lips, with a falling note of confident appeal!

"Suppose a great eagle that was used to sailing over a thousand miles, here and there, lord of everything, were to drop down out of the air, and out of the wind, and down into a quiet little valley — like this, you know — what would he think of the quietness — and the silly cows lifting their heads in the fields to watch him coming down with his great spread wings — and the silly people, all gaping and wondering at him — wouldn't the eagle think it a very dull life, and a very stupid lot of creatures?"

She meant that for him, of course. A great eagle — that was Eddie Clewes! He felt that he could understand a good deal of her attitude of the night before. Because he *had* come like an eagle into her life. Dropping down out of the central sky with blood and battle about his name! And so she had shrunk from him at the first and suspected him afterward.

Well, it was all very easy to understand, now that he had the clew of it! It made him feel rather magnificent. And charitable, too. Like a great king, who pities the little village maiden who wonders at him as he rides forth to war!

Such thoughts of strength and of grandeur swelled in the bosom of Eddie Clewes, and yet there was a melting softness in the very core of his being also.

"I've never been chummy with eagles," said Eddie Clewes. "I can't guess what one of the old boys would think. But I suppose he'd think that the quiet was a wonderful thing, and the smell of the good green grass would mean a lot to him, and I suppose that he would want to flirt his wing in one of these quiet little lakes."

"And then fly away at once, of course!"

Yes, she seemed quite anxious, saying that, with her head canted a trifle to one side.

"Or perhaps he would forget all about the upper air," said Mr. Clewes. And he felt again as though this was a charity from the magnificent strength of his heart. Charity, you see, to the simple little village girl!

Oh, Samson, beware, beware!

She sat back in the canoe with her eyes closed, her lips smiling a little. How unconscious she seemed, with her head thrown back just a trifle, and the delicate roundness of her throat in view against the lake water, blue as the pure blue heavens! How unconscious and how unsophisticated — poor child!

Samson, Samson, the scissors are in thy hair!

And his heart was quickening, and quickening, and that singular sense of something melting in his heart of hearts — deliciously melting —

She opened her eyes suddenly with a slight start.

"Have you *ever* been just a boy like other boys?" she asked him. "Weren't you always as self-possessed, and as calm, and as sure of your strength? Were you ever running into the house for bread and jam — "

"Ah, a thousand times!" said Eddie Clewes

gently. "Of course! Of course! A thousand times. Except that there was often no bread, and never any jam!"

"They didn't believe in letting you have things between meals," she nodded. "And that's right. When I have babies" — and she blushed just a bit — "I'm going to raise them strictly like that!"

"Well, it wasn't exactly strictness. The bread and the jam were often not there, you know!"

"Really? Then you were poor? I'm so sorry! Not for grown people. Because they have things in their minds which keep them busy and happy. But for little children poverty must be a dreadful thing — not to have hobby horses, or soldiers!"

"You can make them, you know. Soldiers out of pieces of tin can, if you get a tin shears in the junkyard. And horses out of a potato, with matches stuck in it. Oh, I was happy enough, you know."

"And yet," she said, "I really thought that every home west of the Mississippi had more comfort than that."

"West of the Mississippi! Well, perhaps. But this was east of it, a good ways."

"In that cold, barren, Yankee land — I know!"

"No, in that fine Maryland with the most

beautiful hills and trees that God ever made. Ah, but I can see it clearly! When you've lived fifteen years of your life in one little village, making a living in spite of bad chances, you know, and putting in for a bit of education, too — why, under conditions like that, everything around a boy is burned into his mind! Except that the off thing is that the unhappy part begins to disappear, after a time. I never think of the winter ice on the river, but of the yellow summer sun. And I never think of the naked autumn days, but all the gold and amber and russet and crimson and purples in October. And a thousand times I dream of the station platform as it was the day that I left forever that town of Comp — "

His teeth closed with a little click. The softness fled from his eyes. Like chilled steel his glance went through her.

But she only murmured, "What a queer name for a town — Comp!"

CHAPTER FIFTEEN
Archie McKenzie Takes the Trail

There were no more sentimentalities to be extracted from Mr. Clewes on this occasion. His attitude had changed as suddenly and as decisively as that of a sleeping wolf when up the wind comes the scent of "bear." He was wakened, now, and it was all that clever Dolly Exeter could do to maintain her own dreamy, attitude, or to slip slowly from it back to a normal wide-awakeness by the time the canoe touched the shore. For Mr. Clewes had suddenly recalled something that made it necessary for him to return to the house.

And it seemed that a premonition had been working in him, for when he reached the house it was to find none other than Sheriff Boots Askew waiting impatiently for him.

Dolly Exeter left them together, and five minutes later her horse was flicking her over fences as she took the straightest cut across country toward the house of Oliver Portman.

She found him supervising the building of

133

the skeleton of a barn, and he walked beside her toward the house.

"It worked better than I could have hoped — better than I dreamed, Oliver!" she told him. "But, oh, it was a dangerous business!"

"Dolly," said the big man with a touch of sadness, "this is the worst thing I've ever heard from you. I wouldn't believe it from any other person. You don't mean, though, that you've been really — er — sentimental with Larned?"

"Don't I mean it, though?" she flashed back at him, and then with a sigh: "I was trembling in my boots! There's nobody else like him! He's just as sharp and as keen as a wolf's tooth. And I could only keep up the play-acting by sort of pretending, Oliver, that I was on a stage — you understand? — and that there was an audience out there to watch, and to applaud if I did the thing well! But all the while, I could feel his mind working at me, puzzling over me, trying to understand why I had been one thing last night and another thing today. And sometimes it seemed that he came perilously close to guessing!"

Oliver stared at the ground and kicked a stone viciously from his path.

"Well?" he asked curtly, at the last.

"Well, my dear big furious Oliver, there was no real harm done. If you have the courage to put your hand between the bars of the cage and pat the head of the tiger — why, it's a reward for courage when you hear the big brute begin to purr and close its eyes and thrust out its claws into the wooden floor — "

"Will you tell me actually what happened?"

"I don't know what did it. Partly because I was playing the game my level best. And partly, I think, because the air was soft and warm, and lazy, and luxurious, he began to soften! I didn't have very long, but the instant that I saw the mood working in him, I tried to flatter him into talking about himself. It wasn't easy — but finally he *did!*"

"And said that he was a liar, a thief, a gambler, a robber — all the things that you suspect him of being?" asked Oliver critically.

"Heavens, no! Not a word of that. But I made him talk about himself when he was a boy — and he fell into the trap far enough, finally, to let me learn these little items about him:

"That he was born and raised in Maryland.

"That he was so dreadfully poor that often there was not even bread in the home.

"That he lived in a town on the banks of a river that froze in the middle of the winter.

"That he left that town and never went back to it when he was fifteen years old.

"That, finally, the name of that town began with Comp. C-O-M-P. He pronounced it perfectly distinctly. I couldn't be wrong. But just in the middle of pronouncing it — why, it was a wonderful thing to see how he recovered himself. They say that a rolling wheel can touch the side of a sleeping wolf — and yet the wolf will waken in time to jump out of harm's way. Well, it was like that. His teeth clicked over the last part of the word. And then he sat there quite out of his dream, glaring at me with dreadful, glittering eyes. It made me positively sick with fear. Positively sick!"

She paused and laid a hand upon the sleeve of Oliver Portman.

Then she went on: "But I managed to stand the strain, and though I presume that he *suspects* that I was pumping him for information, still, I think that he cannot be quite sure. And yet, whatever rascality there may be in his mind, he's apt to rush it through quickly, now, so that we haven't much time to act! We must hurry, Oliver!"

"Hurry to do what? Accuse him of having been poor — and living in a Maryland town which begins with Comp — "

"Oliver, Oliver, Oliver, how can you be such a stupid silly? *Dear* Oliver, don't you see what we must do? We must start to work instantly to find out if there is any little town in

136

Maryland whose name begins with C-O-M-P. And when we find it, then we must send telegrams, instantly, describing Mr. Larned from top to toe, and asking if such a young man was raised in a poor family in that town, and what his reputation was in that place — "

"Nasty work! Nasty work!" said Mr. Portman. "I don't know that I care to take a hand in this sort of thing — eavesdropping on the secrets of a man's past. Besides, you'd probably learn nothing!"

"If there was nothing to be hidden — if there was nothing worth running down, then tell me why it was that Ned Larned was so shocked when he caught himself giving the name of his native village? And why was it, that all the way to the house he kept probing at me with his eyes. Such eyes, Oliver! I have never seen anything like them! Like cold fire — as they say in books. It — it makes me shudder even now, just thinking about it! But — I want you to tell me that you'll go to town and send the telegrams, as soon as you've located the place — "

"I'd rather cut off an arm," sighed Oliver Portman. "But if you could twist such a person as Larned around your finger, how can *I* possibly hope to hold out against you?"

You may be sure that Mr. "Larned" was no

more in the mind of Dolly Exeter than she was in the mind of Mr. "Larned," for all the way to the house he had been weighing the possibilities of the thing. And he told himself that it really could not be that such a slip of a girl had dared to try to work her wits against his own. He writhed in an agony of doubt and cursed himself for a sleepy daydreamer for having allowed his tongue so much liberty, at such a crisis in his life!

But before his thoughts could dwell too long upon this point, they reached the house, and there was the sheriff with such news for him that he could not afford to speculate longer on the wiles of Dolly Exeter.

For the sheriff took him to one side and gave him the whole tidings in a breath.

"Ned, there's bad news for you. The younger brother of Murdoch McKenzie is coming this way for your scalp!"

Eddie Clewes raised his sensitive brows.

"Now?" he asked.

"Just when, I don't know. All I know is that I had a long wire from an old partner of mine, Sheriff Cliff Matthews, over the mountains. And he tells me that the news has come to him that a gent has killed Delehanty and Murdoch McKenzie in a fight, hand to hand, and that he hardly can believe it, and that he wants me to shake hands for him with the

winner. But he says that young Archie Mc-
Kenzie, when he heard about the death of his
brother, went raging on the warpath, and put
a pint of whiskey under his belt, and polished
up his guns, and grabbed his best and toughest
horse, and swore that he'd never stop long
enough to shave before he had killed Ned
Larned! There's the whole packet of news,
and here's the telegram that it come in!"

He handed it to Eddie Clewes, and the latter ran his eye through it carefully. It merely
reiterated what Askew had already told him
by word of mouth, and he asked, "What do
you know about young McKenzie?"

"Ah," said the sheriff, "I knew that you'd
take it this way. Some of the boys swore that it
would only make you laugh, because if you
was able to handle two like Delehanty and
Murdoch McKenzie at a crack, you'd never
bother your head about one like young Archie!
But I guessed different. You got a head on
your shoulders, old son, and it's a safe bet that
you'll think everything over and throw away
no chances!"

"Askew," said Eddie Clewes with a heart-
felt solemnity, "let me tell you that there's
nothing that I hate worse than the mere
thought of a gunfight!"

"I knew it," nodded the sheriff with much
sympathy. "It takes a brute or a fool to figure

139

the game any other way than that — a brute or a fool or a rattle-headed kid that wants to make himself famous! Now, Ned, what'll we do about this McKenzie?"

"Tell me first what sort of a fellow he is."

"I don't know him. But you see in the telegram that Cliff Matthews takes it pretty serious. And Cliff is one that knows men. He's got a head on his shoulders. Slow but sure, is old Cliff, I can tell you! Well, sir, I don't know Archie, as I was saying, but I know the McKenzies, and they're a rough lot. There never was a one of them that didn't know how to ride and shoot extra prime. And there was never a one of them that didn't have a sort of a relish for a fight on foot or on horseback, with knife, fist, club, or gun. And so I take it for granted that Archie is one of the same kind, big, and strong-handed — though not so strong-handed that he could master a gent that could handle Delehanty and Murdoch at the same minute!"

"Do you know what I wish?" said Eddie Clewes gently.

"Tell me, son, and I'll try my best to help you out."

"Well, this fellow Archie McKenzie has been heard on the far side of the mountains to swear that he would have my scalp."

"Yes."

"And now he's headed for us, riding hard and meaning business, no doubt?"

"That's clear."

"Why, then, Askew, what's to keep you from putting him under arrest if you can block his way? Arrest him and put him in jail for a day or two to cool him off, and then bind him over to keep the peace, you know. But sometimes a sight of the inside of a jail will do a great deal to take the bad humor out of a fighting man!"

The sheriff scratched his chin.

"It seems queer — but there ain't any reason why it can't be done," he said thoughtfully. "You don't mind what folks might be tempted to say when they hear? But no, nobody in this neck of the woods would be fool enough to think that you wanted to dodge Archie McKenzie except because you pitied the poor kid!"

And Sheriff Askew straightway mounted to return to Culloden, for he was anxious to lay his plans as thoroughly as possible for the interception of young McKenzie.

CHAPTER SIXTEEN
Sweet Fortune

From the viewpoint of Eddie Clewes, it was a day thronging full of important events, beginning with that odd talk with Dolly Exeter, and continuing through the warning which Sheriff Askew brought to him; and the next step in his history was when the colonel, returning early from the bank, walked up and down the orchard paths with Eddie and unburdened himself of some novel ideas, which were to the effect that he, the colonel, growing old apace, had no one near and dear to him whom he could take into his business. And therefore, why should not Ned Larned be the man?

"For, if you consider," said the colonel, "that I have known you only a short time, on the other hand, it is perfectly true that I have known you through extremely important events. If you wish to know a race horse, it's no good walking him in the pasture; and if you wish to know a man, it's no good seeing him for a thousand humdrum days, one after the other. One critical test is worth more than a hundred thousand years of walks and talks. I have the proof of how you were tested, Ned. Besides that, we like one another, don't we? So what more can I ask? Nothing, my boy! So tell me what you think of the plan."

What did Eddie Clewes think? Of going into a bank and starting in the proverbial way at the bottom, and working his way up, even with help from above to raise him?

But he swallowed his smile. He thanked the colonel with a quiet warmth. He was very tired of wandering, he said. And now a chance to settle down, and with such a friend as the colonel —

As for Colonel Exeter, he was as delighted as a boy. He ran up the stairs and rapped eagerly on the door of Dolly, and when she came he caught both her hands.

"Dolly, my dear," said the colonel, "I've caught him! I've landed him!"

"Landed who?" said Dolly, her heart falling with a quick premonition.

"Why, Ned, of course. I've talked to him about the bank and banking in general. He's interested. He's tired of wandering about. He only wants to settle down steadily. And tomorrow morning we go down the hill together and I introduce him to his work! Start him at the bottom — that's my scheme, my dear. And now, what do you think of it? You've always accused me of putting mollycoddles and old hens into my bank. Will you call Larned a mollycoddle, my child?"

And he laughed with an extravagant happiness, for, in spite of his years and his real dignity, the colonel was a man with a great deal of the child in him. But Dolly was alarmed. She drew her father into the room and closed the door and put her back against it, as though she were afraid that he would try to break out again.

"Now, Dolly." He frowned at her. "What's wrong? What's wrong with this scheme of mine?"

"I can't give you any facts, yet," she said, "but you've always trusted a great deal in the instinct of women."

"Prehaps I have. Well?"

"I can only say this — and I know that it will make you furious — don't trust Ned Larned!"

The colonel stared at her, to make sure that it was really his daughter who had said such a thing.

"And not a scruple of taint attaching to him?"

"Nothing real enough to point out, but — "

"Then I don't want to hear you. Slander is a

devilish engine, Dolly. Once planted, it works like a disease in the blood. I'm sorry that you've spoken like this to me. I'm mightily sorry. Because now, in spite of myself, I shall not be able to look at Ned without a question. I'll begin to doubt him and question everything that he does. And for nothing! Dolly, tell me frankly — are you saying this because I've made such a fuss over Ned so soon? Are you jealous of him, child?"

Something which might have served as a reasonable base for her suspicions, even in the colonel's mind, had been upon the very lips of Dolly, but he could not have found a surer way of silencing her. She threw up her head, very crimson in the face, and she silently stepped aside for her father to pass out when he would.

And out he went, down-headed, and in silence, as though his fine dream for the future of his bank and his family had already been pricked like a bubble and dissolved away to nothing!

Dinner that night was not a great success, for, though both the colonel and his daughter strove to be cheerful, there were shadowy times of quiet when each looked down, and Dolly, with a frown, turned an emerald bracelet on her wrist.

That bracelet fascinated Mr. Clewes. He

knew something about precious stones, because everyone in his general profession had to acquire a knowledge of such things early, or else miss many delightful business opportunities. There were ten square-faced stones, all of a size, in the circle that ringed the wrist of Miss Exeter, and, though it was a reasonably small wrist, still each of those stones was a great beauty and the sheen of them lured the eyes of Eddie Clewes to that side of the table again and again. If this were a sample of the treasures in the jewel casket, then it was very likely that the clever Dick Pritchard had not made an underestimate! There might well be half a million dollars of treasure, at the rate of this sample!

Those little gloomy stretches of quiet interested Mr. Clewes, also, because he suspected that they had something to do with him. When he noticed that the colonel could not meet his eye with any steadiness, then he was sure of it.

It was vastly alarming to Eddie, though not a change appeared in his face, for it meant either that the first suspicious news had arrived, or else that something in his conduct had mysteriously and suddenly displeased the banker.

At any rate, he resolved on a counterstroke which, if there were any chance whatever, would balance matters on his behalf once more. And the chance was offered to him almost at once by Dolly herself, saying, "If you're staying on in Culloden, Ned, you'll be wanting to invest your fifteen thousand in the valley then?"

He thought that it was a bit pointed, this remark, and he could not help glancing quickly aside at her, to see if there were any additional meaning in her expression, but she met him with a perfectly serene smile. And he had come to know that, no matter what he did, he could not deprive her of her poise.

"As a matter of fact," said Eddie Clewes, "I'm not the owner of fifteen thousand dollars."

"I mean the reward money, of course," said Dolly.

"That," said Eddie Clewes, "is to be invested in a hospital."

"A hospital," cried the colonel. "Gad, Ned, you interested in a hospital somewhere?"

"Yes," said Eddie, "almost anywhere a hospital interests me. Because I can't take the fifteen thousand, you know."

"You can't take it? You can't take it?" echoed the colonel. "Hey, bless me! Ned, what do you mean by that?"

"You understand," said Eddie Clewes with a little gesture of abhorrence, "that it's blood-money, and I can't take it! I've thought it over. No matter what Murdoch McKenzie and Delehanty may have done, I don't want to feel that their deaths have been mixed into my own life. I'd rather have clean hands!"

It was a great sensation. It was the very thing that Mr. Pritchard had advised him to cast about for — some startling achievement which would bring the colonel and his family completely into camp!

And now the thing was done!

As for Dolly, she sat with her hands clasped, and her eyes big and bright, and the colonel gripped the edge of the table and leaned forward a little.

"You paid for that money by endangering your life, my lad," said he. "You should be very careful before you decide on such a thing as this. Fifteen thousand dollars is a neat little fortune, at your time in life, and you can invest it at ten percent in Culloden Valley as easily as not. I could *guarantee* you such a rate. Remember, my boy, you're not simply throwing away fifteen thousand dollars; you're tossing aside an income of a hundred and twenty-five dollars every month of life that remains to you!"

"I've thought of it from every angle," said Eddie modestly. "I like money very well — but not that sort of money, sir!"

"But — " began the colonel.

"Don't!" cried Dolly. "Don't try to persuade him from such a fine thing. Ned, what a fine clean, clean heart it takes to have such a thought!"

And she leaned toward Eddie Clewes with such joy in her throat and beauty in her face that he knew, suddenly, that she *had* been merely playing a part with him that same morning.

Yonder was a very alluring girl, but this was Dolly Exeter when her heart of hearts ran over.

It unsteadied him, and he looked down to the table with a sudden hot flush on his face. I think it was the first time in Eddie's life that he had ever been shamed!

"I won't," the colonel was hastening to say, triumph in his face as he nodded to Dolly, "I won't try to persuade him, because I *couldn't* persuade him. When a man has founded his integrity on bed rock, he cannot be altered by every wind that blows. It simply cannot be, my dear. However, I won't talk like a banker any more, but as a friend, and I tell you, Ned, that this decision of yours means more to me than you would guess. And if you'll let me say so, in addition, I don't think that you'll lose by it! Not in the long run. Because courage is golden, but a clean soul is a shining diamond, by the eternal heavens!"

The colonel was prone to these rather rhetorical flights, but there was so much real emotion in him that it was hard to tell where feeling ended and words took command.

And Eddie Clewes was not entirely interested in this. What he knew was that he had gained the point for which he had been willing to make this sacrifice. Fifteen thousand was a greater stake than he had ever hauled before. But what was it compared with the sweet fortune which lay in his hopes at the present moment? So, like a good gambler, he sweetened the pot with a smile on his lips, and shrugged away the thought of what it had cost him.

But after dinner the colonel could not help taking a moment aside with Dolly in the library.

"Now, my dear," he began, "I want — "

"You don't have to say a thing," said Dolly. "You're right, and I'm wrong. You're an old dear, and I'm a dusty, earthy, sooty creature, all filled with unworthy suspicions of everything. But now I see the truth about Ned, and what a thoroughly fine fellow he is — and no matter what I was thinking before, I'll *unthink* it. I will, Dad. And I would *fight* any man who dared to suggest a thing against Ned Larned!"

CHAPTER SEVENTEEN
New Suspicion

Rewards came quickly to Eddie Clewes, and the first test of Dolly Exeter's new enthusiasm arrived almost at once, for big Oliver Portman dropped in a little later in the evening. He had been so long a friend of the family and so long an open suitor of Dolly, that he was acceptable without an invitation, always.

Now he took his first chance to talk apart to the girl.

"I searched through the atlas. There was no town beginning with C-O-M-P. None that answered the rest of the description. But after a time I started the telegraph working and finally I landed what I think will be the right trail."

"Do you think so?" asked Dolly. "But I tell you, Oliver, that since I talked to you before, I've changed my mind entirely about Ned. I doubted him, and I'm ashamed of my doubts, and I'll tell you why."

And she launched with shining enthusiasm

into the story of the renunciation of the reward.

Oliver Portman listened, with his fine large head bent forward, studying every word with an attentive frown, and that frown did not disappear when the tale ended.

"So you see, Oliver, that Father and you were right, and I was simply silly; because, of course, a man who can do such a thing has nothing wrong with him — nothing important, that is. Why are you still frowning?"

"Because," said Oliver, "it seems just a little too good to be true!"

"Stuff!" said the girl. "Are *you* getting silly ideas in your turn?"

"With all my heart I *hope* that they're silly," he answered her. "But I like to see a normal man doing normal things — and fifteen thousand dollars is an extraordinary lot to throw out the window — even for a rich man, and this Larned has always been poor!"

"It's not that. You have a starved imagination, Oliver, if you can't picture to yourself how such a person as Ned Larned thinks and feels. You see, he's all fire, under that quiet outside. That's his hidden strength that enabled him to master two giants like Delehanty and Murdoch McKenzie — "

"I hope," said Oliver Portman, "that it will enable him to master Archie McKenzie, also!"

"Archie McKenzie? Who is he?"

"Haven't you heard? I thought that it was all through the town — I mean, the news that Archie McKenzie has started across the mountains to revenge his brother Murdoch and kill Larned, if he can!"

She looked wildly at Oliver.

"Why, he himself hasn't heard this terrible thing, Oliver!"

"Ah, but he has! The sheriff came up here today to tell him about it — "

"*That* was what brought 'Boots' Askew to our house — at the very time when I was riding helter skelter away to let you know my ridiculous suspicions, and Ned hasn't parted his lips about that dreadful news! One of the murdering McKenzies! Oliver, what will be done?"

"I don't think," said Oliver Portman, "that a man who killed both Murdoch McKenzie and Delehanty will be worried when a single gunfighter comes on his trail. But in the meantime, I want to tell you what I've learned, which is that the little town of Marstonville, in Maryland, was formerly called Compton, until the name was changed — "

"I don't care a whit about Marstonville and Compton, Oliver!"

"And," he went on, "I am opening up telegraphic communication with Marstonville to learn — "

"Telegraphic communication! You sound like a mine disaster, Oliver! But don't you see? No matter what can be found out, it won't shake my faith in our Ned — "

"Our Ned?" said Portman slowly. "Has he — well, let it go! And so you're through investigating?"

"Absolutely, and I want you to drop it."

"I would have liked to," said Mr. Portman, "but the fact is, I've changed my opinion about all this."

"And this morning you were so eager to avoid eavesdropping on any man's past!"

"It's not logical. I'm sorry for that. But you see, the very thing that makes you so sure of Larned is what makes me a bit suspicious — fifteen thousand dollars thrown out the window. Suppose that one of the farmers should touch a match to his ranch and send it up in smoke, because he found out that his grandfather had done something wrong — Why, Dolly, that would be on a par with what Larned is doing now!"

She snapped her fingers and merely laughed.

"What could his purpose be? I defy you to find a wicked purpose in such a thing, Oliver!"

"I'm a simple fellow," said he, as gravely as ever. "I don't pretend to have wits enough to

154

follow the twists and the windings of those clever fellows, like Ned Larned. But I do know that I'll have to stick with this little investigation until I learn what is happening at the farther end of the wire — and all that they can tell me about Mr. Larned, of their town!"

"I think that you'll change your mind again about it," she told him, growing sober enough at this.

"I'm reasonably sure that I shall not, however."

"Oliver, you make me angry — you really do!"

"I should be sorry to do that, but — "

"Oh, be a little less like granite; be human, Oliver, and tell me that you're not going to try to stir up mud in the river!"

"Ah, are you afraid that I *might* learn something?"

"I don't know — I really don't care. Except that I know he's not a common fellow. And being what he is, he *may* have done something a little wrong. But that doesn't matter. Not what he was in the past. That doesn't count. It's the present and the future that really tells what he is, and we know what he is — a hero — with a soul as pure as snow! A man so fine, Oliver, that I feel ashamed of being what I am — so silly, and so weak, and so girlish! He makes me want to be older and bigger and stronger and better — and — it brought the tears to my eyes when he said at the table, so quietly, that he was going to give that great sum of money away, to a hospital!"

Oliver Portman hung his head as he listened.

And then he muttered, with a sigh: "I wish that once in my life I had been able to get a tenth of this enthusiasm out of you about me! But there's nothing rare about me, Dolly. Well, what I am can't be changed!"

"But this last silly idea of yours *can* be changed! You're not going ahead with the thing?"

He hesitated, as though he knew that the matter had become a grave one between him and her.

"I'd like to please you, Dolly, but, now that I've started on it — "

"You'll finish it! I can almost hear you say that!"

"I like to finish what I've put my hand to!"

"Will you let me say one thing to you?"

"Yes, of course, if you wish."

"It will almost make me hate you, Oliver, if you keep on mining in poor Ned's past to find out something wrong about him!"

He looked steadily into her face.

"Very well," said he, "then it will have to

make you hate me. I'm not a spectacular fellow, Dolly. I don't throw fifteen thousand dollars out the window with a fine gesture, but you know that you mean more to me than anything else in the world I can think of. And still, I'm not going to be bought off by the fear of your anger!"

She stepped back from him, standing stiff and straight.

"Then perhaps you'll pay attention to the anger of someone else!"

"You mean what?"

"I mean, what if Ned Larned comes to know that you're playing the spy on him?"

"Ah? Well, Dolly, I never expected to hear you threaten me. But I'll really be glad if you *do* go straight to Larned and tell him everything. You can leave yourself out of it entirely — for starting me on the trail, I mean. The important thing is that I suspect him and that I'm investigating him. And it's best that he should know, and not be struck in the dark unexpectedly."

"Would you *dare* to let him know?"

"Gad, Dolly," said the big man quietly, "you mustn't take me for a welcher and a coward, you know!"

"Then you'll do it?"

"I shall, most certainly!"

She turned sharply away from him, paused

157

at the door with a word on her lips which remained unspoken, and left the room. And Oliver Portman knew that he had sunk his ship beneath him. However, he took up his hat without manifest excitement and left the house with his square jaw set. He was not one who was easily beaten, even by his own sentiments. And he went out to complete his appointed task as resolutely as though he had received nothing but encouragement from Dolly Exeter.

She, for her part, went to find her father and Eddie Clewes, and she discovered them making a brief tour of the house, her father with a jingling bunch of keys in his hand.

"I've been giving Ned his set of keys," said the colonel. "The same one which Tom carried! And we've about finished with everything except the safe. That's this little key, Ned. I showed you the safe, you remember — "

"I remember," said Eddie Clewes.

It gave Dolly Exeter a strange thrill to think that the fortunes of their house had been committed so resolutely to the hand of this man, so nearly a stranger to them. And yet she agreed with the colonel, in her heart of hearts. With such a man, it was impossible that they should go too far!

"And what's up now, Dolly?" asked her father. "You look worried!"

She stood before them with her hands clenched at her sides. She was rather ridiculously like a small schoolgirl, about to speak a piece and by no means assured of her audience.

"I want to say that this morning, Ned, I was playing a very bad part — because I suspected you, and I was trying to draw you out. And when I stumbled on part of the name of your home town — why, I went to Oliver Portman and asked him to investigate you — and just now I've seen him — "

She paused an instant for breath. The colonel, very red, was watching Eddie Clewes with a guilty side glance, as though he himself were responsible for his daughter's behavior. But Eddie Clewes was as calm as stone, to all appearance.

"And I've asked Oliver to stop his investigation — no matter what he might find out, but he's refused to stop — and I wanted to tell you and confess, though you'll despise me for having suspected you, Ned!"

He had a rare smile, had this Eddie Clewes, and he turned the full brightness of it on her.

"I don't despise you, Dolly," said he. "I respect you — as a good housekeeper, you know!"

CHAPTER EIGHTEEN
The Leaven Works

Eddie Clewes, confidence man extraordinary, as he advanced to his room that night, felt that nearly all had happened that well could happen in a single day. But one more thing remained, for as he opened the door of his room he was aware of a faint scent of cigarette smoke.

And so, stepping in, he glided deftly to one side as he jerked the door shut — as a man would do who half expects a bullet to meet him.

He had not forgotten the warning from Sheriff "Boots" Askew, and, though the younger McKenzie could never have arrived by this time on a horse, he might readily have changed his horse for the first train, and that would have eaten up the distance easily enough.

However, it was not the voice of a stranger that addressed him from the darkness, but the familiar tones of Mr. Pritchard.

"It's no good, Eddie. I can see you against

that white wall, and, if I wanted to plug you, I could do it out of hand!"

Eddie Clewes, thus reassured, snapped on the electric light, and yonder he saw Pritchard, lolling in the most comfortable chair in the room, looking bigger, stuffier about the shoulders, fatter about the belt than usual. But Eddie Clewes knew that that seeming fat was in reality the hardest and most efficient muscle.

He respected Pritchard, in a way. It was into that man's hands that he had fallen when he was making his first acquaintance with the shadier side of the world, and much, much had he learned. If, in a good many ways, he had far surpassed his master, that was rather a credit to him than a criticism of his teacher. He knew that Pritchard was a criminal so thoroughgoing that, in many of his paces, he could never be equalled by himself, for what Pritchard lacked in wit he more than made up in a certain ruthlessness.

Eddie admired his old companion, therefore, as he turned on the light and regarded him.

"All right, kid," said Dandy Dick, growing a little uneasy beneath that pale, steady eye. "What're you trying to do? Stare me down?"

"I'm only looking you over," said Eddie.

"And — "

"And an odd idea came to me. Have we ever been really at outs?"

"Not exactly, since the day when you decided that you knew so damn much that you didn't need me for a sidekicker. But that wasn't a fight. It was just a decision."

Mr. Clewes felt somewhat expansive. And now he settled down into a chair, lighted a cigarette of his own, and crossed his lean legs.

"Just a decision, Dick," he agreed. "Between you and me, I've always rather liked you. Admired you Dick, d'you understand?"

"Hello, hello! Soft-soaping the old man?" asked Pitchard.

Nevertheless, he grinned, very well pleased.

"It was the blood that I never liked."

"Ay," said Pritchard. "You always wanted to stop before your hands got dirty. Until you ran into Delehanty and McKenzie, eh? Then you seen the need of being thorough. And I hand it to you, kid, that thorough you was, and done the job proper! That was my old schooling speaking!"

"Perhaps it was," smiled Eddie. "But, speaking of quarrels, Dick — "

"Well, what of them?"

"If you and I were ever to fall out really, what a grand, hundred percent, thorough-going, hair-raising, uprooting fight it would be!"

And he shook his head a little.

"Now, d'you think so?" said Pritchard, lifting his big chin and looking down a little at the smaller man.

"Yes, I think so, decidedly."

"Fighting with what?" asked Pritchard.

"Whatever was handiest, I suppose."

"With guns," said Dandy Dick, "you know what I can do, and there ain't many outside of you that *do* know how good I am. Because them that could tell about it are dead, kid! But I don't think that I'd have much trouble with you at the guns!"

Eddie Clewes shrugged his lean shoulders.

"Or with bare hands," said Mr. Pritchard, "I wonder how far I *could* send a fist through you, kid! So I don't think that I would have much trouble with you so far as the fists go!"

"Perhaps not," agreed Eddie Clewes again.

"And what's left?" asked the older man. "What's left, kid? What other ways of fighting?"

"When you ask it that way," said Eddie, "there isn't much for me to say. But if you look at it in a different manner you'll see what I mean."

"I dunno that I follow you," declared the yegg.

"Consider, Pritchard, that in your life you've worked with some rough fellows."

"As hard as they come — that's the kind that I've roughed it with."

"And right now, Dandy, you could name a few hard ones!"

"Oh, I could do that. I'm a traveling directory of the hard nuts, lad, and you ought to know it! No matter where I land, I hit right on my feet, because I know where the tough mugs are, and which ones I can team with! That's my policy. But where does all of this drift to?"

"Why, Dandy, if you look over that same directory that you are speaking about, and if you run your eye back on the list through living men and through dead ones, can you find a single one of the lot whom you wouldn't much rather tackle in any sort of a brawl than to have me after your scalp?"

Mr. Pritchard began with a snarling and sneering response. But, after a moment, he dropped his head forward and scowled up through the thick brows at the youth.

"You got your head turned by the luck that you've had with a couple of the thugs out this way," he declared. "You forget what I *am*, kid!"

"You're a bad one," admitted Eddie Clewes readily enough. "Murder is nothing to you. And you're well up on the ways of doing it. But think it over, Pritchard. Of the entire list, is there a single one you wouldn't rather

164

tackle than to stand up to me?"

Dandy Dick's eyes wavered to the side. He ran the point of his tongue across his lips and then lolled back in the chair, his eyes closed in thought. Or was it to shut out the keen, quiet, penetrating stare of Eddie Clewes?

"I dunno — I dunno!" said Pritchard. "I see what you mean, though. No, I wouldn't especially remember your number if I was out looking for trouble. I'd pick up something easier. But what started you on this line tonight? What got you going on this gag, Eddie?"

"I'll tell you frankly. I simply want to let you know that there may be the worst kind of trouble ahead for us two!"

"Hit me, kid. I'm steadied for it. What's the news?"

"Nothing clear, up to the present. But what would you think, old-timer, if I chucked this entire deal?"

"What would I think? I wouldn't think nothing. What would I *do* is what you mean?"

"Put it that way, if you wish to."

"I'd — lemme see — I'd croak you, kid, I suppose," said Mr. Pritchard with much thoughtfulness. "It would have to be that! Because I stand to clean up something worthwhile in this little job that we have on hand — though God knows that it's nothing compared to what *you'd* make! But tell me, are you figuring on something that freezes me out?"

"There's no use talking about that," said Eddie. "It's something else. A thing that you wouldn't understand!"

"You try me. You've always put me down for dumb, kid. I dunno how you get that way. What's the gag?"

"You want to see my cards?"

"You've seen mine. I've held nothing up."

"No, you're frank enough. But what would you say to this Dick? Suppose that I decide to go straight?"

Dandy Dick raised his heavy brows — he raised his head — and he sank back into the chair, smiling, at his ease.

"Is this stringing, or have you gone batty?"

"I'm not batty," said Mr. Clewes.

"Straight?" Mr. Pritchard indulged himself in a luxurious though silent laughter. "You couldn't keep as straight as a snake's track. It ain't in you. But even if it was, how you gunna amputate the things that you've been from the things that you want to be?"

"You mean that somebody would run me down, sooner or later?"

"I mean that, of course."

"They couldn't put me away for more than five years — because I *have* kept my hands clean."

"You mean that you'd stand for a fiver —
you mean — "

Dandy Dick pointed a forefinger like a gun
at his companion.

"I see what it is!" said he. "But go on!
You'd stand for a trial and take a sentence.
What for? To dodge this here McKenzie?
Hell, boy, while you're with me, you don't
need to fear him. I'd eat six or seven of these
Western four-flushers on toast like quail. You
dunno me, Eddie. You dunno me!"

Eddie Clewes smiled.

And he held up a bunch of keys.

"The little one opens the safe, Dick," said
he.

"Lemme see, will you?"

But Clewes dropped the bunch back into
his pocket and smiled again.

"Hungry, aren't you, Dick? Red-eyed, eh?
Those are the keys, old fellow. And they're
not stolen. They're given. Now, old fellow, I
want you to think it over. Am I to rob a man
who would *give* me the keys to his house?"

"Rob? Rob? Hey, Eddie, for God's sake —
this here ain't any low down common robbery. This is the sort of a thing that books is
wrote about. This here — why, Eddie, it's a
sort of a financial manipulation. It ain't robbery. It's for a cold half million, at the bottom
figure. Why, kid, there ain't any time for you

to get a conscience in a deal like this! This here is art — it's science — it's — it's — hell, boy, are you really getting soft?"

"Perhaps," said Eddie. "Mind you, though, I haven't made up my mind. I'm just thinking things over. I know it's half a million. And that means peace for me. And if I try to go straight, it means that the law swallows me up, even if you don't kill me first — but still, I'm thinking — "

"You ain't!" snarled Mr. Pritchard. "Damn you, you're turning woozy and worse than batty, and I'll tell you what it is — it's the girl that's done it! She's knocked you dippy! Damn a picture face like that! It always raises hell with the best men!"

CHAPTER NINETEEN
The Fly in the Ointment

Honest indignation is always a little infectious, and Mr. Clewes looked back into his mind, toward the image of the girl in question, with a flushed brow. And then, suddenly, he remembered that the viewpoint of Pritchard and his own outlook might not be the same.

Mr. Pritchard, in the meantime, expanded upon his inmost thoughts with a swift and dynamic tongue.

"I'll tell you how it is, old-timer," said he. "I want to do the right thing. You know what you've always meant to me — why, you was like a son to me, kid, when we first met — "

"I know," said Eddie Clewes. "Those good old days when you first showed me how to pick a pocket and work sleight of hand — and the little arts of blowing a safe — "

Mr. Pritchard closed his eyes with the sad, sweet memory.

"Ah, kid," said he, "in those days, when I seen the real talent that was in you, I used to tell myself that my working days was soon to be over, because when you began to get going, you would open up the Bank of England and ask me to help myself. Because it looked like nothing would be past you! And then — "

"And here we are, down to considering half-million dollar lots!" murmured Mr. Clewes.

Dandy Dick opened his eyes more fully.

"Now about this fool talk of going straight — now lemme ask you if you ain't ashamed for having turned loose such talk as that, kid?"

"Perhaps," nodded Clewes.

"And something is sticking in your craw — the girl, eh? Or else, Eddie, it's because you want to close the door on this here job and close me out of it; and after I fade, then you'll turn the trick by yourself and not have to make even the measly split that you planned to do with me!"

Again Eddie Clewes nodded.

"I thought of that, too," he admitted.

"You did! Why, damn me, but you're kidding! You're gunna get murdered one day for that kidding habit of yours, Eddie. But you tell me straight, now — you're gunna go through with the deal?"

"Otherwise, you go to the sheriff and tell him that I'm Eddie Clewes, the confidence man, that has just broken away from Cliff

170

Matthews. And 'Boots' Askew puts me in jail. That's your game, isn't it?"

"That's my game," growled Mr. Pritchard. "You know me, kid. Soft as a woman to a bird that plays straight with me, but harder than steel when it comes to taking a double cross."

"I know you," said Eddie Clewes. "And now I want to be alone. Trot along, Dandy, and if you let anyone see you coming to this house or leaving it, I'll take a bad job out of the hands of the law and kill you, you hear me?"

Dandy Dick leaned back in his chair again, nodding with something like sympathy toward the younger man.

"I remember how I was taken, about the same way, when I got my first case on a girl. She was a snappy blonde that done a turn on the Small Time. She had me faded. And I walked around in a haze for a couple of months, taking her all the profits that I made on every deal that I pulled off in all that time. And then she handed me over to an elbow when she got tired of me! Love is that way, Eddie. You think that you're walking straight toward heaven, and then you wake up bumping your head against jail bars. Love is a sort of a dope. So I don't hold you responsible for what you're saying and doing."

"You've settled it, Dandy. I'm in love, am I?"

"You are, kid. You're deep as any that I ever seen. No, you ain't noisy about it, and you ain't gay, and you ain't foolish on the surface. But love is like booze. It affects fellows different ways. Mostly, it makes a man cut loose with a lot of high stepping and wild talking, and noise, and such. But the worst booze-hound that I ever knew was a bo that used to stand up and drink by himself at one end of the bar, and never say a word to nobody, and keep his eyes turned down, and keeping getting paler and paler, but inside of him he was filling with hell-fire. And finally, he *would* look up. And then he'd start for the door, and before the morning came, you could be sure that there would be a first class horror-crime for the papers to write about. And it's the same way with you, kid. You deceive yourself because you're so quiet, and all that. But there's a lot of misery piling up in you all of the time, and pretty soon it'll bust loose and swamp you! You take my word for it. This pretty girl, the colonel's daughter, will make you wish that you'd handled fire sooner than the thought of her."

Dandy Dick, having finished this speech, gathered up his hat from the floor and lighted another cigarette. And then he leaned a hand

172

upon the table and looked firmly into the face of his former pupil.

"What's the result, kid?" said he.

There was no answer. The eyes of Eddie Clewes were far away.

"You go to jail by yourself, or you get rich with me. Which will you choose?"

"Jail without you is a temptation," said Eddie Clewes coldly. "However — I suppose that I'll sell out. Except that I want you to understand that there's nothing in this 'love' idea of yours. I never heard such sappy talk!"

"Didn't you?" grinned Dandy Dick. "All right. I'll lay off that line. But when does the job come?"

"When do you suggest?"

"As soon as you get the lay of the land at the bank."

"The bank? What do you know about that?"

"Nearly everything, old boy. This whole town here is watching you close, and they know that the colonel is taking you into the bank with him. He's given you the keys to his house. And then how long will it take before he gives you the keys to the bank?"

"You want me to clean him out entirely?" smiled Mr. Clewes.

"Why not? You think that he's gunna keep right on loving you after you slide away with his jewels? No, kid. And the best thing to do is to clean him out so complete that he'll have a sort of an awe and a respect for you. A little crime gets you into the jail. A big one gets you into the newspapers. The bird that kills only one poor sap, he's sure to get strung up. But the guy that runs amok and drops a dozen or so, he's made a hero of, and the reporters worship him and all the little boys wish that they could grow up to be terrible and grand like that! Same way with you. Smash the colonel as flat as a pancake and he'll know that he had his dealings with a real man!"

This advice he delivered in a soothing tone, with inviting gestures, and a smile like a light to show his great inner wisdom.

"Keep your profession out of your Bible," advised Eddie Clewes. "Sometimes you give me the creeps, Dandy. You've killed your dozen and more, and still you're not in the newspapers, except a police report now and then. When they get on your trail, though, what a lot of bones are going to be turned up!"

"They can't hang me more than once," said Dandy Dick, shrugging his shoulders. "But now tell me what's up?"

"You think that I ought to wait until I have the colonel right inside my rope?"

"Of course, if you ain't a fool."

Eddie shook his head.

"You wouldn't understand," he declared, "and so I won't try to give you any reasons, but I'll just have to tell you that I'm not cleaning out the bank. Only his private safe, old fellow. I stick at that."

"Nothing budge you?"

"Nothing!"

Mr. Pritchard sighed.

"Then clean the safe out tonight — the cleaner and the sooner the quicker. Clean it out and make the get-away. I'll have two horses ready in an hour, out there beyond the trees. Two real horses, kid, that will take us kiting through the hills, and away to good luck as long as we live!"

"Not tonight," declared Mr. Clewes with finality.

"And why the hell not?"

"Because you've made me curious, old fellow. You're so positive that you've made me very curious. And now I'll never rest happy until I've found out whether or not I'm really in love with the colonel's daughter."

"You don't even know your own mind?"

"Not a bit."

"Then don't get curious. Let the wasps sleep. Grab the stuff and come away, lad."

"I might," nodded Mr. Clewes. "I'll try to see her on the balcony in a few minutes, and then I'll have a talk with her. I ought to be able to decide then if she's what's the matter with me."

"You want to wait till you find out, and when you learn that I'm right, then you won't have the nerve to leave, and you'll start thinking about wedding rings, Eddie — "

"Do you think that I'd stay on after I knew that I loved her?" asked Eddie Clewes.

"Why not?"

"You wouldn't understand that, either, so I won't explain. Now I'm tired to death of you, Dandy. Slide out of here. Get the horses, and bring them over there behind the trees, as you suggest. The great probability is that I'll be out there to join you, in a couple of hours, and if I do, we want to be ready to cut loose. So long, Dandy!"

Dandy Dick, at the window, paused to give a little more advice, but he changed his mind again and slouched suddenly away into the night beyond, lowering himself over the outer balcony with the agility of an ape. For the strength in his arms was proverbial through the whole underworld.

Eddie Clewes, however, watching him depart was not particularly eased, except that he felt it was now more possible for him to concentrate upon the problem before him. As for the technicalities and the moral questions, he could not spare any energy for them. All that was of importance was to find out whether or no he really was deeply entangled with Dolly Exeter as Dandy Dick himself had so confidently suggested.

From the window, he watched Dandy glide like a beast across the garden and reach the trees, then he turned away. And consequently he had not the slightest idea that Dandy, having reached the trees, had doubled back again and was approaching the house from a different angle. In two minutes, he was crouching again beneath the balcony!

CHAPTER TWENTY
Unknown Under the Balcony

All the evils which philosophy had attributed to money, Dandy Dick Pritchard laid to the levity of woman. That was the reason he had cast about to find some source of feminine influence through which to explain the unaccountable behavior of that ordinarily level-headed young man, Eddie Clewes. And when he learned that Eddie Clewes now insisted upon a final interview with the girl, all his fears for the future of their plans were awakened. He determined straightway to overhear as much of that interview as possible, and for that reason he had stopped his arguments and had consented to leave the room.

Now, crouching beneath the balcony, he waited for the first telltale sound above him.

The balcony extended across the side of the house, and the climbing vines which twisted their strong brown stems around its pillars spread above into long green arms which wound, on wires and trellises, toward the eaves above, and even spilled across them, washing a scattering green spray up the roof of the house. So that the balcony and its railing composed a pleasant arbor, all overstarred with blossoms. Their color was gone, now, but their fragrance was all the richer. Even Dandy Dick Pritchard, kneeling on the garden sod beneath, breathed of it and felt a little of the grimness of his humor depart from him.

At the same time, a step crunched ever so lightly on the balcony above him. Dandy Dick at once put to use the apelike power of his arms and swung himself as silently as a shadow, hand over hand, up the first post of the veranda, until he reached the broad arms which curved out from it, holding up the roof. In that position he came to rest, one leg hooked through the fork of the beams, and one leg dangling free. Swayed out as he was from the perpendicular, it would have been more than another man could have endured for five minutes. But Dandy Dick held himself tirelessly in place.

For he guessed that, if his old pupil wished to talk with the girl, this was the time for him to be at it!

In fact, he had not waited there for half a minute when there was a little creak as of a door opening, and a dim shaft of light passed out into the darkness just above the head of Pritchard.

He heard Eddie Clewes saying, "I hoped that you'd come out."

"I saw you wandering up and down and wondered what was wrong," answered the voice of a girl, "because you look romantic, Ned, straying around this way, with the wind in your hair — *very* Byronic!"

"You're comforting in spite of what you say," he told her. "Sit down here."

"It's too chilly for sitting."

"I'll get you a wrap."

"Something has been in my mind about you for the last few hours."

"Tell me, then."

"When you were a youngster, Ned, according to your report, you did nothing but break windows and steal apples, and such. What else?"

"Nothing very much besides!"

"You must have, though."

"And why?"

"You've picked up an education."

"A shoddy one."

"But you know books, I mean — and the things in books."

"Why, perhaps a few. I've read a little."

"But if you were so busy getting into scrapes, when did you find time?"

180

"I just filled in the nooks and the corners, and that was all. But about my real education — I can't tell you, I'm afraid."

"That sounds mysterious."

"It's more mysterious than you guess."

"Something that no one can ever know?"

"Except my wife-to-be."

A little silence fell between them.

"It is a serious thing, then."

"Yes," said Eddie Clewes, "and there's no one to whom I'd rather talk about it than to you, Dolly."

She made another pause before she said, thoughtfully: "I think that I ought to let that remark slip. I shouldn't ask you to explain it."

"Why shouldn't you?"

"Very well, then, tell me what you mean."

"I'm glad to. I mean, Dolly, that I'd like to regard you as the girl who'll marry me, one day."

"That's a very small new moon, yonder, but you don't need a great deal of moonshine, I see, in order to be romantic."

"I have learned the art of becoming serious since I reached Culloden," answered the voice of Eddie Clewes. "But, if you wish, we'll suppose that I have been only joking. Does it embarrass you?"

"I'll tell you the truth," said Dolly, "which is that I'm never quite sure about you. Because most of the time it seems to me that you're the last man in the world to lose his head about anyone."

"Do you think that I was very steady this morning?"

She was silent.

"Before I go on, I want to tell you more about myself," said Eddie Clewes. "But the fact is that I'm a bit giddy tonight. And though there isn't much moonshine, as you say, it's addling my wits and confusing you with these flowers around us, Dolly, and the sweetness of them — and in another minute I shall be talking about stars, and such rot. You see, Dolly, that there isn't much question about it. I've lost my head, and lost it permanently, I'm afraid."

Now, almost any other person in the world would have held that the quiet and almost matter-of-fact tone in which Eddie Clewes made these remarks indicated that he was not more than a quarter in earnest, but Dandy Dick had known him through long years, and he detected a most vital ring of sincerity that made him scowl. If Clewes had wished to remain until he knew whether or not he was in love with the girl, this single glimpse of her seemed to have decided him. And even Pritchard, soul of steel that he was, was tempted to lift his face above the edge of the

182

rail and steal a look at her. But he controlled that impulse, for he was one who threw away no chances.

"*Are* you serious?" asked Dolly Exeter with a suddenly changed voice.

"I am."

"Then I think — " she began, and paused.

Mr. Pritchard waited for Eddie to speak, but he waited in vain.

"I think," went on the girl, more unsteadily, "that the best thing will be for all three of us to sit around in a circle, and talk things over."

It seemed to Dandy Dick a complete surrender, and he expected rather tensely an ardent outburst from his ex-pupil. But in some things Mr. Clewes forever failed to come up to the expectations of his old tutor, and now he answered gravely: "Of course that would be the best way. Because the colonel should hear what I have to say to him about myself, before I talk to either of you again."

"I have an idea, Ned," she said, "that you're going to tell some unpleasant things about yourself. Have I guessed right?"

"You have," he answered. "I am going to make a full confession of things that will probably sink the colonel's friendship in deep water. Now I suppose that I should let you go to bed!"

"Good night, Ned."

"Good night."

Mr. Pritchard could hardly believe that the matter had ended in this fashion. Was there to be *no* concession to romance? No panting voices? No echoes of poetry? No, there was not one, except that, as the door creaked again, the footfall of Dolly Exeter paused.

"After all," she said, "if Dad is flurried a bit — you have to remember that he's not the final judge in this!"

And the door closed!

Another moment, and Pritchard heard the soft whistling of his former pupil, as the latter strolled up and down the balcony with a hardly distinguishable, catlike step.

No, nothing in the world could be farther from Romeo and Juliet, and yet Mr. Pritchard felt that he had overheard a love scene just as convincing and just as decisive as more famous and more wordy ones — some of his own included! There was no doubt about anything. Eddie Clewes was in love. And by that last speech of Dolly Exeter, she had confessed her love for Eddie as clearly as though she had promised in definite words to marry him.

CHAPTER TWENTY-ONE
One of the Chosen

What became of the celebrated jewels of Exeter, then?

Why, they remained safe and snug in the safe of the colonel, for why should Eddie Clewes rob a house which contained a treasure that he would eventually inherit?

When these ideas had been firmly lodged in the mind of Mr. Pritchard — and they flashed home to him instantly — he lowered himself softly to the ground and sneaked away behind the same trees through which Eddie Clewes had watched him disappear earlier in the evening.

Then he went to the livery stable.

He had chosen his horse long before. It was a big dapple with black points, and it had a depth of chest that promised a true heart and plenty of staying powers, even though it might not have speed. Strength and patience were what Pritchard, with his bulk, wanted in a horse. He would leave speed to men of less bulk, and they could mount such an animal as he had picked out from the lot for Eddie Clewes, at the time when he had sincerely hoped that the younger man would be his partner in crime and in flight. It was a leggy bay, with a head like a deer, and Mr. Pritchard looked upon it with an eye of longing. He hired the gray for the whole night, and then rode it back to the shelter of the trees which looked out upon the house and the garden of the colonel.

He had consumed a half hour in this, and as he looked at his watch, squinting at the dial by the dim moon, he estimated that it would be necessary to wait for another hour, at least, before making his attempt on the house.

Dandy Dick was impatient as a man could be, but he knew the times when he should control his desires, and this was one of them. So he steeled himself, and sat down in the mellow gloom beneath a tree and watched the dial of the watch, with the second hand ticking round its little circle, and the minute hand crawling behind with imperceptible motion, and the hour hand with less movement, it seemed, than a fixed star.

Every ticking second might take a life or give a life, thought Dandy Dick. And every minute might be an ample frame inside of which to construct the picture of a great conception — such as this one of his for the looting of the colonel's safe! And every hour could contain such a conception carried into execution, and finished, or ruined, with the executor dead or escaped past pursuit.

Something whispered through the trees, and Mr. Pritchard slowly raised and turned his leonine head, not with fear but with keenest attention. The big dapple had lifted its head, also, with pricking ears; but then, its animal wits piercing the mystery before the man's, it lowered its head once more and went on cropping the rich grass which grew there. Dew was beginning to form on it. It was icy-cold, luscious beyond telling, to the dapple, and the bit clinked softly against its teeth as it ate greedily.

Apparently that whisper was only the wind in the trees. So Dandy Dick turned his attention back to the watch which he held in his hand.

Only five minutes had passed!

He recalled the happy night when he had gained this watch. There had been a moon in the sky, no larger than this and in the same quarter, but not, like this one, washing a naked sky with its light. Instead, it sailed upward like a boat, cleaving a path through piled clouds which puffed away into vast masses of bow-spray, and then rolled off into the eternal

187

darkness of the outer spaces of the heavens.

Such a moon had ruled the world on that other night, and there had been a winding road that twisted down a hillside and into a clump of trees in the hollow at its foot, where a pool left by the afternoon's rain gleamed like a dim dark diamond through the shadow.

And when the man for whom Pritchard waited approached, he was singing a soft song between his teeth — half singing and half humming. Pritchard had waited until he was past and then used a slungshot. He was fond of a slungshot. And more than once he had heard bone crunch and felt it spring away beneath the shock of that little weapon.

He had struck just a little harder than he intended, and the man was dead. But Pritchard had not been greatly bothered. It gave him more time to go through the pockets of the deceased. His disappointment was intense. Instead of the well-filled wallet upon which he had so carefully planned, there was only a scattering of small change to be had. And you may be sure that, no matter how scattering and small, Pritchard had it! That bit of money and this fine Swiss watch were his prizes.

It had seemed to Pritchard, at the time, a beggarly small prize. Now he felt that it had certainly not been time wasted, and he looked down upon the little timepiece with a certain awe. Just as a pagan might have looked to the oracle which had regulated many of his actions. So it was with the watch. He knew what great events had been measured and molded according to the seconds which it spelled out. None other could know, saving he!

For two hours and a half, by the never failing hand of this watch, he had worked in the basement of the Rochester Bank, drilling at the safe with his electric drill. For six terrible hours, by this same regulator of his fortunes, he had sat at roulette and gathered a great fortune, and tossed it back again. And again, in five sweet minutes, as related by the same reliable watch, he had entered a certain Brooklyn house by night and taken from a bedroom a string of pearls which had afterward paid for a frolicsome journey around half of the world!

Full of these thoughts, the time passed for Mr. Pritchard. And as he looked at the little watch and thought of his greatness, he felt a sort of melancholy pity that others in the world should not have brains great, like his, for huge conceptions, and strong, like his, to persist in their careers of lonely glory. He was troubled with a sense of vague regret. Something should really be done to tell humanity what it was missing.

And then he laughed softly to himself!

Because, after all, the world cannot well be

peopled with tigers. There must be sheep and silly lambs, that the creatures of tooth and claw may have a prey. He who created this world, how wisely he planned and made it, electing for some the great rôle of conqueror and destroyer, and for the rest, the parts of slaves, laborers, nameless creatures.

Once, happening into an old museum filled with Egyptian relics, Mr. Pritchard had run his eyes over the translations of various inscriptions, in which the monarchs related, one after another, how they had gone forth to battle, and made the Ethiopians or the Asiatics as dust under the wheels of their chariots, and how they had gathered them after the battle like sheaves after the reaper, and how they had struck off hands and ears, to mark them, and how they had brought them by tens and by hundreds and by thousands and by tens of thousands to show them to their people, and to set them cruel labors all the days of their lives for the glory of their conquerors!

Mr. Pritchard had read, and he had understood, as brother understands brother! And his very bowels yearned with envy of those lucky men of another day. All that Mr. Pritchard needed was an ampler field and a little more in the way of tools for the performance of similar glories. For he was one of the chosen!

Dandy Dick, raising his head again, looked up past the dark and slowly moving plumes of the trees to the quiet stars of the sky, and beyond them he comprehended the universal spirit, the transcendent mind!

He was at rest!

When he looked at the watch again, behold, the hour had elapsed, and Dandy Dick arose and looked to his guns.

He carried two, always. The first was a good, long-barreled Colt of forty-five caliber, which shot almost as true and as far as a rifle, and the spat of whose heavy slug would knock down a strong man like the blow of a fist. He had also, for quick work and at close quarters, a little snub-nosed weapon which looked like an abbreviated toy. But in the handle of that toy were seven cartridges, and one brief pressure upon the trigger launched the whole seven in a closely compacted spray of death. It was a neat little gun, and Mr. Pritchard had a special affection for it. Particularly, in a crowded room!

Then he took off his shoes, and, tying them together, he draped them over the pommel of the saddle. That done, he arranged the reins of the horse, tying them to a branch, in a slip-knot, so that they could be freed with the slightest pull. After that, he regarded intently his means for flight.

There were two courses open to him. One was to break down toward the river and then to wind along its banks. The other was to canter straight across the open fields and jump the fence beyond to the higher valley road.

He decided that if he were pressed he would head for the river. But if he had plenty of time, he would go for the higher road, because he could make far better mileage along it.

Next, as he advanced toward the house, he examined the way across the garden, because, when he returned, he might be running in his stocking feet, and aiming to make the best possible time.

It took the great Mr. Pritchard a full half hour to complete all the necessary investigations, and if you ask why he did not make these surveys before, it may be answered that this was because Dandy Dick always left the last calculations until the last minute, because he was a freehanded genius, a sort of inspired improviser, so to speak.

In the meantime, he reached the side of the house and, as he laid his grasp upon the veranda pillar, he gave mute thanks for his stocking feet. For his own part, he would have been very happy if the tyrant fashion had permitted men to go always with bare feet.

That was the style of the Egyptian kings, and see what results they had obtained!

So he worked his way softly, softly, up the pillar, until he reached the edge of the balcony railing. There he paused, crouched low, his heart trembling, for he remembered that, great as Dandy Dick was, he was about to move against a greater than himself!

CHAPTER TWENTY-TWO

In the Dark

When he raised his head above the railing, all was mild darkness along the row of opened windows and doors which gave upon the balcony; but, though that blackness surely meant a great deal, so far as the rooms of the members of the family were concerned, it might mean nothing at all for young Eddie Clewes.

Going back over his own actions of the evening and the words which he had used to Eddie, he found that he had much to regret. And certainly he had said enough to put Clewes on his guard. On the other hand, he felt that two great forces worked to dull all suspicion in the mind of the great Eddie.

The first was that, for his old teacher, the confidence man felt nothing but contempt, which he rarely cared to so much as casually veil. The second was that Eddie had certainly fallen in love, and love, as Mr. Pritchard knew, was a great stupefier.

"Almost like beer," said Dandy Dick in his philosophical moments.

Now the secret fear of Mr. Pritchard was that, when he entered that darkened chamber of his disciple, he would be walking upon a dreadful danger — Eddie Clewes lying in the dark with his eyes opened and his ears listening. What Eddie could do, unarmed as he was, was not the point. Mr. Pritchard did not analyze. He only knew that, as Eddie himself had said, there was nothing in the whole world which he feared with such thoroughgoing intensity as his young scholar.

The corresponding secret hope of Mr. Pritchard was that Eddie, excited, delirious with happiness after his interview with the girl, would have completely forgotten the ring of keys which the colonel had given to him earlier in the day.

From the balcony and through the door went Mr. Pritchard.

There he paused like a great squat spider, its claws upon the nerve-threads of the web. So did Mr. Pritchard pause, and, with his raw soul open to every whisper of sound, every hint of movement, he probed the blackness before him.

The glimmer of the stars and the radiance of the moon at length no longer left their images in his eyes, and he could see what was before him with as much distinctness as he could hope.

There was the bed, a faint outline against the wall. Yonder was a chair, here a table, here another chair, and there the closet door, its polished knob shining with the single ray of a star like an infinitely distant eye.

Mr. Pritchard gripped his Colt, but he changed his mind. For yonder wild devil of a boy, he would not trust the slow action of a Colt. He took the automatic.

And then he remembered that an automatic will jam.

With nerves that prickled up and down his spine, he sneaked to the closet door, opened it a fraction of an inch at a time, and felt for the coat that was hanging inside.

He found it at once. His huge hand became more delicate in touch than the fingers of a great musician. So he explored the pockets and almost instantly he reached the thing that he wanted — the ring of keys!

In the keen relief of that discovery, he leaned for a moment against the jamb of the door, breathing heavily, for he could realize, now, on how small a chance he had been depending. It was a ten-thousand-to-one shot that Eddie Clewes would be guilty of a carelessness so criminal as this! And yet here was the thing accomplished! Another catastrophe that could be attributed to the malign influence of love!

The confidence of Mr. Pritchard increased enormously, after this first success.

To be sure, Eddie Clewes was drugged with love and sleep, at the present time, and his regular breathing, from the bed in the room, could be distinguished; but when Eddie wakened and learned what had happened, that would be a different matter. Oh, very different indeed!

And Mr. Pritchard had no intention of being trailed across the country by this sinister young smiling man!

He changed his mind, therefore, and crept with tigerish caution toward the bed. He would not use the gun. Guns might fail, and besides, the noise of the explosion would spoil everything that remained to be done. Instead, there was the slungshot.

A quick flexion of his hand threw it down from the rubber band that held it close to his wrist. He held it with the tip of his thumb against his flattened fingers, a small weight to do such great things as it had accomplished in the past. Now he planned, with one blow, to crush the intellectual forehead of Eddie Clewes.

But as he came closer and closer, he could eventually see the silhouette of the sleeper quite clearly, and it happened that Eddie lay upon his side, with his face turned straight toward the advancing enemy!

A small thing, surely, to stop such a person as Dandy Dick Pritchard, but then, he knew more about Eddie Clewes than has been related. And when he was sure that the face of the sleeper was turned toward him, it seemed certain to him that Eddie had not been sleeping any of the time, but that he had been lying there wide awake, listening, and smiling to himself.

That was typical of Eddie, to smile and nod his head, with secret knowledge of which Mr. Pritchard could not even conceive. There was a mysterious invincibility about that young man, and now a flood of fear poured out upon Dandy Dick and made him shrink away toward the door of the room as fast as he could go.

He knew that the knob turned softly, because he had tried it before, earlier in the evening. Yet he spent a whole quarter of an hour of sweating anguish opening that door without a sound.

Eventually he was in the hall, beyond, but even there he hardly dared permit himself to breathe. For behind there was stalking the image of Clewes slipping from bed, picking up a weapon, and walking with the silent step which Pritchard had so often admired, so often striven to imitate, and always in vain!

He shook this phantasm out of his brain and was about to turn down the hall when he heard the crash and the thrill of an electric bell ringing through the house —

It seemed to him that every soul in the place must instantly be on their feet, shouting, "Burglars!"

Certainly it was an alarm which had entrapped him.

He waited, his shoulders flattened against the wall, murder in his hand and in his heart. The bell rang again, and now with less tension he could understand. It was the telephone ringing in the lower hall and who would go to answer it? Why, young Eddie Clewes, of course, anxious to be of service to this new family into which the scoundrel was insinuating himself! Eddie Clewes, of course, awakened by his hair-trigger nerves the instant that the bell rang!

Mr. Pritchard glided down the stairs to the lower hall. He thought of attempting to get on down to the cellar where the safe was kept, but he hesitated as he heard a door open above him. That meant that his time might be very short for investigating the safe with any security. And there were all of those keys to be tried in the lock!

So thought Pritchard, and he slipped into the dark mouth of the next doorway and shook his fist at the clangor of the telephone, which was ringing for the third time.

A light snapped on in the upper hall and crossed the lower floor with bars of shadow from the railings of the stairway, and a moving shadow floated swiftly down across those bars and turned, a white-robed figure, into the hallway.

It was Dolly Exeter, first in all that sleepy house to waken. And Pritchard wondered again, and heaved a sigh of relief. If it were she, so much the better — so infinitely much the better!

She was at the telephone, now, while he shrank deeper into the shadows of his doorway and listened.

"Hello! Hello! . . . Well, Oliver, at such a *late* hour! . . . Oh, yes, I've forgiven you, of course. I was rude to you, and I'm sorry — but just now I'm shivering here in my nightgown. It's dreadfully c-c-cold! Of course I forgive you. Is that all?"

The telephone's snarling, metallic murmur answered through a long moment.

"You want to talk to the colonel? So late — so very late? . . . Well — of course — if you really have to; but you know, when his sleep is once broken, it's gone for the entire night, he's so high-strung."

Another pause, and another murmur of the phone.

"Very well," she answered. Then, in the act of turning away, she whirled suddenly back. "It's about Ned! You've found out something about Ned!"

She waited, her ear pressed hard against the receiver.

"Ah, well, I'm glad of that! You promise? Yes. Good night, Oliver. It isn't about Ned, then? Good night, good night. I'll call Father at once! . . . No, not a bit. . . . Yes, you *must* come. I haven't any bad feeling about it. I'm only ashamed that I was so rude to you, I should have known that you wouldn't do anything except what your best conscience told you to do! Good night again!"

She placed the telephone carefully on the stand, and then turned away, and into the arms and the coat which Mr. Pritchard held in waiting for her.

She had no chance for movement or sound.

One long apelike arm had crushed the breath from her body, and the folds of the coat closed at the same time across her face.

That accomplished, all that Mr. Pritchard had to do was to wait until the struggling inside that coat ceased, and he minded the kickings and the beatings of the hands no more than rock minds the flurrying wings of a moth.

When she struggled no more, he carried her back into the dining room, which was the nearest door, and laid his ear to her heart. It was still beating, and he rather regretted it. It made him take more time, and time was precious to Mr. Pritchard, just now.

CHAPTER TWENTY-THREE
Luck with Him

Strong men or weak women were all one to Dandy Dick, when they came in the way of his projects. He bound and gagged the unconscious girl with enough thoroughness to have held a giant helpless. Then he stepped out into the hall again, in his stocking feet.

Yonder was the phone still waiting, and Dandy Dick grew nervous at the sight of it.

If he let it hang down, with no answer, Mr. Portman was fairly sure to grow suspicious, and if he grew suspicious, being such an old friend to this family, would he not instantly decide to start for the house? And if he lived in one of the near-by places, which was most likely, might he not arrive before Dandy Dick's work was completed?

So Pritchard took up the receiver.

There was one vast difference. The colonel's voice was rather light and high; his own was abnormally rough and deep. So he pitched his tone high in the scale and said:

"Hello; hello, Oliver!"

"Are you there, Colonel?" answered the voice of Portman. "I'm sorry to get you out of bed at this hour."

"That's nothing," said Pritchard.

"Hello! Hello!" said Oliver Portman hurriedly. "Is this the colonel?"

"Yes," said Pritchard, growing more uneasy.

"I can't recognize your voice," said Portman.

"That's a cold that I caught this evening," said Pritchard.

There was a little pause, during which the beat of Dandy Dick's heart quickened.

"Very well," said Portman. "What I want to tell you is that I've been in telegraphic communication with the town in Maryland which formerly was called Compton, and I've learned such things about Larned that you ought to know them at once, because the valuables in your house, sir, are in danger as long as he's under your roof!"

"Hey?" exclaimed Dandy Dick. "Go on, Portman!"

He should have said "Oliver" and he bit his lip with vexation.

"My informant," went on Portman, "could tell me all about Larned, and it seems that Larned is not his name at all, but Clewes. Edward Clewes. Does that name mean anything to you?"

"No," grumbled Dandy Dick.

"Then I'll tell you something about him. He's called Eddie Clewes and he's well-known as a confidence man. He was recently arrested by a Sheriff Matthews, but he escaped from the jail cleverly, and got out of the county and disappeared. Hello Colonel. Do you hear me?"

"I hear you," said Dandy Dick.

"I can't place your voice at all," said Portman with some irritation.

"The phone's not clear, maybe," said Dandy Dick, carefully pitching his voice up the scale again.

There was another silence, and then:

"I advise you to send for Sheriff Askew at once. Or shall I pick him up and bring him to the house?"

Dandy Dick was on pins and needles.

"It ain't necessary," he said finally. "Because I'll handle this here job — "

"The devil!" muttered the voice of Oliver Portman. "Who is speaking?"

Exactly what was wrong, Dandy Dick did not know, but he guessed that his last speech had not been in quite the language which the colonel might have used. He held the receiver, shifting his weight from one foot to the other.

"Hello! Hello! Hello!" Portman was calling. "This is very queer! I want the colonel!

Who has been speaking to me in his name? Hello!"

He was fairly shouting across the wire, and Dandy Dick cast a troubled glance over his shoulder. Then he let the receiver fall to the length of its cord and turned hastily down the hall.

The mischief was done now. In another moment, Oliver Portman would come plunging through the night to investigate the mysterious answer which he had just received. And perhaps all of the good work of Pritchard would be undone in a moment!

But he had no thought for a moment of giving up his task without another firm attempt at pushing it through.

He knew where the safe stood in the basement room. So down he went, with the dim, round eye of his electric torch picking out the cellar steps for him. He stepped down into an atmosphere of damp and gloom, and there he found that the door to the room which he wanted was firmly locked.

It doubled the task before him!

There were more than thirty keys on that ring.

He went through the entire list of them, but not one had turned the lock!

The sweat of anxiety was pouring down the face of Pritchard.

He began again, remembering the old proverb, that more haste makes less speed, and now he tried each key firmly and strongly in the lock. The fifth fitted, the lock turned with a little groan, freeing itself from the rust that bound it, and the door opened with a lurch.

With more than a lurch, too! For, forced in by the haste of Pritchard, its old hinges screeched so loudly that it seemed to Dandy Dick like a set of hoarse trumpets blown on purpose to alarm the house.

Not that the rest of the house really mattered, except for one man in it. And at the thought that Eddie Clewes might have heard this noise, he turned his head, with lips snarling back like the lips of a dog, and shook his fist up the passageway in token of defiance.

Then he shot the ray from the torch ahead of him, and it centered at once upon the black-painted steel front of the safe itself.

Instantly Pritchard was on his knees before it and working at the keys with trembling hands.

There was no need for the larger keys, now. It was only the smaller ones which could be possible, but there were more than enough of these!

He had used six or seven of them before luck came, and the lock turned, and the safe door opened. Instantly the clutches of Pritchard were in the drawers with which the old safe was lined.

He jerked them open, from top to bottom. Luck was with him again. For the third one, deeper than all of the rest, held the jewel casket. He drew it out with a gasp of joy and opened the lid. The light of the electric torch was thrown back to him, reflected in a thousand points of green and yellow and crimson fire, and moonlight pearls, and diamonds like liquid points of flame.

He turned the casket on its end, and sluiced the contents into the little canvas bag which he had prepared for the purpose, but one great sparkler, an unset stone, clicked on the floor and rolled away toward a corner.

He cast the ray of the torch frantically after it. But it was not in sight at the first glimpse.

He would not wait to look longer, not if that one diamond had a price equal to all the rest combined. The strain was telling heavily on Dandy Dick. The automatic was in his hand as he stepped back into the passage. At the same time, he heard above him the soft sigh of air drawn in as when a door is pushed open suddenly, and then soft, soft steps came down through the darkness.

The heart of Dandy Dick stood still.

There was no other human being in the

world, he was assured, that would go to investigate such an affair in the black darkness. No human being other than Eddie Clewes! And Pritchard crouched back against the wall, and there squatted, low down, waiting breathlessly.

That soft step went by him, paused — then continued into the room where the safe stood. As for Pritchard, he had risen at once, and now he began to steal up the stairs, thanking God for this good fortune. He reached the top of the flight before he heard the scratching of a match beneath.

But he waited to see and to hear no more. Before him was the hallway. He hurried down it, leaped through an open window to the garden beneath, and then raced for the thicket and the horse he had left in it.

So utterly shaken was the nerve of Dandy Dick, that when he reached the spot where he had tied the horse, his heart leaped with thankfulness to find the big dapple still there. He was in the saddle at once, and his mind made up. The river road might be a trifle safer, but it was far too slow for him in his present mood. He wanted to put long miles between him and the house of Colonel Exeter, and the faster he could consume those miles, the better!

At the same time, he saw a horseman race down the upper valley road at a speed which the dapple, he was sure, could never equal. He saw that horseman turn in toward the house of Exeter. Then Pritchard gave the gray the rein and galloped across the field.

When they came to the fence, the big horse took it in fine style, and now they swung down the road at a smart clip — not too fast, because Pritchard guessed that he might have before him a very long and a very hard trail.

But he felt that this matter had ended almost too luckily for him. There must still be some sort of disaster waiting for him around the corner. It was the experience of Pritchard that great things cannot be brought to pass like simple ones. Only a huge effort brings a huge return. Unless, indeed, his reward were given to him because he had had the courage to stand up to Eddie Clewes and take his chance of what might happen in the fight!

The town of Culloden lay before him. He carefully took the narrow lane that curved around it upon the right hand, and, following this, he hoped that he would be able to escape all observation.

Troubling news had already reached the town, however, he could make sure. For, as he passed, he heard a noise of shouts, and then a rapid trampling of horses that disappeared up the valley, in the direction of the house of the colonel.

CHAPTER TWENTY-FOUR
The Iron Trail Once More

It is well known that a mother can sleep through all the roar of a city's traffic, but at the first whisper from her baby she will be awake and on her feet. And a soldier in action can be sound asleep among the roaring of guns, and yet a whisper from his mate on the gun crew will rouse him.

So it was with Eddie Clewes. For the clangor of the telephone, though it penetrated quite clearly to his room, did not disturb his slumber for an instant. But when a little later, there was a creaking of hinges far down in the house, a noise that came so faintly to the upper rooms that Dolly, lying gagged and trembling in the dining room, was the only other person who heard a hint of the sound, Eddie Clewes was instantly awake and sitting up in his bed.

For this was the sort of noise to which he was accustomed to attach some significance. And it drove straight through the guards which kept him unconscious, and brought him up, listening as keenly as though he had been awake by broad daylight for an hour.

There was no other sound to follow on the heels of the first groan of hinges. He settled back for an instant against his pillow and told himself that he was a fool for keeping such hair-trigger nerves. And he slipped his hand beneath his pillow, merely to make sure that the bunch of keys was there for security.

The sweep of his hand touched no metal, and Eddie Clewes was instantly out of his bed, for he could remember, now, that he had taken no precaution whatever about that bundle of keys — even though the light-fingered Mr. Pritchard knew that it was in his possession.

So he gritted his teeth and leaped for the closet and his coat.

One pat of his hand was all that he needed to tell him of the worst. Then he stepped into his clothes faster than a fireman answering an alarm. He was reasonably sure that he was much too late, or he should not have waited even for this. But then down the stairs he went with that same silent, catlike stride which big Pritchard had so often envied and had so often labored in vain to imitate.

He went straight for the cellar room in which the safe was, and there, as Pritchard had seen, he scratched a match and the flame of it was blown out by a draft before he could see. He scratched another, and this one showed him what had happened. That deep drawer, which now lay on the floor, had once been filled with the jewel casket which lay beside it, its lid open, and its interior vacant.

Something like a little eye of light winked at him from a corner, and he spared a glance for it. It was a diamond of great size and beauty. He saw that much, and somehow the presence of this abandoned treasure showed him the greatness of the haul which Pritchard must just have made.

Other things loomed swiftly in his mind. That safe had been opened by a key, and the keys had been given into his keeping. There was no use remaining to protest innocence. His place was surely on the road trailing Pritchard.

And yet his disappearance would look exactly like the flight of a thief! It would seem so to the colonel. It would seem so to Dolly Exeter, as though he had weighed his love for her against this opportunity of stealing half the wealth of the family, and had chosen the latter way!

He did not give himself time to grow sick at heart. Neither did he become bewildered by this crushing stroke and all of the consequences which it was sure to bring upon him, but he stood for a moment with his hand on the door knob, his head thrown back, his eyes closed, and on his lips that little, mirthless smile which Pritchard hated and dreaded more than all things in the world.

The Jew. That was his first goal. To reach the Jew before Pritchard could get to the famous fence!

When he reached the floor above, there was a rushing of hoofs up the road outside, and then a thundering hand against the front door.

What other thing could be wrong, tonight, he wondered.

And then, from the floor above, he heard the kind and cheerful voice of the colonel calling: "Hello, Ned, my boy. Will you go down and see what's up below? There's someone at the door, and I don't want to get rheumatism in my hip again — Hello, Ned! Are you there?"

And his hand tapped again at the door of Eddie Clewes.

Now the cheer and the kindness of that voice came very near to unnerving Clewes. And he was on the verge of rushing up the stairs to confront the colonel, flood his ears with the tale of what had happened, protest his innocence, and then to disappear.

214

But even the courage of Eddie Clewes was hardly sufficient for such a crisis as this, and as the loud hand beat at the front door again, he went back, issued from the kitchen entrance, and turned away into the night.

He did not have to ask where to go.

The railroad was his charger, to take him to his goal, sooner or later, and he swung away across country as straight as a die for the nearest line.

It took him two hours of hard work to get there. His wind was gone, and he was trembling with weakness from his exertions. But he had not wasted his time, because he had not crouched on his heels for five minutes when the distant headlight glittered down the tracks, and then the rumble of the approaching train poured at him with a growing voice. It did not matter in which direction the train went, because in either eastern or western journeys it was certain to pass through the underworld of crime and criminals.

He saw the headlight of the train reeling with speed, but, striking this steep grade, it slackened rapidly and slowed under the strain until the driving wheels were shuddering and groaning against the steel tracks.

Still it was hurtling along at a swift rate; enough, indeed, to have made another man dizzy. But Eddie Clewes had been too long a knight of the Iron Trail not to know exactly what he could do and what he could not do.

As soon as the flaming, crashing engine was past, he turned and sprinted at his full speed along the cinders. There was fair footing for him, here, and he made the most of it. The suction of the air around the driving of the train drew him along faster and faster, and, as car after car jerked past him, but with diminishing speed, he turned his head and threw a glance behind him.

He could see the observation platform in the rear, with its attendant cloud of dust flapping behind it in the moonlight. Surely there would be no occupants upon it, at this time of the morning. So he gathered his strength, set his teeth, and, swinging sideways, he leaped straight at the shooting bulk.

That is the expert's method. Your clumsy amateur tries with a single foot and hand, sidewise. If he misses, he slides under the hurtling cars and the next day he has become: "Unknown Man Found Dead." But Eddie Clewes, driving with feet and hands closely bunched, struck at the observation platform, and, though one hand and one foot missed, the others got a grip that held him safely.

He swung back hard along the railing with the impetus of his flying weight and the speed of the train pulling against it. For an instant he thought that his grip would fail, as his fingers trembled and threatened to open. But then he righted himself. And now he was holding firmly, easily, and wondering how it happened that the sane, normal men on that platform had not been able to see him jump. For even at this hour, there were two of them studying the stars and smoking their cigars.

The arms of Eddie Clewes were growing tired. And so he worked his way up the side of the platform until he had reached a point at which he could venture to try to climb it. Yet it was hard work and most dangerous work, for there was hardly more than the heads of rivets to cling to!

Up the side, then, he went, and he was already reaching the curve which turned toward the roof, when he heard the whistle for a tunnel, and looking ahead of him, he saw the round black mouth waiting like a throat.

Eddie Clewes clung as he could. Even if his strength had been fresh, it might have been an ordeal, but as it was, his arms were already shaky and his fingers more than half numbed. Yet he held to his place and waited and thought of only one thing — that he must not give up till he was beaten.

They struck the still air in the tunnel; it was as though a strong hand had beaten against his side. A vast roaring rushed against his ears.

But blackness and confusion, and the lung-choking masses of oil smoke that blew back to him could not break his spirit.

They lurched in the darkness around a curve that brought him to the trembling verge of falling. And he made sure, twice, that his utterly numbed finger tips were slipping. But still he clung as a cat clings. Then the open stars began once more to dash across the sky. Sweet, fresh air filled his lungs and gave him power to pull himself up to the roof of the car.

There he lay sprawled on his face, realizing that he was on the Iron Trail again and with a vengeance.

CHAPTER TWENTY-FIVE
Reading Signs

He dropped off at a water tank the next morning because he saw under it a small group of the people he most wanted to see — denizens of that same underworld which draws into pools in the great cities, and which is otherwise spread out and streaked across the continent in dwindling lines which follow the railroads, only dripping aside from them now and then.

There were four in this group, and as Eddie Clewes nodded to them and then fell to work brushing the dust from his clothes, he marked them down in his mind. Two bindle stiffs well past middle age, and dyed in the wool. A young boy of fifteen or sixteen, asleep in the shadow of one of the iron poles which supported the tank. And another, somewhat like himself, who might be a tramp royal — one of those superior beings who use their wits in the place of a roll of bedding and a pack filled with food and cooking utensils.

He drew aside and, taking out the little

pocket kit which always was with him, he made his toilet, and shaved with deftness and incredible speed. The others paid no attention to him, continuing their talk of odds and ends, while Eddie Clewes drew up his belt a notch and examined the sign on the posts of the tank.

Stray wolves and traveling bears leave token of themselves at calling posts here and there; and stray tramps will do the same. It is a habit of which they can never break themselves. For the chances are that each man of the underworld belongs or has belonged to some coterie, large or small. And these, when they come across his marks, will understand the hieroglyphics.

Many a compressed letter is told by this means, and many a message sent to eyes which are friendly. The trouble is that some eyes which are *not* friendly will be sure to read and understand bits here and there. And more than one officer of the law gives up his life to the study of these signs, mastering by the dozens the signal codes which are used along the Iron Trail. There are many signs plain enough for the most untutored eye to follow, however. And now Eddie Clewes saw an arrow in red chalk pointing west and under it: " 'Missouri Slim,' with luck to his pals!" And again, a free-hand sketch of a man walking and carrying a pack was labeled to indicate that "Dago Charlie" had passed this way — recently, by the freshness of the chalk marks. There were scores of other tokens, as blatantly open and staring as these. But Eddie Clewes gave little heed to them. He was interested in a smaller writing.

And here and there, on the under surface of the iron crossbeams, or openly on the pillars themselves, or on the concrete foundations into which they were sunk, he saw little cramped groups of hieroglyphics, done with red ink or blue, with pencil, or with crayon; or, most often of all, indelibly scratched into the iron with the point of a knife, until the next coat of paint, given to the water tank and its supports, should cover all the mass of this literature, never to be brought to light again!

Many a curious hour had Eddie Clewes worked over these systems of writing, and he knew that, beneath the complicated exterior, there was often a great simplicity in the hidden codes. And yet, so compact were they and so crowded with meaning, that it was usually a keen pleasure to make out their significance.

He saw, for instance, a K, then the figure four and a half, followed by a direction check, in front of a little circle, with radiating spokes, like a child's picture of a wheel, and beneath these items was a letter N followed by a brief wavy line, and at the end a tiny sketch of an open hand.

It might have puzzled a Solomon unless he had had long experience in the reading of these tokens. But Mr. Clewes had that necessary learning, and he deciphered the message with the greatest ease. The K obviously stood for "Kid." The hieroglyphic of the "wheel" was meant to be a representation of the sun. The N must be held to stand for New York, city or State, and the wavy line indicated in dreadfully real symbolism, Salt Creek. While the open hand at the end was the age-old symbol which forever means: "Help wanted!"

Even with these clews supplied it might be difficult for the uninitiated to understand the little sketch in faded red ink, but Eddie Clewes instantly translated to himself as follows:

"Four and a half months after the beginning of the year, that is to say, about the middle of May, I, the San Francisco Kid, heading west, stopped at this place. I am flying from the result of a crime committed in New York, and if I am followed and caught, it means the electric chair for me. Help me, friend, if you possibly can!"

All of this was included in that minute sketch, smaller than half of a thumb nail. And others were crowded around it. A surface no larger than a single sheet of letter paper was compacted with a hundred or a hundred and fifty of these minute messages. Not that Eddie Clewes could read them all with the same fluency with which he had been able to interpret the message of the lad from the City of the Setting Sun — San Francisco. But as he ran his eye through the lot of them, he was quickly able to see those items which might be of direct interest to him. And it was for news of the Jew that he was casting about.

That vagrant receiver of stolen goods, wanted as he was in a dozen cities on account of as many convictions, wandered through the country keeping strictly to the underworld, and usually venturing onto the Iron Trail only when it was absolutely necessary. Then, always with a prize in his clutches, he turned and fled back to one of his many coverts. The money which he had made was believed to be almost past computation. And still he would not retire from his dangerous life. He loved it for its own sake, and clung to it desperately.

And the Jew was somewhere in this region, probably, waiting for the chance that should put the jewels of Exeter into the hands of Dandy Dick. The desire for a prize so great would have led an ordinary man to wait in the immediate vicinity of Culloden. But the Jew was not such. He kept to a safe distance until the prize was ready for him. And then, like a falcon out of the heart of the sky, he swooped upon his quarry, seized it, and was gone again to dispose of it. The jewels of Exeter, in due course, would be brought by him to some dealer in precious stones, from whom the Jew would extract the ultimate top price, and then, with his profits sent to join his already overswollen bank accounts, he would go back to one of his coverts and wait for the intimation of the next prize.

Yet it was necessary for him, from time to time, to distribute little tokens of his presence here and there about the country, so that the initiated, who were very few in number, could tell where to find him and take their goods to him. Dandy Dick, fresh from conference with the man of money, would know exactly where to find him. It was the task of Eddie Clewes to pick up signs by the way. And in an instant more he had found the hieroglyphic of the Jew himself, a little intricate scroll, like a loosely written "t" passing through a narrow loop, and beneath that signature was the message that the Jew was bound for Omaha — but alas, that message had been written in the first month of the year and it could have nothing to do with the whereabouts of the great "fence" at this season. And yet it was an immense satisfaction to Eddie Clewes to know that his quarry had actually come this way, and had crouched here by this pillar, and worked at the inscription with his long, bony fingers, and then squatted cross-legged, after his Oriental habit, and turned his skinny, yellow-brown face toward the parched desert. Months might have passed since that moment, but it gave Clewes a sense of security.

He sat down with a smile which he could not restrain, and one of the bindle stiffs, looking at him askance, murmured: "You got your orders all right, then?"

"I got my orders," said Eddie Clewes. "Who belongs to the kid?"

"He's flying it alone."

Eddie Clewes picked up a small pebble and tossed it accurately upon the pale forehead of the boy. He sat up instantly and broke into a torrent of curses, his half-smoked cigarette, which all during his sleep had been adhering to the corner of his mouth, wabbling up and down like paper floating in a high wind.

"Who pulled the joke?" he snarled. "Who done that dirty trick?"

He scanned the group with a malevolence truly animal. He stood up and inflated his narrow chest, and his eyes glittered.

"Because I don't see nobody here that I take nothing from!" he declared.

Confused and smoky rage blurred his senses. He jerked out a murderous little automatic and waved its muzzle toward the group. The three of them shrank from him, but Eddie Clewes merely smoked his cigarette thoughtfully. And that calmness infuriated the youngster more than ever.

"It was you!" he snarled suddenly at Eddie.

"It was I," said Eddie Clewes.

"You admit it, eh? Why, you — "

He had not time to pour out his curses at full ease. For Eddie Clewes raised a gentle hand.

"Sit down and forget your troubles," he said. "New York has stopped talking about you days and days ago. And I'm not going to tell the flatties where they can pick you up."

The effect of this brief speech was wonderful. It deflated the viciousness of the boy at a stroke. He glanced a little wildly about him, guiltily at the three who watched and listened to him, and then in terror and wonder at Eddie Clewes.

"You was there!" he breathed. "Oh, you was there!"

Mr. Clewes finished his cigarette and snapped it into the distance. He exhaled the last cloud of smoke.

"We had better step over there and have a talk," said Eddie Clewes.

The automatic disappeared, and the mur-derousness slipped from the eyes of the youngster and left the blank of terror there. Meekly he followed the older man to the far-ther side of the shadow of the tank.

"Now," said Eddie, "my first bit of advice to you is to learn how to smile and forget how to curse. And my second bit of advice to you is never to pull a gun without using it. And never to use it unless you have to."

"Say," said the boy, a little awed, and very frightened still, "d'you mean that I should of *shot* you — once I had the gun out?"

"Yes," said Eddie without hesitation, "be-cause that would have kept you from a bad habit. But remember this: We're west of the Rockies, and people who use guns for bluffing purposes out here, die young. That's all of that. Now tell me what you've been doing and who you've seen on the road, since the big day."

CHAPTER TWENTY-SIX

Into the Arms of the Law

The boy, who had lost more confidence with every moment, was now in a state of complete surrender.

"The big day?" he echoed feebly.

"Your one big day," said Eddie Clewes. "I suppose the police call it a rather large-sized day, too."

The youngster looked at Eddie Clewes wistfully, for the wisdom of the ages seemed to be seated upon the calm brow of the confidence man.

"Say," he remarked at last, "would you tell a fellow who you are?"

"You've had enough good advice from me," said Eddie. "I think you can call me a friend."

And he smiled faintly on the other.

"Ah!" sighed the boy, "don't I wish that you was!" And he added, half curious and half sad: "I dunno how you got all the dope on me, though. Is it spread all over?"

"Some of us know," said Eddie Clewes, "because we get word when something big has been done."

Again the eyes of his companion opened. But the memory of the things he had done and been through suddenly drowned his wonder at the information which this chance acquaintance seemed to have concerning him.

"They nearly had me in Pittsburgh, that night," he said.

"You had your luck that time," nodded Eddie.

"Didn't I though?" chuckled the boy. "If I hadn't been watching when I turned that corner — but I'm always watching. They ain't going to have me like a sleepy pig, y'understand? And when the finish comes, I'll have my teeth in some of 'em, too!"

He curled back his lip from yellow fangs, as though he meant the threat literally. There was much danger in this young man, as Eddie Clewes could see at once, but it was not the first time that he had ruled greater force than this by the power of wit and quiet self-control.

"The word I was to pass along to you," said he, "was particularly to have you mind that you don't show your teeth unless you have to. Haven't you been told that before?"

The sharpness of this schoolmaster tone did

not offend the youth. He merely shrank as under a whip.

"That's Talbot," sighed the boy. "Yes, he was always saying that! When I tackled the job you know what he was always saying: 'No guns, kid! No guns!' But how could I help it? You know how the cards went against me!"

Eddie Clewes nodded.

"That's something that's happened. Forget about it. What's to come is the important thing now." He was more interested every moment. Because he guessed that he knew this same Talbot that had been named — big, florid, jolly, and deep as the sea, he had engineered some of the cleverest jewel thefts on record. And Clewes could imagine at once that if Talbot had had a hand in the matter, then it was a jewel theft which had furnished the motive for the boy's "big day." So he went on: "But after this, you take the advice of 'Pinkie' Talbot. And remember that, on the big day, if you had really kept your head, you wouldn't have had to use guns!"

"You know Pinkie?" asked the boy, throwing down his last reserve. "Then you know everything. Tell me, where is Pinkie now? I was to meet him out here. I dunno why I couldn't of met him in Brooklyn as well!" He shaded his eyes and squinted across the sands, blazing with the sun of the morning. And he

230

shuddered, as though these great open spaces were a torture to a soul reared in back alleys. "But here I am, and still I ain't found Pinkie. Where is he? Lord, how I want to find him!" he concluded, almost with a sob.

"Look here," said Eddie Clewes, almost in a tone of reprimand. "You know that Pinkie has his reasons for what he does? He had a reason, too, for coming out here!"

And he listened eagerly. That reason was one that he already half guessed, but he was feverishly hungry for confirmation.

"Why, it was the fence, of course," said the boy. "Because Pinkie said that there was only a few fences in the country big enough to handle that much of the stuff. But the point is, here I am waiting for my split! And where's Pinkie? Where's Pinkie?"

It was the guess and the wish of Eddie Clewes come true. Pinkie Talbot, then, was in this part of the country to meet a fence of rare importance. And considering that the matter was jewels and the size of the transaction was great, was it not likely that the fence in question was none other than the famous Jew? It all seemed to Clewes to dovetail together.

But how much more could he draw from this lad?

"Well," said Clewes, "you've asked, I suppose?"

"All up the line. Everywhere! I've described Pinkie, and questioned bums and everybody about him, but never had no luck at all."

He seemed close to tears again — tears of fear, and disappointment, and weariness, and savage anger.

"I went up to Denver, just the way that Pinkie told me to. And then I headed south for here. He spotted this on the map. I know this is the right place. But how can I wait for him here? What's there to do — excepting go crazy, looking at that desert! And I'd head for El Paso, because if he ain't in Denver he must be down that way. But how would I know that I wasn't passing him on the trip — and how — "

His voice trailed away, and his lips trembled.

Mr. Clewes broke off the conversation. He had learned about all that he hoped to gain from this young murderer and jewel thief — this poor tool in the hands of smug Pinkie Talbot, who had pocketed the proceeds of the bloody work and gone off to find the Jew, or one of the Jew's ilk! But though the boy might not dare to leave the water tower which had been chosen as a trysting place, Mr. Clewes dared to leave it. And half an hour later he was winging west on a heavily laden freight.

He took the trail for El Paso and rushed

down it with only two stops. The first was in a "jungle" outside a small town, and there he found three tramps "boiling up," but, he got no information from them. The second stop was a quite involuntary one, impelled by a furious brakie, who tried to brain Mr. Clewes with a heavy signal lantern. So he left that train the first time it slowed down and saw another vagrant dismount at the same time, with much expedition. They crouched in the brush and watched the train hurtle by. Then they brushed dirt and cinders from their clothes, and exchanged opinions of the brakeman on that train.

"What's your game?" asked Clewes.

"What's yours?"

"Looking for an old pal of mine — Pinkie Talbot."

"I dunno that I ever heard that moniker, but I been coming up and down this line for a month on a little job. What's he like?"

"Big, and pink around the gills. That's where he got the moniker of Pinkie."

"Kind of a dude?"

"That's it."

"I saw a bo that had that look this afternoon, docked in a jungle fifty miles back. He was playing a harmonica."

"That's good old Pinkie! What was the lay of that land?"

"You can't miss it. There's a town in a hollow, with two valleys pointed at it out of the north. I remember thinking: Suppose that a flood was to come down those valleys! Well that's it! This side of the town is the jungle. Big and comfortable. And handy to the chicken yards. They're surely great on chickens in that town, and the dogs aren't so very bad, either!"

These friendly items had hardly been communicated before Mr. Clewes was listening to the thrumming vibration in the rails, announcing the coming of another train. And as it slowed for the bend on that staggering upgrade, he caught it — a flying engine dragging a crashing, roaring procession of empties.

Lost in that Niagara of sound, Eddie Clewes was rushed away for the town of the two valleys, and in little more than an hour he had sighted it from the top of the caboose. The freight took a siding at the town, and there Clewes dismounted and stepped straight into the arms of a robust gentleman in a blue coat with brass buttons down the front of it and a stout truncheon swinging on his hand.

"Clewes!" he shouted, and gripping that young man by the collar he tried for his head with a crushing blow with his club.

It might have been the end of Eddie Clewes, if that blow had landed. But he ducked neatly below the stroke, and the policeman found himself standing awkwardly, holding an empty coat, while the fugitive streaked off into the mass of freight cars in the little railroad yard.

A .45 caliber bullet bored the air above the head of Eddie Clewes as he dodged behind the end of the first car. And then the policeman and the half-dozen onlookers plunged into pursuit, with the man of the law shouting: "It's Clewes — him that robbed Colonel Exeter of Culloden."

Others joined them, rushing among the freight cars. But Eddie Clewes, seeing the coast clear, crawled out from beneath the first refrigerator car around which he had fled, and, picking up the coat which the policeman had dropped, he crossed behind the station house, unobserved, and sauntered straight down the main street of the town.

He felt very much at home, and invigorated by this little encounter, and he stepped into a tobacco shop to buy cigarettes.

"Have you heard the news?" bubbled the clerk. "It just came over the telephone to me! They've caught Eddie Clewes, the great crook, down in the yards!"

"That's a good thing," said Eddie. "How did they do it?"

" 'Buck' Jones, the cop, knocked him down

with a bullet. Fired twice over his head to warn him to stop, and then punched a slug through him. Buck is a great fighter!"

"He is!" agreed Eddie Clewes. "And I'll tell you what. If there were more cops like Buck, the crooks would go out of business!"

He leaned by the door a moment and lighted his smoke. It was a bright, warm afternoon. And the stir of the town drifted dreamily to the ears of Eddie Clewes — the tapping of hammers, and the jolting of a loaded cart, and the chorus of voices, and even the barking of a far-off dog, all united in a drowsy humming that increased the content of Eddie Clewes. And he felt that it was a kind world, and a good world.

"That Clewes must be a bad one," he said over his shoulder.

"Bad? He's a wicked devil!" said the clerk with feeling. "Why, the way he double crossed Colonel Exeter — "

"Rotten!" said Eddie Clewes, and he stepped leisurely forth up the street.

CHAPTER TWENTY-SEVEN
Pinkie Turns Up

A creek, twisting around the shoulder of a hill, left a sandy stretch strewn with big boulders and girded with trees and sheltering underbrush, an ideal spot for a jungle. And Eddie Clewes, working his way to the edge of it, found Pinkie Talbot and two unshaven tramps in the midst of it, making busy preparations for a meal around a battered wash boiler from which issued the steam of a fragrant mulligan. Patient as a cat at a mouse hole, Mr. Clewes waited and watched. For he was amused, quietly, to observe Pinkie Talbot trying to be democratic with the pair of hobos. He looked like an elderly and somewhat debauched king's son in the slums, or a millionaire trying to masquerade as a worker.

But presently he picked up a tin and started for the creek to get water, and the moment he entered the trees, Eddie Clewes was behind him, admiring the plump breadth of those shoulders and the strength which he knew them to contain, for Pinkie Talbot, soft as he looked, was a proved man. He admired, too, a little lump that showed against the coat tail of Talbot just over his right hip.

And now one of those talents which had been developed in him by the old tuition of Dandy Dick Pritchard was brought into use. And never more expertly! It is one thing to pick a pocket in the midst of a jostling crowd, but to perform the act with a solitary man as victim in the watchful silence of the western forest was quite another. It needed softness of step — and not a stone stirred under the catfoot of Clewes, and not a twig crackled. It needed the sleight of hand of a conjurer. And that skill was his possession. So he took the lump from the pocket of Pinkie Talbot and now he stepped behind a tree carrying the heavy automatic which he had taken from the jewel thief.

He watched Talbot fill his tin at the brink of the stream, straighten and admire the sunset colors which were forming on some western clouds, and then turn to go back to the camp, and at that moment Clewes stepped from behind his tree.

"It's Eddie!" gasped Talbot and twitched his right hand back to his hip pocket.

He brought it forth again — empty — and the plump face sagged into lines of stricken grief and fear. His weapon was no longer visible in the hand of Clewes, but Talbot did not have to ask questions about where it had disappeared.

He forced an expression of cordial cheerfulness and stretched out the hand which had just been fumbling for a weapon.

"Hello, Eddie," said he. "But I might have known that we'd drift together when — "

"Wait a minute," said Clewes. "We'll have our talk Chinese fashion."

Talbot halted, perplexed.

"What's that?" he asked.

"Walking in single file. And you lead the way — down the side of the creek, old fellow."

Talbot hesitated an instant.

"What's up, Eddie?" he asked in a shaken voice.

"No trouble — I hope!" said Clewes. "But I like to be sure of privacy!"

Mr. Talbot turned with a sigh and led the way down the bank of the creek.

And as he went he said: "I've got news that you'll want to know, Eddie."

"Thanks."

"But before I tell you — why, perhaps we can have an understanding?"

"Perhaps we can," said Clewes. "This is something that you'll have to take a chance on, though. Tell me the news if you wish, but I won't drive a bargain."

Talbot sighed again.

"You drive a hard bargain, Eddie," said he. "Well, what I have to tell you is that a young bull of a fighting man by name of Archie McKenzie has swung up in this direction looking for your trail. He's left horses and taken to the railroad. I thought that you'd be glad to know!"

"I am," admitted Eddie Clewes. "Is that all?"

"Except the reward that Exeter has posted."

"Well? I haven't heard that."

"Twenty-five thousand. That's a good bit, eh?"

Clewes whistled through his teeth. For twenty-five thousand there was hardly a man in the underworld that would not gladly sell his soul. And every step that Eddie Clewes took thereafter would be in the utmost peril, unless he could avoid human beings. And who that travels the Iron Trail can avoid other men?

"We stop here," he said.

They had entered the cool dimness of a little grove on the banks of the creek. And Talbot faced around on him.

"Now, Eddie," he asked nervously, "what's the great mystery? After the Exeter job, you're fixed, of course. But if it's cash that you want I can fix you for the sake of old friendship."

"Not cash, but information, to begin with."

"I've told you all that I know, old man. I'm not holding out on you. Unless you want to read what's in this paper — that has the full account of your job, and may give you some pointers that you'd like to know."

"Thanks," said Clewes. "just throw it on the ground, because I like to keep my hands free — for conversation!"

Talbot bit his lip and tossed to the ground the rumpled newspaper which he had taken from his pocket.

"What else?" he asked.

"Where's the Jew?" asked Clewes gently.

Talbot did not blink. Never had he showed a readier presence of mind than he did now.

"The Jew's in Santone," said he.

"What address?"

"Two hundred and twelve Rushforth Avenue."

"A good lie," smiled Clewes, "but not good enough — "

"Look here, Eddie — "

"It won't do, Talbot. It won't do at all. I partly know where the Jew is. But I want the facts in small print as well as headlines. I've got to make sure of reaching him."

"As sure as — " began Talbot loudly.

241

But Clewes shook his head and smiled again.

"Besides," he said, "you shouldn't have told it so easily. A man fights for news like that — about the Jew. And if you had fought for time, I might have believed you — if I hadn't known beforehand nearly the exact truth."

He changed his tone just a trifle and stepped a bit closer.

"Now I'll have the exact facts, Talbot. I'm on this trail to win."

"Lay off, Eddie," breathed Talbot. "I was only stringing you a little. As you say, you can't expect me to bring out the straight dope about a guy like the Jew at the first crack. Fact is that he's not in Santone but down in El Paso, and — "

Now Eddie Clewes knew that there are times when a man must leap in the dark, and he felt that this was probably one of them. It might very well be that Talbot was telling the truth now.

But on the other hand, he knew something of the hidden talents behind that pink-cheeked face. And he decided that probabilities leaned a little toward the side of a second lie.

So he interrupted that glib speech by dropping a significant hand into the side pocket of his coat.

242

"Pinkie," he said sternly, "it's your last chance!"

"All right, all right!" groaned the jewel thief. "I knuckle under. Blast you for the most knowing kid in the game! The Jew's in a little dump called Almadera."

"Go on."

"I'm telling you what I know — confound you, Eddie! He's on the edge of the town, somewhere. A shack with a brick chimney. That's all that I know. I've been floating around waiting to get word, and this was the last news that came. I was about to string out for the town. I suppose that you want him to handle your stuff, Eddie! And there you are!"

Even this might be a lie, but Clewes felt that he could go no farther.

"Now put your hands out in front of you, old-timer," said he.

"Hey, Eddie, Eddie! Is it rough stuff, after you've pumped me? No, Eddie, you're too white for that!"

"I'm not going to kill you," said Eddie Clewes. "Put out your hands — and jump to it!"

Talbot, literally, jumped to it. And he stood with his arms rigid before him, while Eddie Clewes, one threatening hand still buried in his coat pocket, with his left

243

wreathed a stout cord expertly around the wrists of the other, and then drew the cord snugly tight.

"That will be about all for the present," said Clewes. "But before I left, I had to delay you a little, old fellow, to keep you from crowding in word to the Jew before I got to him. Of course you want him for yourself!"

"For myself? Well, I've got a little stuff planted that I wanted him to handle. But the Exeter stuff will fill him up."

"Not him. He has pockets too deep for us to cram. But about that last big deal of yours back in New York — that was poor stuff, Talbot!"

"What deal?" asked Talbot, a glitter in his eyes.

"You know what I mean. The kid and the killings."

It seemed to freeze Talbot so stiff he stood for a moment. And then he burst out with: "Who hitched me to — " He recovered himself and went on: "I don't know what you're talking about, Eddie!"

"Of course you don't! Until you stop to think. I mean, Talbot, that it's well enough to get another fellow to do the dirty work. But he ought to be of age! Eh!"

"Lord," cried Talbot, "I've no idea what you're driving at!"

244

"Haven't you? I'm not arguing. I simply tell you that it's low, Pinkie. I know your jobs; they've always been clever, and you've usually worked out of cover. But this is pretty bad. Murder, Pinkie, ought to be left for the fools. And you don't belong in that class! And when you let a skinny kid do your killings and collect the stuff, and then leave him flat, waiting for you when you never intend to turn up — you might as well have tied his hands and turned him over to the hangman, or delivered him postmarked: Salt Creek!"

He had poured forth in this speech about all that he had been able to infer from the remarks of the youngster whom he had met at the water tank. But Talbot had heard enough, and he muttered:

"I'll tell you, Eddie, I was the worst staggered man in the world when I heard the news. I didn't expect any killings. I warned the fool kid! I told him beforehand that there wasn't to be any blood. I hate blood, Eddie, as much as you do!"

"You took a rattlesnake," said Clewes, "and you told it not to bite? Was that square?"

"How could I expect that he would lose his head, though, with an old man, like that, and a twelve-year old kid who — "

"Twelve years!" breathed Eddie Clewes,

and then he gritted through his teeth: "You dog, Pinkie! You hound! Now be quick and back up against that tree!"

"Eddie, what're you — "

"Shut up and keep still!"

Mr. Talbot backed against the tree without another word, but with his eyes staring and a white face, and Eddie Clewes tied him, hand and foot, and gagged him securely.

After that was accomplished, he said grimly: "I intended to pump you, if I could, Talbot. But I didn't think that I'd have to do this. But it seems that you've turned loose a little murderous rat of a kid where he was tempted to kill, and he bumped off an old man and a little boy. All right, old man. This is where you pay — the first small install-ment."

He slipped his agile hand into the breast of the other and instantly drew out a wallet — and then a soft chamois bag.

There was a stifled groan from Talbot, and a writhing of his body, but Eddie Clewes stepped back and sneered at him.

"And after this — there'll still be more for you, Pinkie. But if it'll do you any good, I'll let you know that you're not making this pay-ment to *me!*"

CHAPTER TWENTY-EIGHT
A Race for Life

Whatever consolation might have been derived by Pinkie Talbot from this last remark was removed a moment later, no doubt, as young Eddie Clewes turned the chamois bag upside down and poured forth into his hand the few contents. There was not more than enough to fill the palm of his hand.

But what there was made even the cool nerves of Eddie Clewes jump. There was no jumble of colors. All were diamonds, and all were of a well-proportioned bigness. There were enough stones, here, to make the pendant part of a wonderful necklace.

The unimportant stones could easily be graded down at either end to complete the circle. But each gem, it seemed to his practiced eye, was of a perfect color. They were beautifully cut according to the most modern methods, which exhibited the full splendor of the light which was locked up in each of the diamonds. And Eddie Clewes, closing his hand over this little cold heap of wealth, said grimly to the bound man:

"And the collection of stuff like this, you turned over to a half-baked kid, that looked as steady and as trustworthy as a mad dog! And you expected him to keep his head when he saw *this* sort of loot?

"I don't know that I can make you feel any worse, Pinkie, but I can tell you now that I never had even heard about the robbery, until I pumped the kid for it. And then I pumped you until you confirmed it. So that you've acted like a fool, Pinkie, and I suppose that you won't believe me if I tell you I would never have touched your loot if I hadn't got out of you a confession that you had murdered for it. And even then, Pinkie, I would not have taken it if it had not been that it was a secondhand murdering, so that your own hide is safe, and a poor, half-witted little devil will have to swing for it, one of these days, or sit in the electric chair and have the current shot through him for your sake. So long, Pinkie. Perhaps I ought to tap you on the head and drop you in the creek, with stones in your pockets. But, as it is, the hobos will probably hunt for you tomorrow morning, and then you'll have your chance to get on my trail."

With this, he turned away and walked swiftly down the bank of the stream toward the town where men must still be hunting for him, and where every train would be watched.

He made a long detour and cut in toward the tracks in the dark, far on the other side of the village. Five miles up the Iron Trail he jogged until he reached a grade which would slow a heavily laden train enough to permit him to hook aboard it. And there he waited and watched two fast passengers roar past, too fast for him to take either of them. It was close to midnight before the slowness with which a train thundered up the grade warned him that his chance had come again. It was a loaded freight that picked up Eddie Clewes, and on it, he journeyed until the gray of the dawn. While the sun was rising, he was safely ensconced as blind baggage on a little jerk-water passenger train which did local duty on a rattling side trail and made the town of Almadera among its stops.

When the day was at its prime, he swung down to the ground on the off-side from the station, as the train pulled up for the stop. But though he had dropped to the ground on the safer side, there were people here, also, and they could not help noticing the dusty figure which landed beside the tracks and sprinted at breakneck speed to keep from losing its balance and toppling headlong. The attention of the watchers was drawn by the uncanny skill of this performance, which was unlucky for Eddie Clewes. And it was drawn next by a sudden whoop from a cowpuncher, who sat in his saddle on the off side of the train to watch it pull into the station. He had eyes accustomed to squinting across the mountain desert to scan the bearing of cattle just visible on the rough horizon. Consequently he was able to look through the dust that covered the slender form of this wanderer, and his shout rang clear and gay through the mountain air:

"It's Eddie Clewes! It's Eddie Clewes!"

And as the spurs drove into the side of his horse, he snatched out his Colt, and charged the fugitive.

That watching group did not need to have the name explained. They had been flooded with information concerning the appearance and the deeds of this same Clewes, confidence man, now jewel thief, and betrayer of his friends. And for the last reason, these Westerners looked upon him just as tenderly as they would have regarded a snake, crawling into their family circle. There was a wild answering yell from many throats. Other horsemen lurched into pursuit.

But he who had sighted the enemy first not only had the keenest eyes, but he had also the best and the quickest horse, and he was hopelessly away in the lead, with twenty-five thousand dollars lying, now, in the capable crook of his forefinger. And the trigger of a tried and trusty Colt resting in the same compass, also!

So he came, yelling with the savagery of a wild Indian, stooping low in the saddle, a tight grip on his mustang, his gun thrust far out before him, for he wanted to make this an aimed shot.

An aimed shot it was. But he rode a racing horse, and at the critical instant, the fleet-footed fugitive wavered to the side. He fired again, and flicked a heavy bullet through the hair of the head of Eddie Clewes. For the third shot there could be no missing.

Clewes had managed to stop his forward impetus by this time. But he did not attempt to turn about and flee; it was as though he realized that there was no hope of matching human fleetness of foot against that of a fine horse. He stood still, lightly, his weight on his toes, ready to dodge the last bullet, if it were humanly possible.

That third bullet never came, for at that critical instant — perhaps the excited rider had attempted to fire too rapidly — the weapon clogged.

The next leap of the mustang carried him past.

But it was a trained cutting horse, and he wheeled it, head down, feet planted in one spot, to try for the criminal again. He had dropped the gun that had failed him and torn out a second.

All this he accomplished in the split part of a second after his third pull on the trigger. And now he was wheeling his mustang back at Eddie Clewes, when a cyclone struck him.

It was Eddie Clewes, leaping forward to take advantage of this hair's-breadth opening! He had half a second, but that time enabled him to spring onto the back of the mustang.

The long Colt flashed in the air and its barrel clicked against the side of the cow-puncher's head. Down he dived from the saddle, landed on back and shoulders, and rolled in the dust. And Eddie Clewes was scooting down the track bent low over the neck of the horse.

There were three riders behind him, but from the first jump it was evident that they could not hold the pace. They began to pump lead. The air was punctuated with the crisp singing of little leaden angels of death, whisking past on eager wings, and then Eddie Clewes, remembering how he had escaped pursuit in his last adventure, turned his mount straight down the first open street of the town.

Three times he turned corners, the mustang taking them with all the practiced cunning of a tried cutting horse, and three times Eddie Clewes barely managed to keep his seat. But he heard the yelling of the pursuit dimmed a bit by distance, and so he sped from the little village into the rolling country beyond.

Behind him, as he took the first hill, he saw the three original riders streaking, but in the little dust cloud which they raised came half a dozen others doing their best, and some of them rolling closer and closer through the dust mist. And farther behind, other riders came snapping out from the town singly or in groups, as fast as they had been able to leap on the back of their horses and make off. Still others, he could be sure, were now flinging saddles upon their chosen mustangs, and they would fall in on the trail.

He bit his lip as he watched.

He knew something about horses, and he knew something about riding. But what was his skill compared with that of the trained range riders behind him?

There was only one thing that could save him — the fine little animal which was working beneath him.

He looked down to the narrow shoulders. He looked back to the sloping hips, and he felt that he was lost. But he looked forward to the high-held head and the pricking ears, and hope entered his heart again.

There was little that he could do. He gave the mustang a free rein. Heavy saddlebags weighted it upon either side. He cut them away. There was a bulky bedding roll behind the saddle. He cleared it off, also, and now the gallant animal flaunted across the miles and kept the pursuit in check.

If only he were not being herded into some blind alley!

He knew nothing about this country, except that a general map of it was roughly sketched in his memory; but that was a map such as one used on the Iron Trail, and on it were marked grades, and "jungles," and towns of all kinds. It was not the sort of map that took account of mountains. For, on the Iron Trail, from the Atlantic to the Pacific there is only one great plain with a few mild ascents and descents, here and there, just sufficient to enable an active man to swing aboard.

Now, however, he needed knowledge of a different kind, and he set his teeth and vowed that if he lived through this scrape he would accumulate information that would make him as much at home in the saddle as riding blind-baggage, or the rods.

As he dipped over the next ridge, a blinding

wind cut him in the face, and with it came a straight-volleyed spray of sand that stung and cut his skin like small razor edges. A norther had sprung up with its usual suddenness, and that wind, combing down the valley, had turned into a typical sand storm.

He looked down from the ridge at the pursuit.

It was streaming closer and closer every moment, and above all a rider on a tall black horse, with a rifle balanced across the pommel of his saddle. Others were working up almost as fast. But the black horse was running strongly in the lead.

And never did a frightened fugitive turn from light to darkness with more joy of heart than Eddie Clewes turned from the upland into the boiling midst of that sand storm.

CHAPTER TWENTY-NINE
The Elusive Jew

He faced straight into it for a solid hour, not attempting to ride; but walking ahead, bowed, straining into the wind, and leading the mustang behind him.

The wind increased. He could not force the poor beast to follow. So he stopped, tore a section from his shirt, and with it blindfolded the little brown speedster. After that, he could make it follow.

His own eyes were in a constant torment, and his face was turning raw, but still he would not give up that march into the wind, until he knew that he had put a pair of miles behind him. For his secret hope was that the posse, when they saw him disappear into the sand mist, would take it for granted that, once hidden from view, he would quickly drift down with the wind at his back.

That was not the view of Eddie Clewes, however, and after he had beaten his way against his fierce opposition, he turned straight to the side and struggled out of the dusty chasm of the valley.

The storm had increased in violence. The whole landscape was now misted over with the effects of it, and the sun looked an angry red through it. But still it was possible to endure through such weather as this, for all things were mild compared with the maelstrom which had raged in the valley.

He got into the saddle again and cantered the mustang on across the storm, depending on its instinct to turn it down with wind enough to bring it back just about at the town of Almadera.

For he felt reasonably certain that he would not be looked for at the point where the hunt of him had begun.

And, as he rode on, he felt more and more convinced that the sand storm and his use of it had beaten the pursuit. There were no horsemen in sight, in this weird land fog.

So he came back to Almadera, and sent the willing little mustang cantering around the outskirts of it. Somewhere on the borders of it, if wily Pinkie Talbot had been forced to tell him the truth, was the shack in which the Jew had taken refuge.

But the first complete circuit revealed no hovel with a brick chimney. He tried again, like a hunter cutting for sign, and this time in a wider circle. And so, as the sand mist lifted and thinned a little, and the sun turned from red to a bright, warm orange in color, he came upon the spot.

By the first look of it, he knew that Pinkie Talbot had told the truth, for it was just such a spot as that Jew would have chosen, according to what Clewes knew and had heard of him.

All was the direst poverty. There was the shack itself, and beside it there was a little shed and a lean-to. As for the stacks, there was no sign of hay, but only a blackened and moldering straw heap, leaning awry. Last year's provisions for the cattle!

It half sickened even the steel-hard heart of Eddie Clewes to note the misery of this place, surrounded by its tangle of broken fences, and littered about with the junk heap of long years of folly and carelessness.

But that was what the Jew would look for. Some miserable weak-spirited man whose very soul he could buy for a hundred-dollar bill, was sure to be the victim of that wily rascal. Here and there about the country he had picked out certain places of abode, and returned to them from time to time, varying the length of his visits and changing often; and though the police had trailed him to half a dozen of these places and extracted from the owners information about him, yet it seemed that by a mysterious power he always knew when a house had become dangerous to him, and he was never known to return to one of these baited traps.

But still he roamed from place to place, moving and living secretly, with no more apparent joy in life than a night-flying owl. For years he had continued, and for more years to come he would maintain his ways, and all the skill of the cleverest detectives, used upon him time and again, had never been able to lodge him in a jail, or to take so much as a photograph of his long, narrow, ugly face.

Even Eddie Clewes felt a touch of awe when he thought that he was probably about to encounter this genius of the underworld.

He drew closer.

Here was the single brick chimney, a badly made affair, apparently composed haphazard from the wrecked foundation of a house which had stood on this site before. But no smoke issued from it. All was still and lifeless, and when he noticed that there were no horses in the corral, he decided that the owner and perhaps the Jew also were probably away from the shack.

He left the mustang at a safe distance and made his approach on foot. Through a window he could make his observations, and he saw that the little house was indeed empty. So he went back to the horse, and, as the sand storm cleared, he made himself secure with the mustang in a little clump of trees and settled down to watch for the approach of the dwellers in the shack.

He had the newspaper which he had taken from Pinkie Talbot to help pass this leisure time, and he found it interesting enough to amuse him. And yet, though he made himself smile, there was a dourness in his heart that perhaps a close and clever observer could have detected at once. Let us say that Dandy Dick Pritchard would certainly have known, and trembled.

For the account opened with a flaring recital of the manner in which the rich jewels had been taken, in the middle of the night, and by means of a key which had been given to the thief by the foolishly trusting banker. And he read how he had brutally bound and gagged the daughter of the house when he found her about to call her betrayed father to the telephone over which, by a strange coincidence, Oliver Portman was striving to give a warning as to the true character of the guest in the house of his old friend.

He read, also, how Oliver Portman, in giving his evidence, declared that he could hardly believe that the voice which he had heard over the wire had been that of the famous Eddie Clewes, alias Ned Larned. He could not believe it, but as the reporter wisely remarked, the voice of a man who has just struggled with a woman, and tied and gagged her, is not apt to be as level and easy as usual. Besides, Mr. Portman had rarely heard Clewes speak. And if it were not Clewes who answered the telephone, then who *could* it have been?

No, the fact must be that Clewes had gone to his room that night confirmed in his purpose to use the keys which had just been given into his keeping, and when the darkness settled and the house was black and silent, he had set to work!

It was a Western paper, and a Western editor. And when the story of the crime was completed, there followed some sturdy moralizing on the nature of this crime, which as the editor said, was blacker than any murder which it had been his misfortune to print in the course of a long and varied experience in journalism. Never had there been a more complete betrayal of trust. And never had a criminal used more dastardly expedients. But above all, never, to his recollection, had a criminal played such high stakes so boldly and well — fifteen thousand dollars thrown away with one fine gesture, and this bait cast out in the mere hope, and by no means the certainty of a richer reward — and all the time working against time so close that, fast as he sped toward the accomplishment of his designs, justice in the person of Oliver Portman had almost outsped him and tripped up his heels at the last moment!

What it showed, according to the editor of that paper, was a mind as cold, as cunning, and as snaky as a new Machiavelli! And such he was, a type of all that was heartless and wicked!

There was more, much more. And last of all, a stirring recital of other crimes known to have been accomplished by Mr. Edward Clewes, and an account of many more of which he had *not* been guilty.

But Clewes, as he read, was more and more deeply conscious that the case was hopelessly black against him, and that the law and its agents would never, except by the aid of a miracle, be able to attach any suspicion to the person of the real criminal.

Somewhere across those mountains rode Dandy Dick Pritchard, without the slightest danger, except for what Eddie Clewes himself could contrive for him.

And that, perhaps, would be very little.

For, from the emptiness of the house, he foreboded that the Jew had already been visited by Dandy Dick, and with such a prize in his hands, he had not waited even for the coming of Pinkie Talbot, but had fled across the country to stow the treasure away!

CHAPTER THIRTY
Archie McKenzie on the Trail

For though trains had been swinging him steadily toward the Jew ever since he left the valley of Culloden, certainly it was very probable that Dandy Dick Pritchard might have winged away straight for the place where the famous "fence" was waiting.

What gave him hope, however, was simply the sense of the huge effort which he had made, and of the success which so far attended him. For it seemed as though some reward *must* be waiting for him.

The wind had fallen away, in the evening, to a mere ring. The sand was gone out of it. Only, now and again, as the breeze cuffed one of the trees in an unexpected direction, a rattle of sand like a shower of rain descended and sent fresh crystals of quartz sifting down the neck of Eddie Clewes.

He was very hungry and had twice drawn in his belt until it sawed him almost in two, but the sense of hunger pangs came to him only now and again, so great was his absorption in the landscape before him.

Then, as the sunset turned toward dusk, he saw three riders loom around the corner of a hill and sweep like three great shadows toward the little shack with the brick chimney. To the left was the bunched figure of the Jew, most unmistakably. The other two, by that light, he did not recognize.

He watched them put up their mounts in the shed. He saw them file into the house. Then a lamp glowed behind the window, and a pillar of thick white smoke rose from the chimney, toppled suddenly to the side, and crumbled away above the tops of the trees.

The ravishing fragrance of frying bacon was wafted forth to the nostrils of Eddie Clewes, but still he remained quiet until the dark was complete. And then when he moved, it was not toward the house!

Instead, he went to the little shed. With whispers he gentled the three smoking horses which he found there and carried away a heavy forkful of hay. He gave that hay to the stolen mustang which waited so patiently beside him in the covert. Then he returned and carried water until the thirst of the hardy little hero was quenched.

After that, he sat down and waited again, and when hunger rose in a besieging wave that made his brain dizzy with yearning, he ruled it away from him with a stern self-control. He had no time for such small torments as mere hunger!

Another half hour. Then, against the stars and the moon, he could see that the smoke which rose from the chimney was a mere wraith. This was the time, if ever in the day, when the three would sit about and stretch their feet toward the fire, and indulge in a few reminiscences and a little jovial talk. So he chose that moment for his approach.

When he reached the window — there was only a crack between the boards that replaced a glass pane, through which he could see — he discovered that all his work on this hard trail had been in vain. For yonder was the Jew, and facing him was the man whom Eddie Clewes had striven so valiantly to forestall — yonder was Dandy Dick himself!

It gave Clewes no sudden pang of hatred to see that burly form. He stared rather with a dull wonder to think that this man, whom he had known so well, should have been able to outwit him!

He turned his attention to the third member of the group. He was the silent one, never speaking except for a grunt when he was pointedly addressed. He was a huge man of twenty-two or twenty-three, with pale red hair, and blond, bushy eyebrows. Though Clewes had never seen him before, he knew him instantly by a most pronounced family likeness. It was young Archie McKenzie, beyond a doubt, and it sent a little shiver through Eddie Clewes to see this youth. Big Delehanty and Murdoch McKenzie had been fearful men of valor, to be sure, but they, were not like this younger Goliath. With his head bowed and a poker gripped in a monstrous hand, he thrust at the open fire in silence. He wore two long Colts, one at either hip. And it was not hard to make out that he carried holsters beneath his armpits. So at least two pairs of revolvers were ready to speak out for him, and in addition, he had a sawed-off rifle leaning against his chair. All in all, Eddie Clewes felt that this man was the grimmest figure of a man that he had ever encountered in all his days.

As for Dandy Dick, he was very much as usual, except that there was a continual brilliant light of triumph in his eyes, and Eddie Clewes needed no other witness to tell him that all things were going very well for Dandy Dick!

"The only thing that I regret about today," said Pritchard, "is that we wasn't able to get near enough for him to recognize us. Because if we had, and he'd seen me, he would near of died with misery and hating the world. I think that he would of turned around and charged us!"

"It was like fox hunting," said the Jew unexpectedly.

"Hey," broke in Pritchard, "what do you know about fox hunting?"

"I've ridden to the hounds in my day," said the Jew. "And I've ridden to the hounds in the galloping counties, too! And been in at the kill, my lads, behind the fastest hounds that ever followed a scent through the dew. However, this today was better. A man is really a better prize than the plume of a fox. And I thought for a time" — he turned his keen eye toward young McKenzie as he spoke — "that our friend Archie would win the race, when that big black horse of his started moving up through the crowd! He was overtaking Clewes with every jump, and if that lucky young devil hadn't struck a sand storm that was as good for him as a streak of dark night at midday — "

"He must of worked up against the wind," said Pritchard. "And if we'd left Archie alone, he would of done the same thing. It's a queer thing about you, Archie — you seem to know just how the brain of that hound will work!"

All of this subtle flattery, did not bring so much as a single touch of color to the face of

Archie McKenzie, or a single ray of light into his eyes. He continued to thrust at the burning wood on the hearth. And then, rearing his bulk suddenly, he stood in front of the fire, his eyes half closed, and his brow a little contracted, as though by pain.

It was perfectly plain to Eddie Clewes that this young man had not heard a word of the conversation that was passing between his two companions. All his abstracted thoughts, therefore, were out on the hills, running again the chase of that day.

And Eddie Clewes groaned with impatience and with disgust, to think that such a formidable character as this had been added to the might and the cunning of Pritchard.

He could remember only too well the gigantic speed with which the great black horse had thrust itself through the press of the posse and gone on by itself to overtake him. Another half hour and he would have been under the guns of this young tiger. And yet he could understand very well how Pritchard and McKenzie might have joined forces, and how Pritchard might have won over the talents of this natural king of beasts.

It seemed to Eddie Clewes merely hard luck — the worst of very hard luck!

"And now this stuff," said Dandy Dick, and he brought out a small leather sack.

"Hello — hello!" breathed the Jew, and raised his glittering eyes toward the somber face of young McKenzie.

"Oh, Archie is all right," said Dandy Dick, and, without more ado, he turned the sack upside down on the table in the center of the room.

The Jew's head sank between his shoulders like the head of a great bird, and a grin stretched back the corners of his mouth. Well might he smile at such a wealth of treasure as the Exeter jewels. And yet his glance shifted like lightning once and again from the jewels to the blank face of young Archie McKenzie.

"Because," explained Dandy Dick loudly, "Archie knows that he could have what he wanted. Eh, Archie? You know that you're free to help yourself to these sparklers, don't you? Anything that I have, it's yours, too. That's the way that I am when I take a fellow into partnership with me!"

Archie McKenzie recovered a little from his trance of thought and blinked at the jewels. Then he made a step forward and scooped up a great quantity of those shining beauties.

Poor Pritchard turned white with apprehension, but there was no need for his fear. He had most delicately estimated the character of his strange young companion, for now Archie McKenzie dropped the rattling handful back on the table and swayed back to his post in front of the fire.

"They're worth something, I suppose," he murmured, and instantly his eyes were half veiled, as before, and his brow puckered with painful thought.

The Jew, seeming to realize the truth about this young man at last, murmured to Dandy Dick, "A little queer, Dandy?"

Eddie Clewes read the faintly stirring lips and those of Pritchard as the latter answered:

"Not so queer as you'd think. But he's only living for one thing, and that's to revenge poor Murdoch, and to kill Eddie Clewes." He added, with a chuckle, leaning forward, "What would you bet on the life of Clewes now, eh?"

The Jew looked again at the face and the formidable form of Archie McKenzie. Then he said thoughtfully:

"I don't know, young man: I don't know. But, after all, the strongest thing in the world is not steel and guns and bullets — the strongest thing is the brain, Pritchard. And the best brain will usually win. It will usually win even in a fist fight!"

Never had Eddie Clewes heard more heartening talk from an enemy, and the face of Pritchard blackened and fell.

However, at that moment, young McKenzie gave them all something to think about, for he stepped suddenly forward to the table and, with a puff of breath, put out the lamp and left the room in darkness, except for the dull twilight cast by the smoldering wood on the hearth. And by that uncertain light, Clewes saw the bulk of Archie McKenzie slide for the door.

CHAPTER THIRTY-ONE
A Battle of Wits

For his own part, he did not wait. He turned and hurried away from the cabin, keeping on the blind side of the window. When he was thirty yards away, he dropped flat behind an outcropping of rocks.

He fell with his face toward the cabin, and at the same instant — while he was still in the air, as it seemed to him — the massive form of Archie McKenzie strode around the corner of the shack. Straight toward the rocks went the big young man. Ten strides away, he halted suddenly. A gun glittered in his hand, and Eddie Clewes made up his mind that it must be a gunfight on the spot — and a gunfight which could hardly have other than one end!

It seemed that there was only a blind instinct working in Archie McKenzie, however. For now he turned away upon his heel and marched around the house, making the circuit on the other side. Eventually, he stamped back into the shack, and the light of the lamp gleamed inside once more.

Eddie Clewes was instantly at his former post.

"Now what was up, Archie?" asked Pritchard, his tone masking a great deal of irritation behind a semblance of good cheer. "What did you hear or see?"

"Nothing," said Archie McKenzie, "but I had a sort of a hunch."

"What sort of a hunch?" asked the Jew with a sudden interest.

"I don't know," muttered Archie McKenzie.

Then he wheeled sharply around and pointed his great arm at the window behind which Clewes was standing.

"I feel as though there's something watching us," said Archie. "And — "

He stopped short and bowed his head in his former reverie. But Clewes, waiting and watching with awe and fear, began to wish that any ten men in the entire world might have been enlisted against him, rather than this one singular youth who lived by instinct far more than by reason and the evidence of his five senses.

Dandy Dick, at this last speech, had masked a smile behind a cough and a raised hand, but the Jew stared long and earnestly at McKenzie.

"I begin to change my mind," he said softly to Pritchard. "I don't think that any one man will ever beat that boy!"

"All right, all right," muttered Dandy Dick. "You can have your own thoughts. But I'm glad to see that you're switching around to my side of the deal. Only — I don't see what can of come into the crazy head of the youngster!"

"A miracle," said the Jew, with his inhuman smile. "There are some of us that never see them. And there are some of us that live by nothing else!"

"Nothing else than what?" asked Pritchard sharply, lifting his head and looking with suspicion at the older man, as toward a suddenly revealed madman.

"Nothing, nothing!" breathed the Jew. "Let us get down to business. I have to revise my offer, Dick. I'm sorry. I hate to change. But when young Exeter showed me the stuff, he did not have time to leave the jewels with me long enough, and I was forced to guess at a good many of them and cast up a general value. As a matter of fact, Pritchard, there are not more than three hundred thousand dollars' worth of stuff in that lot."

"No?" echoed Pritchard, cool and calm, but his eyes very shrewd.

"No, Dick. And — allowing me a decent

profit for my money and my time and the terrible risk that I run — you can't ask me to pay you more than two thirds of the market value of the stuff."

"That cuts me down to two hundred thousand, clear profit?" remarked Mr. Pritchard, without further comment.

"Yes, a grand fortune for you, my lad! I'm proud to think of what a good time you'll have when you retire on this! Two hundred thousand dollars! Ah, ah, if you would let me handle the investing of it for you, I could get you seven percent as safe as the ticking of a clock, and that would give you a reward of fourteen thousand dollars a year, my boy. Fourteen thousand dollars a year! Do you understand what I'm saying?"

"I understand," said Dandy Dick. "But explain how you could have made such a very *big* mistake in valuing the Exeter jewels, will you?"

"I can explain it in a nutshell, my dear boy," said the Jew, stretching out a long, skinny hand and patting the powerful arm of Pritchard with the claw. "I can explain it so that you'll understand perfectly. The fact is, that when I saw all of those jewels in the hands of such a very frightened and inexperienced young man as Tom Exeter — why, Dick, your face instantly flashed into my mind. And

I said to myself, 'Dick as good as has the stuff already!' And I grew so excited that I began to count the chickens before they were hatched, and everything looked so rosy and fine to me that, in short, I could not help overlooking flaws, and seeing more brilliancy than there was actually to be found. For instance — "

He picked up a yellow diamond and held it in the accurate grip of thumb and forefinger, rotating it a little from side to side, so that the light from the lamp should flare back from it.

"When I looked at this stone the first time," said the Jew, "I thought that it was worth a small fortune, all by itself. And I did not have time to see that it had this flaw."

He turned it upside down, and then dropped it rather contemptuously onto the table.

"You see, Dick — ah, but you know without any teaching from me! — that in the old days, when they were collecting family jewels, they had an eye for color and size and brilliancy only in a general way. They didn't have the special knowledge that we have today, concerning gems. Unless you except some of the Arab dealers in pearls, for they know pearls as well as you could know any man or woman. And they have always known pearls! However, in the old days of which I am speaking, the rich folk of Europe knew that jewels were beautiful, but they did *not* know that there are very fine little points of difference. For instance, here is a diamond four times the size and with ten times the splendor of that next little one. Who would guess, then, that the little one is twice as valuable as its big brother? No one, I am sure, in the century when these gems were collected. But if you'll look at the diamond under this magnifying glass — "

"I'll take your word," said Dandy Dick.

"You're a sensible fellow," said the Jew. "As a matter of fact, I have worried a good deal over having to tell you the truth about these jewels and the correct price for them. And since you're so reasonable about it, Dick, I'll tell you what I'll do. I'll cut down my own profit to the bone. I'll grant you another twenty-five thousand right out of my pocket, and we'll call the whole deal two hundred and twenty-five thousand dollars hard cash! What do you say to that, Dandy?"

Mr. Pritchard leaned back and shook his head as though in admiration.

"Damn me if you ain't wonderful!" he declared. "The other sharps, they may have their smart days and their dull days, but there's nobody like the Jew that's always on top of the deck!"

"I don't understand you!" exclaimed the

sharper, canting his head pathetically and wistfully upon one side. "I don't make out what you mean, my lad!"

"Don't you?" snarled the other. "Well, you'll start in making it out pretty soon, I can tell you. I'm going to tell you some hard facts and some mean truths. You offer me two hundred thousand — "

"And twenty-five," said the Jew. "I offered you a handsome fortune in excess of two hundred thousand — without bargaining, either, mark you! Dandy, I hope that you're not going to do or to say anything foolish!"

"You damned snake!" said Dandy, his face swelling and turning purplish with rage. "After some of us go out and risk our lives honest and fair in the open, then we come around to you that never take no chance, except with some of your dirty money — because who cares a damn about your life or where you spend it? — and then you try to beat us down and skin us to the bone, damn you! And damn your whole tribe, too!"

He leaned forward in his fury, while the Jew sank back in his chair, shaking his head a little from side to side, his eyes almost closed. He was the very picture of one who mildly and sadly deprecates the language and the ways of another, but Eddie Clewes, looking deeper than most men could have done, understood at once that there was not the slightest real alteration in the heart of the old fence. This storm of words had injured him no more than a soft shower of rain in spring injures the bald and scarred face of a granite cliff.

"I'll tell you this," said Mr. Pritchard. "I'll just raise your price to seven hundred thousand. And I'll make it seven hundred and twenty-five thousand, you see, so that you can see that I'm not a piker, but that I raise you a solid half million at a time. Now tell me — do we talk business at seven hundred thousand?"

"Dandy," said the Jew, "you will have these little jokes of yours — "

"Damn you, I say do we talk business at that figure?"

"You had better take a walk and cool down your imagination a little," said the Jew.

"When I walk out, I stay out," said Mr. Pritchard, leaping to his feet.

He strode to the door. There he paused.

"I'll tell you what I'll do," he said. "I'll cut out all bluffing and I'll bring you down to hard tacks. I cut myself down to the lowest possible figure. I'll let you have this whole lot of stuff for six hundred thousand dollars, and not a penny less!"

The Jew shook his head still with his eyes closed.

"It is no use, Dandy!"

"Then you can send for the farmer and tell him that the coast is clear for him to come back again, because I'm gone, and I suppose that you go with me, Archie? We want to hit up the trail of that rat, Clewes, don't we?"

Archie McKenzie duly stood up, without a word, still sunk in his deep reverie. But as the pair reached the door, the Jew spread both his hands palm up on the table.

"You win, Dandy," said he.

CHAPTER THIRTY-TWO
An Escape in the Night

So Pritchard turned slowly back into the room. He was not smiling with happiness over this victory, but scowling blackly.

"Six hundred thousand?" he repeated. "It sticks at that?"

"I rob myself," sighed the Jew. "I shall lose maybe a hundred thousand on this deal, but it's the oldness of the jewels that stirs me. Do you know, Dandy, that I think very seriously of keeping these jewels for myself. Of retiring with them, and using them for my own pleasure. Because there is some sentiment in me, Pritchard — "

Dandy Dick glowered without sympathy upon the older man.

In the corner by the fire, with the heavy, misshapen poker in his hands, young Archie McKenzie looked on with the dull face of one who hears other things than meet the ear.

"How have you got the crust to stand there and talk to me about sentiment and such things?" asked Dandy Dick. "And you after trying to beat me down a third of the value of 'em? Yes, less than a third. You ain't fooling me, you damned old crook. You're gunna make something handsome out of this deal — worse luck to you! I tell you, I know that you're gunna clear at least a couple of hundred thousand on it."

"I won't argue with you," said the Jew blandly. "I don't wish to excite you. You may say what you please, Dick."

"But how could you have the front to offer me only a couple of hundred thousand? My God, did you think that I was a plain fool?"

The Jew listened with his eyes half closed.

"Will you answer me?" snarled the thief.

"I won't answer you except to talk business," said the other. "I don't greatly mind the insults. But I suppose that it's better for us to get down to hard cases. Or have you forgotten that Eddie Clewes is on your trail, perhaps?"

That intimation made Dandy Dick flash a sudden glance of fear over his shoulder, and, as luck would have it, he fixed his eyes upon the very window behind which stood Clewes.

"All right — all right!" said Mr. Pritchard. "I ain't forgotten nothing. I suppose that you'd like to have him show up and clean me up, eh? But he ain't going to, old boy. Me and the kid — Archie, there — have gone into partnership, and there's not a chance of him beating the pair of us!"

Chattering after this fashion, he raised his spirits so high that he presently forgot all about the door, which he had left open, and sat down opposite the Jew.

The latter had already scooped the gems back into the bag and securely tied the mouth of it.

"Shut the door after you! Shut the door after you!" said the Jew peevishly. "Do you want to invite the whole world to come and have a look at us?"

"Damn the world!" said Dandy Dick, lolling at his ease, in the midst of his triumph. "There ain't more than one man in the world that would have the sense to get at us here, and he's been chased so close to the edge of the jumping off place that his hair is most likely white. But if little Eddie Clewes could be had, I would like to have him looking in here on this deal!"

"With his guns and all?" asked the Jew, biting at his lip with toothless gums.

"And what of it? I don't believe he ever packs guns. Anyway, he never uses them."

"That's it," said the Jew. "He's saving them for a big occasion, and when that time comes, perhaps you'll be the lucky man and see Clewes swing into action!"

"You think that there's action in him?" asked Pritchard, half nervous and half derisive.

"Never mind what I think," said the other. "McKenzie, will you close that door — or I'll do it myself!"

He started up from the table and turned toward the door, when he saw something beyond it that brought a screech of terror and surprise from his lips.

"It's Clewes!" screamed the Jew.

And at the same instant, Eddie Clewes struck.

Not with a revolver, to be sure, but with a weapon which, for the moment, was even more effective. It was simply a good rough-edged stone, big enough to fill his hand, and heavy. He whipped it over-hand with absolute accuracy of aim that brought it crashing against the lamp.

With a spurt of flame, the lamp leaped into a thousand tinkling pieces, and then the cabin was all blackness, except for the now darkened coals upon the hearth, and these gave only a faint suggestion of light.

In the gloom, the Jew wheeled, still screaming, and caught at the bag of jewels which he had just left on the table, but with a rush a form brushed past him and whisked away again.

Dandy Dick, amazed and staggered by the suddenness of the catastrophe, whipped out a gun and balanced it aimlessly in his hand.

"Clewes — Clewes! My God!" he cried.

And then he saw the rapidly gliding shadow and fired as fast as his thumb could work the hammer of the weapon.

His shots were wild, however. It was not in this sort of a fight that Dandy Dick excelled, but in one where he had ample opportunity to prepare his ground and pave the way, as it were. A style of Indian warfare was most fitting to the talents of Mr. Pritchard. And so his bullets went wild.

Perhaps Eddie Clewes could have counted upon that wildness, too. But there was a second man in that house to be feared. And with the dread of him, Eddie ran out from the shack as a teal flies, darting from side to side as it wings through the air, and dodging the hunter's aim.

Even so, he barely escaped from the sudden torrent of lead which was loosed at him from two chattering guns in the hands of young Archie McKenzie. It had been said of his dead brother that no man in the mountain desert was more capable of giving a finished exhibition of gunmanship than was Murdoch McKenzie. But Archie was just a peg above him. His gun education had profited by all that his elder brother knew, and by much that he did not know. And Eddie Clewes was aware of this as he snatched the jewel bag from the Jew's hands and darted back through the door.

His hat was ripped from his head. Another bullet stung a little chip from his left ear, and a third slug chopped off a lock from the center of his head.

Even as he sprinted for safety outside, Eddie Clewes had time to wonder at the uncanny self-confidence of this youth, who disdained to fire at a larger target, and chose to aim for the head!

From behind him, Dandy Dick was yelling a stream of curses. And the wild, high voice of the Jew wailed to the very stars. But when he glanced back over his shoulder, it was at the great bulk of Archie McKenzie which was sprinting into the lead, gaining upon him at every stroke of his driving feet. Like the great black horse that afternoon, Archie McKenzie ran with a lightness which seemed to defy his bulk.

Not for half a minute could Eddie Clewes have maintained his precarious lead. But he did not have to struggle so long. For just ahead of him was the covert where he had placed the mustang, and now the little horse, as though curious to discover the cause of all of this uproar, had worked loose from its tie rope and stepped out from the trees with pricking ears.

It saw its latest master flying toward it and wheeled away with all of the incredible neatness of foot of a fine cutting horse. There was not room for it to get away from Eddie Clewes, however. He dived at the mustang, sprawled somehow along the side of the little animal, and felt himself twitched instantly away from the great shadowy form which had been grasping for him.

In a hungry desire to take the slayer of his dead brother with his bare hands, young Archie had dropped his first pair of revolvers. And, now that the speed of the mustang was snatching his prey from under the tip of his fingers, he had to pause and snatch out the guns which he carried beneath his armpits. As he swung them into play, the mustang swerved out of sight behind the trees.

By the time that Archie McKenzie had his prey in line again, the mustang and the crouched rider along the side of the horse were already twinkling into the distant starlight. McKenzie dropped upon one knee and, steadying his revolver, tried three long-distance, aimed shots.

Every one of the three whisked hornetlike past the body of the fugitive. But neither he nor the horse was touched, and Eddie Clewes, at last, could pull himself up into the saddle and draw back the mustang to an easy canter.

He would have a three-mile start, perhaps, before Dandy Dick and young McKenzie could manage to get back to their stable, and put the saddles on their horses. And, in the meantime, Clewes headed in the vital direction, back toward the Iron Trail.

Let others tread the wilderness with horseflesh. That was too slow and uncertain a method for Eddie. He wanted the trembling, shining rails of steel once more beneath him, and the chucking and rattling of the trucks, with their ponderous, whirring wheels.

It seemed to Eddie Clewes that there was such a power and a lightness of happiness in him, now, that nothing could prevent him from winning through to eventual complete success. The Fates, surely, had taken a hand in his affairs, and had delivered the enemy into his hands. And still he wondered and laughed, remembering how the Jew had been twice robbed of illegal profits by the machinations of Eddie Clewes. And he thought of Pinkie Talbot, too!

Certainly the work along the Iron Trail would become very hot for him, now that he had added these bitter enemies to his old list.

He turned aside from the direction of his flight toward the railroad in order to advance upon the first yellow ray of light that issued from the window of a farmer. In the kitchen of the shack, he stole enough cold, clammy bacon and cold pone to make himself a meal, and tucked a dollar bill under the edge of the shelf paper to pay for it. Very rough food, but the soul of Eddie Clewes, on this night, supplied spice and sauce no matter what the dish that might be set before him.

CHAPTER THIRTY-THREE
In the Valley of Death

West and south in the light of the next morning went Eddie Clewes, headed toward Culloden Valley, and as he rode, his heart was blithe as the heart of a blackbird. For he felt, now, that his work was as good as done, and that in a few days, at the most, he could place the stolen goods back in the hands of the colonel. And a richer repayment than millions would be sight of the banker's gratitude! But when his mind turned toward Dolly Exeter, there his imagination failed him quite, and he left that happiness floating like a bright mist in the future.

Not that he was purely interested in the welfare of others, either. For, as he cantered the mustang along the trail toward the heart of the mountains before him, other thoughts flickered up in the mind of Mr. Clewes and obscured the pure philanthropy of his first ideas.

He had jogged on in this fashion for an hour

or more, perfectly pleased with himself and the world, when he found himself passing through a long cañon, with steep rock-faced walls on either hand, and before he issued from the gorge, the rapid rolling of hoof beats sounded in his ears, made thick and confused by the echoes. He turned his head hastily and had a beautiful picture of three big men on three big horses rushing behind him down that narrow pass!

One was Dandy Dick Pritchard, and another, somewhat to the rear, was Pinkie Talbot. But these counted as nothing in the eye of Mr. Clewes.

For riding first by several lengths, and rapidly increasing this advantage, came the man whom Clewes most feared — that strange youth, Archie McKenzie, slipping over the ground at an unbelievable rate on his great black horse.

In the first whirl of fear, Clewes gave himself up for lost. Before him stretched a vast rocky tangle of mountains, with the railroad cleaving through it somewhere miles ahead. And behind him came a better horseman on a finer horse than the mustang.

He looked back again.

Heavy men run slowly uphill.

He could remember that from his boyhood. The fat constable who had captured him easily, running on the flat, was left gasping and panting behind the next time, when Eddie Clewes had turned into the hills.

And so he headed the mustang at the steepest slope in the tangle which rose before him.

He had a reward at once.

When he reached the top of that upward pitch and glanced down, he could see that young McKenzie had gained little if anything on him, and the great black horse was burnished over with sweat that flashed like dark crystal in the morning sun.

The others had stood the running much better, and now Pritchard and Pinkie Talbot were not being thrown so far behind by every stride of the black. But still, to the mind of Eddie Clewes, it seemed hardly less terrible to face the three together than to face young Archie McKenzie by himself. And if he could only stave off the attack of that dreadful youth — !

He rode with his mind concentrated with a naked fierceness upon the effort which was before him. He rode with his mind melting into the mind of the little mustang, and his soul joining that of the fiery little mountain horse. And he obtained results! The scientist may belittle the brute mind of the animal and range it close beside the sticks and stones, but still it remains true that, in spite of this, there are certain sympathies that will thrust in from the clinging knees of the sympathetic rider to the very heart of his mount, and there is a certain mental lightning forever flowing up and down the reins that a great horseman grasps, telling the horse certain things about the man, and the man certain things about the horse.

Not that Eddie Clewes was a great rider, so far as practice went. The ridiculous manner in which he bounced about in the saddle would have proved that point against him, certainly. At the same time, horsemanship is far more instinct than practice, and, though long labor may teach a man how to follow hounds, it will never finish him first at a great run. And Eddie Clewes was making a great run for his life — his ignorance and his poorer horse against the craft, the skill, the instinct and the magnificent stallion of Archie McKenzie.

Now, with just that difference in poundage to balance the scales and keep them from turning too heavily against him, Eddie Clewes maintained that struggle.

They reached a down slope.

From the ravine floor he looked up and saw the mighty mass of the black horse and his giant rider toppling above him like a falling crag that rolled down into the cañon, scattering rocks and thundering fragments before it.

And Eddie Clewes sent his own mount up

the farther rise with a sinking heart. To attempt to escape from this young McKenzie was like attempting to escape from three-forked lightning, thrown from the hand of a god.

Still he rode his valiant best, and felt the mustang quiver with intense effort beneath him; but when he looked back again, half way up the slope, he was paralyzed with fear to see that, even on the up slope, Archie McKenzie was gaining with a dizzy speed, and gaining by such tactics as Clewes, for all of his sharpness, would never have dreamed of.

For McKenzie had dismounted, and now he sprang up the mountainside with an agility that made his body seem a dancing shadow rather than a solid bulk of flesh and bones. And the stallion, lightened in this manner, was making wonderful progress up the steep.

Instantly Eddie Clewes was on the ground, also, leaping and climbing and plunging ahead. And when he looked back again, he could see that he was again holding the other even.

He could follow a good example, and he could set one, also, so when the mustang topped the next rise and started a descent down a dizzy precipice that seemed to offer no foothold for even a mountain goat, Eddie Clewes cast himself out of the saddle again, almost before he had remounted, and down he went, sliding and clutching, and saving himself from dreadful death by inches, time and again.

An avalanche of stones and gravel showered before him. And another avalanche of the same kind was showering like a waterfall not far from his side, loosened and cast down by Archie McKenzie, who was traveling toward the bottom of the gulch in exactly the same manner, with greater skill and strength, of course, but also with the far greater problem of handling his tremendous weight.

Clewes had almost reached the bottom of the descent when a booming voice called him from behind and above. It was rather like the imagined articulation that sometimes seems to come roaring down upon the wind than like the tones of a mere man. But looking back across his shoulder, he saw a pinnacle of rock straight above him leaning from its base, while Pinkie and Dandy Dick pried at it.

Dragging the mustang by the reins and certain, as he scrambled to the side, that he could not miss death now, he saw that lurching ruin descend. It fell two hundred sheer feet, struck a sloping rock surface, and exploded outward like a high-power shell, breaking into a thousand pieces, each big enough to have killed horse and man. But that outward impulse saved Eddie Clewes. He saw a brief rain of the splintered boulders pour past his face.

A moment later he was in the saddle and fleeing up the easier slope across the ravine, and then winding in toward the higher heart of the mountains.

All that day, until the dropping of the dusk, he dodged, ahead of his pursuers. Half a dozen times he gave himself up for lost, seeing the black horse verging nearer, and noting the drooping head of the mustang. But still the little hero found an unsuspected bit of strength reserved in its heart and staved off each challenge, until now they were winding rapidly down from the highland toward a long valley, and the dusk was deepening over the ravines, while the summits were still bright with the last light of the day.

Half an hour more and he told himself that the shadows would have deepened to such a pitch, in the lowlands, that he could surely hide even from big McKenzie. And so with a greater courage he rode forward, and the little cattle horse rocked down the incline with a tireless canter, regaining wind and strength and heart with every moment of this easier going.

There was no sight or sound of the pursuit behind him, and Eddie Clewes could afford the luxury of a moment's reflection, during which he asked himself how it happened that McKenzie had shouted that warning while his two companions were on the very verge of ending the chase. He could not arrive at any satisfactory explanation except for the gruesome one which had occurred to him before — that young Archie wanted no ending to this man-hunt, except the one that should come when his hands were on the throat of the fugitive. It was his own peculiar personal revenge toward which he was looking!

There was no great comfort in that thought for Mr. Clewes. And now, as he brought his horse to the head of a hill, and watched the distant, dim streak of light that slid down the valley where a train was speeding, he told himself that if he could ever bring this trail to a lucky termination, he would never again trust himself a hundred yards away from the Iron Trail!

Most good resolutions are made when it is too late.

And the next moment, looking behind him, it seemed to Clewes that the end had undoubtedly come. For behind him he saw all three of the pursuers coming at full speed, Talbot on one side, Pritchard on the other, and of course the great black horse speeding straight toward him in the center, and far ahead of the other two!

CHAPTER THIRTY-FOUR
A Leap for Life

He could not dodge, now. There were no highlands before him to which he could run.

He thought, as he started the cow pony ahead, of risking its life and his in an attempt to pass the river. But he only needed to give that idea a single thought to know that it was the worst of follies. For, in the first place, the white gleam of the waters as they twisted along under the evening shadow promised a rushing speed that would roll horse and man under the surface instantly, like helpless pebbles. And, in the second place, what could he and his horse manage in the water that would not be easy for the black stallion and the omnipotent McKenzie?

He looked back, revolver in hand.

He had never in his life aimed a bullet seriously at a human being, but he was prepared to shoot, now. However, he knew well enough that in a matter of gun-play he would be a child in the hands of Archie McKenzie.

What rescue was there for Eddie Clewes, then?

There was needed a yawning of the earth to hide him, or the hand of God out of the skies to pluck him away from this danger, so it seemed. But he carried with him something almost as potent as either — wits as steadily and keenly working as though he were sitting securely at ease in a room, planning for himself.

There was one moving thing in the head of that valley which could move faster than the black stallion, even with all the wits of Archie McKenzie to urge it along. It possesed a power that would not falter. Its knees would not weaken and bend beneath it. Its wind would not fail nor its eyes grow dim. It was a mighty force to which he had trusted his life more than once. And he knew it out of years of long experience. It was that same streak of moving light that swept along beside the river — the passenger train which was curving down the slope at full speed!

There were two great questions.

One was — could the strength of the cow pony last long enough to get him to the train before the black stallion overtook them? The second was — could he reach the train at all, whether he were pursued or not?

He had to lay a course at an angle and hope

300

to come up with the line of the railroad just as the train came by. And then he could only pray that the little horse would not be too terrified by the roar and the thunder of the passing express, and the fires which flew from the spinning wheels, and the moaning song which goes up from the Iron Trail. But if he could crowd the mustang near enough, then he would venture his life in a leap for the train.

If he missed, the wheels would have him, and the Iron Trail would see the end of him. But even that was better than to die under the hands of Archie McKenzie.

So he made his determination, and laid his course, and drove the tired little animal beneath him on the last lap of their journey, no matter what the termination of it might be!

All the steel of resolution in Eddie Clewes was being tried now; and, in the horse, four hundred years of an ancestry which had learned to run on the great plains with muscles of leather and lungs of brass.

So they stretched away and, glancing back, he saw that the pursuers understood the meaning of all this. They, too, were jockeying their horses with a reckless speed, and flying after him in a great wedge, of which the foreward point traveled far faster than the two rear points.

That was Archie McKenzie, making the

proper finish to the ride of his life. And the long leaps of the great black horse were making a pace against which the mustang could not possibly compete.

Still, he had a fairly long lead, and the race in this final stage was not to be long, no matter how desperate. So, though the black gained, it was not gaining fast enough to run Clewes into the ground before he had his chance to risk his neck in boarding the train.

He could tell that, as he felt the last remaining strength in the mustang working steadily for him. So he put all the thoughts of Archie McKenzie from him and concentrated upon the remaining half of his problem — the train!

Its headlight was blindingly in view, now, pouring up along the tracks and turning them to two molten streaks of silver through the night.

Behind the headlight was the glow of the engine. And then a few long sections of darkness — the baggage and mail cars, at which he hoped to be able to aim his leap. And behind them, again, there trailed the long succession of passenger coaches, their sides checkered with soft yellow squares of light.

It made a very wonderful picture to any eye; to Eddie Clewes it was a bolt of beauty from the very heart of heaven!

And he was nearer, now, and sure to reach

it at whatever point of its length he chose to strike! The headlight dazzled him and then darted past as he swung the mustang in beside the train.

Alas, the heart of the cow pony, which had sustained him through many perils, and had enabled him to endure even the supernatural blast of brightness from the single eye that burned in the forehead of this night monster — that courage of the mustang gave way at last when he heard the grinding and the roaring of the coaches that followed the panting engine, and he swayed far out to the side and shortened his gallop.

Terror blinds most of us. It freezes our nerves, and a film of darkness passes across our eyes. But it was not so with Eddie Clewes. For danger merely screwed him, suddenly, to a higher peg — a more useful tension. Danger was what gave the perfect temper to that soul of steel.

And so it was that as he dragged the head of the little horse back toward the train, he had the sense to lean far forward as, throwing his heart into his voice, he shouted a hoarse, ringing, cheerful word of encouragement.

It acted on the cow pony like brandy on a failing man. Up went its head again. Once more it was driving its body along with all its former speed and willingly allowed its rider to swing it in close and closer under the flying walls of the train.

But that loss in momentum told dreadfully against them, now.

One after another the baggage cars and their safe darkness were snatched past, with a brief glimpse of the white river beyond and a breathless roar of air for the interval between the coaches. One after another the passenger cars were jerked away from Eddie Clewes. And, though he dared not look behind him, he knew by the way the roar of the train increased ahead of him, and by the way in which it fell away behind, that he was rapidly nearing the very end of the long procession!

Still, he would not think of failure. He had worked the horse to its full speed. He could only pray that it would continue to run true and straight as he made his leap. And he shouted to it, once and again, and saw the gallant ears flick forward each time in response to the master's voice, though they were instantly blown back again by the wind of his gallop and the desperation of his effort.

Oh, if he lived through this adventure, would he not find a way to come back to this horse and buy it or steal it, and make the rest of its life a heaven upon this earth?

Then Eddie Clewes made his effort.

He abandoned the reins altogether, simply

looping them over the pommel of the saddle. His left leg — for his right was nearest the train — he swung over the withers of the straining horse.

He had kicked off his shoes long miles before, in anticipation of this great instant. Now he suddenly planted his left heel on the withers of the pony, and, shaking his right foot loose from the stirrup, he heaved his entire body up, jammed the right foot against the cantle, and for an instant stood upright — he who had never so much as ridden bareback in his life, to say nothing of such circus tricks as this one!

As he lurched up, the pony wavered not at all, but hung to the line of his race beside that perilous mass of lighted thunder as though strong hands were on his reins!

It was only for the split part of a second, but long enough for Eddie Clewes to see, just on his right hand, the naked tracks. And he knew that he was leaping at the very tail of the whole train!

Then he sprang, and as he did so, something like a hornet's sting ripped across the skin of his cheek.

He was scarcely conscious of it, so great was his concentration upon the final peril of this adventure; and, even as he hung in the air, he had time to fix his eyes more keenly upon the

305

hands and footholds which he had selected.

He struck.

Hands, legs, body, turned numb with the shock. Would they hold by instinct? They would and they did, and, after all, there was no need for the helping hands that stretched out to him and dragged him aboard.

He beat them aside most ungratefully and, leaning out from the railing, regardless of one on a great black horse just to the rear, rifle in hand, he screeched, "*Adiós*, old pal!"

That was for the mustang, stopping now, with falling head, utterly spent, perhaps even exhausted to the point of death.

It seemed to Eddie Clewes, at that moment, that it would almost have been better to remain back there in the desert and take his chance of life and death with the horse rather than to abandon such a companion in the midst of such a chase!

CHAPTER THIRTY-FIVE
Eddie Turns Detective

He turned back from this wild thought — how wild it was you could never guess unless you have stepped fully into the mind of the criminal — and faced the nearer and the crisper facts of his existence.

Those facts consisted of a constantly thickening group of men blinking as though a great light had just been flashed upon their well-fed faces.

There was no light at all, but what held them was the sight of a slender young man with a haggard face encrusted with the salt of evaporated sweat and with the accumulated layers of mountain and desert dust; and down one cheek there was at the present moment a thin trickle of blood, rapidly coagulating, as soot and dust settled in it.

This young man wore no hat.

Upon his feet there were no shoes.

His naked toes thrust out through his socks and gripped the floor of the platform as it heeled along in full flight.

His trousers were scrubbed through at the knees, as though the foolish man had been trying to slide downstairs on them — which was true, except that some of the flights of those stairs had been several thousand feet long!

His coat was a matter of tatters, in an appalling condition.

On the whole, if one could imagine a creature dipped for an instant into hell and then plucked forth and jerked back into the midst of us, one might very well imagine just such a terrific figure as Eddie Clewes made at this moment.

For he had been facing imminent death for so many successive hours, on that day, that something like death itself had been written into the expression upon his face.

And he had not yet had time enough to smooth his expression back to its usual mildness and innocuous cheerfulness.

There was such chattering of voices, at first, that even his rapid-fire ears could hardly keep track of everything that was said, except that one tall, fat man kept shouting:

"Say, do something, somebody! Stop the train! We ought to get and bring in those two who were trying to murder this poor fellow! We ought to stop the train. Where's the cord

— or the button? There's some way of stopping this train, I tell you! Hey — "

"Friend," said Eddie Clewes, "after you stopped the train, how would you catch mounted men on that desert?"

The fat man started to reply, discovered that he had no good answer, and remained with pursed lips ajar, indignant at Eddie Clewes for having thus looked into his vacuous mind — and he a leading member of a flourishing community in central California.

"There's no use stopping the train," said another man, with a good deal of authority, "but I think that we can all be glad that we've seen a circus trick that wasn't performed under a circus tent! Have you been with Barnum and Bailey, my friend?"

And a woman's voice broke in, shrill, cutting through the tones of the men just as the upper register of a soprano will ring above the whole crash of a chorus:

"We're all going to be murdered! There's more of them! Maybe this one is in the plot! They're going to derail the train! Oh, that ever this should happen to *me!*"

"This is something that we need a police officer for. Where's the officer that's aboard this train?" asked another man.

"Here he comes now!"

"Clear a way for him! Here you are, Officer! Here you are, Gregory!"

Detective Gregory came through the crowd and, planting his feet far apart, he confronted Eddie Clewes.

Gregory, of the plain-clothes force, always followed a system, faithfully.

First he examined the suspected man. Then he examined the environment of the crime.

He was never in a hurry. He believed in making haste slowly.

"Time will beat the fastest crook in the world!" Mr. Gregory was fond of saying.

Now he examined Eddie Clewes, according to his maxims. Here was the man, evidently just through a very rough passage — but amazingly cool in spite of the trial which he had been through. But as for environment, there was only the black of the night and the cinder dust whirling up behind the flying train and blurring the faces of the lower stars.

It was very odd, to think that this fellow could have come into the train — this train, which was being hurled across the mountain-desert like a black thunderbolt, with flickering yellow fires within it! One would hardly expect him to be a real human creature, but merely a shadowy silhouette blown aboard like a bit of paper and apt to vanish again, spinning head over heels.

So Gregory stepped closer. He looked at the

cheek of Mr. Clewes and saw a drop of blood beginning to ooze through the coagulated streak along his face.

Then he pointed a sudden finger at Eddie Clewes. He believed in surprises and used them whenever he could. Lay your ground with all the care possible, but when the moment comes, use a surprise if you can.

"I know you!" said Detective Gregory, and he examined the dusty face with an increasing intensity. There was not the slightest change in the expression of Eddie Clewes, and the detective felt that that was much against him. For one of the first things that Gregory had learned, in his life work of matching wits against criminals, was that the nerves of an honest man are most easily upset but the nerves of a criminal are usually as strong as chilled steel.

"Are you sure?" asked Eddie.

And then something about his smile threw an electric shock into the brain of Gregory, and he gripped his gun as he barked: "You're Eddie Clewes!"

There was such a gasp from the men standing around that it was plain the record of Eddie Clewes was known far and wide, by this time. The newspapers were still making copy out of his exploits, real and imaginary.

"I am Eddie Clewes, am I?" replied the suspect.

"You are! You are!" snarled Gregory, and he placed the muzzle of an automatic suddenly within a hand's breadth of the chest of Clewes.

"Confound you!" cried Clewes with a burst of honest indignation. "Confound you for mixing me up with a little shriveled sneak of a rat like that Eddie Clewes! You beef-headed second-guesser! Is he within fifteen pounds of my weight? Or within two inches of my height?"

And his breast, swelling with an honest anger, pressed fairly against the muzzle of the gun, as he leaned forward.

"You mind yourself," said Gregory, not quite so sure of himself. "This trigger is light!"

"Damn the trigger and you!" exclaimed Eddie Clewes. "You're a detective, are you?"

"I am," said Gregory.

"Have you got a badge on you?"

"It's here," said Gregory, and, opening his coat, he showed a glinting face of metal.

"Very well," said Eddie Clewes. "But you're a new man on the force or you'd know me. Here's my own sign — "

And he held open the breast of his coat.

"Ah — well? What sign?" inquired Gregory, looking and finding nothing.

"What sign? Why this — The devil! It's gone!" burst from Eddie Clewes.

"It's gone — if you ever had one," said Detective Gregory. "And you'll have to give me better proof than talk, young feller! I want to know — "

"You're going to make me make a fool of you, in another moment, my friend," said Eddie Clewes, apparently controlling himself with a great effort. "I don't want to, and I'll tell you, frankly, that I *do* look a bit like Clewes, and that was the very reason that the chief sent me on his trail, but I'm Thompson, of South Bend."

"Eh?"

"That's it."

"It's easy to say who you are," protested Gregory. He looked uneasily about him. It was plain that the sympathy of the crowd was most decidedly with the stranger. And yet the detective was worried. It still seemed to him that the flash of recognition had something behind it, and his eyes rarely failed him in such matters. "It's easy to say who you are. How am I to tell? Have I got to wire to South Bend to find out what — "

"I've stood enough from you," snarled Eddie Clewes suddenly. "And I'm going to tell you what I hoped nobody but my chief would hear straight off. I was sent from Indiana to get this same Eddie Clewes. And I got him, Gregory!"

"You what?"

"I got him, and those were his pals who were giving me a run for my life!"

"What pals? What — "

"And as a proof that I fixed Eddie Clewes so that he'll never steal again, I'll show you what I took from him, Gregory. And perhaps that will talk for me!"

Suddenly a stout chamois bag was produced from his pocket. He reached into it and brought forth a handful of glittering, glowing, colorful stones, set and unset.

"Do those look like the Exeter jewels to you?" asked he. "And would I be getting them from anybody other than Eddie Clewes?"

Mr. Gregory was convinced. He held out both hands as though to warn back all others.

"Put 'em up, Thompson!" he gasped. "Put 'em up. I've been wrong and I admit it! I've been a fool! But don't take a chance on having that stuff snatched!"

CHAPTER THIRTY-SIX

A Play for Life

"And you've taken Eddie Clewes!"

"And where did you leave him?"

"He was dead, of course!"

"And who were his friends, who were trying to run you down?"

"We thought that Clewes played a lone hand."

"And how did you manage to get on the trail of that slippery fox, to begin with?"

Eddie Clewes turned to Gregory.

"Look here, Gregory," he sighed, "I'm done up. I've had a couple of hundred weight of lead squirted at my face by dead shots, in the last day or two, and I've had the hardest and the longest and the wildest ride that any man ever took across the mountains. Get me away from these people, will you? I've got to rest. God knows what else lies in front of me before the finish!"

This appeal was taken in the very best part by Mr. Gregory, for he was an officer with the best of hearts, and he only desired an opportunity to make himself useful to any good cause.

He cheerfully inquired from the conductor the best available place to take his companion minion of the law, and presently Eddie Clewes was resting in a luxurious drawing room, stretched out upon a couch, eyes closed, body relaxed.

"How long before the train makes a stop?"

"Another eighty miles, Thompson."

"Eighty miles? Eighty miles? How long is that?"

"We'll be pulling over some heavy grades and doing some sharp turns. It'll be two good hours before the finish, I suppose."

"I've got two hours to sleep, then. Thank God! Gregory, it's a lucky thing for me that I've met you and that you're the sort of a man that you are! I'm going to expect you to watch that door and let nobody enter, up to the devil in person. And I'm going to lie here and sleep and know that with all of my stuff I'm as safe here as though you had surrounded me with stone walls. Good night, Gregory!"

Detective Gregory's heart swelled with pride. He was glad to have his honesty recognized, in this fashion, and, if "Thompson" had spoken to him a little harshly, a short time before — why, every man is angered when he is taken for a crook!

So Gregory convinced himself and, having done that, he felt that there remained nothing for him except to stand guard like a faithful watchdog, while the curiosity of the entire train raged outside the door of the drawing room.

Not even the conductor himself dared to show more than a nose at the door of the little room where the great "Thompson" was resting. And when the noise grew too great, Mr. Gregory softly opened the door. He stood in the aisle and said in soft and stern tones to the pushing men and women:

"Ladies and gents, I've got to tell you that inside that room there is lying my friend Thompson, who's just done one of the finest and the biggest things in the whole history of crime. Now I leave it to you to say whether you're going to make so much noise that he can't rest, or not! Are you going to give him a square deal, friends? Because he's got a lot of responsibility in his hands, still — as everybody on this train knows!"

This earnest appeal saved Mr. Clewes from being disturbed. So he enjoyed two hours of the most beautiful sleep in his career and did not so much as open an eye until the brakes ground and the car rattled as the train slowed up at the end of the eighty miles.

"Why you're gunna get off the train at this little jay town, Thompson," said Mr. Gregory, "I dunno and I can't guess. That's your business, and you've showed that you know what to do with yourself. But, just the same, if I was you, Thompson, I'd pretty seriously consider getting off farther down the line, because the news can't help leaking, from the porters and what not on this train, that you're getting off, here, with the whole load of the Exeter jewels aboard of you!"

"It's true," sighed Eddie Clewes, holding his head, which still whirled with sleep such as he had never in his life before enjoyed to such a profound degree. "It's true, Gregory. You've been a Godsend to me, and I've got to admit to you that I must get off the train at that next town. You understand? Wait a moment! Just make the conductor open a door on the blind side of the train, and I'll slip out quietly there; that's the best way!"

It was done, of course, exactly as he wished, and, as the train slid into the station yard, Eddie Clewes gripped the hand of Mr. Gregory very hard. Then he dropped off into the black coolness of the night. He was lost to view, as the train rolled slowly on toward a stop; and who could have followed the intricate movements of the shadowy figure which ducked under the line of freight cars that stood on the next pair of rails, and then raced ahead until he came up with the head of the train from which he had just dismounted?

He waited until an engine had been coupled on for the beginning of the next division, and, as the train pulled out again, quivering and laboring, Eddie Clewes was aboard it once more, but this time as invisible blind baggage.

So when the "wise" heads of the police in the town began to look for the reputed slayer of Eddie Clewes, the bearer, unquestionably, of the famous Exeter jewels, though they used every device at their command, they closed their hands upon nothing but thinnest air.

And Eddie Clewes, dismounting in the gray of the morning from the "blind baggage," found himself in the capital city of the state, toward which he had drawn so long a bow the evening before.

It was very cold, because of the altitude. A fine, steady rain was falling, blackening the paved streets and making the reflections of the yellow street lamps run in long brilliant streaks up and down them.

Eddie Clewes marched steadily across the business section of the town. When he came to the residence portion, he found a spacious avenue, with one side being ripped up by a big gang of night laborers — the night shift, laying pipe. Bunched into a wet, wretched figure, as he huddled beneath the branches of a tree on the sidewalk, he began to talk with a brawny fellow who had paused in his labor, with steam going up from his neck and his bared chest.

"Ain't it a sweet night for the likes of us?" said Eddie Clewes. "Here we got to sweat and be miserable while the rest of the world is lyin' over yonder taking their ease in their damn fine beds, and us out here, and slaving — and why? Is they any better than us? No, they ain't!"

The big man turned and observed Eddie Clewes, in the shadow of a tree, leaning upon a long-handled shovel.

"It ain't easy," said the laborer, with the tolerance of the strong. "For some, it ain't easy to stand up to this work. But I dunno. We about get what we're fit for, in the long run of things, I figger."

"The hell you do!" snarled Eddie Clewes. "You figger wrong, though! There's the governor sleeping in his house, over yonder, with no more care nor thought for what the poor devils that may be — "

"Hold on a minute," said the worker. "What house? That one? That shows that you dunno what you're talking about. *That* ain't

320

the governor's house! Who told you that it was? Why, the governor lives right over in Whitney Street in a neat little red house with a fir hedge, old style, in front of it, and nothing fancy about him, at all. That governor is a real man, I can tell you. And he ain't one that would huddle himself under a tree and whine about his hard luck!"

With this, he turned his broad back upon Eddie Clewes and, whirling his pick, drove it home six inches through soft sandstone, in the fine heat of his scorn and his anger.

But Eddie Clewes had learned what he wanted to know.

It took him half an hour to find Whitney Avenue, but on the way he encountered a prosperous-looking kitchen, at the back of a great house, and presently introduced himself to a smell of cleanliness and newly roasted pies and cookies, and other delights. He found cold ham and chicken in a pantry, and he helped himself largely to all that he required before he was ready to continue his journey.

And he sat on the back steps and smoked a cigarette and smiled at a patch of stars which were beginning to show in a distant corner of the sky. For they showed that the luck of Eddie Clewes was beginning to change. At least, so felt Eddie himself!

Then he went back to his task of searching for the street. He had turned into it when it seemed to him that, as he was passing across the mouth of a narrow alley, a great, bulky, shadowy form of a man slipped away into the darkness at one side.

And for an instant a thrill of dread came into the mind of Eddie Clewes — that the shadowy monster might be Archie McKenzie.

However, he dismissed that thought at once. Because how could Archie McKenzie possibly have followed him, fast as his flight had been?

So thought Eddie Clewes, and reassured himself, and went on again with his caution relaxed, and no more wary than a hungry falcon, or a lean wolf.

So he went down Whitney Avenue until he came to a high, old-fashioned fir hedge, and behind the hedge he saw the low, broad front of a house built substantially but in cottage style. That was the home of the governor!

He stood inside the gate and looked at the narrow, black, recessed windows, with a few high lights cast upon them, now and again, from the nearest street lights.

There was something about the very modesty of this governor's house that filled the heart of Mr. Clewes with a certain awe, but that emotion was never very long resident in him. He shrugged his shoulders. The awe fell away, and he advanced to explore his future and mold it to his hand if he could.

CHAPTER THIRTY-SEVEN
An Interview of Import

It might have been a lesson to the clever constructors of locks and bolts and bars, if they had noticed how Mr. Clewes, in spite of a watchman who constantly went the rounds of that building, melted his way, as it were, past all guards, and then ranged through the house at will.

In the very last room he searched — an upper, small, dormer-windowed room — he found what he wanted — the governor! By the dim light that came through the rain-streaked windowpane he made sure of that. Then he drew the shade, and turned on the electric light.

The sleeper had been a good rancher before he became a politician. And as he wakened he automatically reached under his pillow and brought forth a revolver before he realized that he was already covered by a formidable Colt.

He recognized the weapon and the face behind it at the same instant.

"You are a bold rascal, Clewes," said he, putting down his useless weapon and hunching himself up against his pillows.

"Thank you, sir," said Eddie Clewes.

"The last that I heard, in the evening," said the governor, "you had been killed, and your loot taken away from you by a brave detective working in plain clothes."

"Did that news come here so soon?"

"We follow your movements as closely as we can," said the governor, "and I went to sleep hoping that I should be able to pay the reward for your capture — or for your death — in a day or two!

"It seems that you have won again, and on that train there was only a most colossal liar!"

Eddie Clewes said nothing, but watched. He was interested in the governor. He liked the lines of that big, bold face.

"However," said the other, "I hate to think that such a bold horseman and daredevil as the chap who caught that train when it was traveling at full speed could have been a rascal and a liar, also!"

"You're right," said Eddie Clewes. "He wasn't so much of a rascal, after all. And not a great liar, either."

"You know him, then?"

"As well as I know myself!"

325

"And had he actually met you?"

"Yes, he had."

"I begin to grow excited, Clewes. Did he have the jewels, too?"

"Yes."

"He took them away from you, but he couldn't keep you?"

"You see, sir, I was the man who caught that train."

The governor was too bold and strong a man to care to conceal his emotions. And first he stared, and then he laughed softly.

"Clewes," said he, "I see that you're one in a million!"

"Thank you, Mr. Harkness," said Eddie.

"I've had my own days of excitement," said Governor Harkness, "but I don't think of anything that rates above the present five minutes. How did you pull the wool over the eyes of the detective who was on board that train?"

"He was a good man and a good worker," said Eddie Clewes, "but he was a little too honest to catch me."

"Humph," said the governor. "I suppose that that's a doubtful compliment. However, I wonder at you, Clewes — running your head into a good deal of danger to come into my house, when you must know that I'm a poor man. There's no plunder here that's worth your collection."

"You're wrong," said the thief. "You have something that I put above everything else."

"And what's that?"

"You can make me an honest man," said Eddie Clewes.

The governor smiled, as one prepared to see a jest, if possible.

Then he said: "I'm one who takes his office very seriously. But I've never aspired to any miracles. You'll have to explain yourself in words of one syllable, I'm afraid."

"Certainly," said Eddie Clewes. "I'm glad to do that. For the point is this: I'm through with my adventures, Mr. Harkness, and I'm ready to settle down. But every place that I'd like to sit is on fire. You can put the fires out, sir!"

The governor blinked a little, and then he nodded.

"I can pardon you," he agreed.

"That's it!"

"And what should induce me to pardon you, Clewes?"

"Is my case very hard?"

"You have courage," said Governor Harkness. "You've shown a lot of that, and I'd go ten thousand miles to meet a really brave man. But I'm afraid that there's one thing that rather spoils the picture, so far as you're concerned — which is that I'm afraid you're a bit hard-hearted, Clewes. I have known murderers that I have even respected for their murders and the way they did them. But I have never had any use for a fellow who broke the faith he had given to an honest man."

"You mean the way that I treated Colonel Exeter?"

"I mean exactly that."

"Why," said Eddie Clewes, "that sounds like a hard thing against me, I admit. But suppose that I could wipe that out?"

"I'd still need strong reasons in your favor."

"Here is one, perhaps," said Eddie Clewes, tipping up the muzzle of the gun, so that it was accurately trained upon the head of Harkness.

"Yes, that might be an argument of weight, with some!"

"But not with you? No, sir, I'm not fool enough to come here to threaten you. I'm working on a different principle, tonight."

"What principle, Clewes?"

"I'm going to buy you off."

"Ah," said Governor Harkness, and he smiled again, with his eyes very cold, indeed. "I didn't know that I had a price — perhaps I've been wrong!"

"I don't think that you can resist this offer," said Clewes. "It's about a half million, or perhaps more."

He passed a heavy, little chamois bag to the governor. And Harkness, opening it, peered with a frown of intentness into the contents. He reached in a hand and brought up a little heap of priceless beauty, shimmering under the electric light.

"And this is for me?" he asked, as he closed the bag.

"The same as for you," said Mr. Clewes. "It's for one of the citizens in your State. Name of Exeter. Colonel Exeter."

"Ah, I see, I see!" said the governor. "The trail has been too hot a one even for you, Clewes! You're back against the wall, and you're willing to surrender. Is that it? I mean, you're willing to surrender your profits if you can get a pardon? Perhaps you have the proceeds of some other little jobs waiting for you. Enough to live on comfortably, eh? Enough to retire on — with a new name — is that it, Clewes?"

"Well, and what if it is?"

"Then," said the governor, "I should be sorry to have Exeter lose his jewels. I see that they're actually worth a fine fortune. But I'll make not a single concession to you, Clewes. No man can buy off justice in this State!"

His voice had raised a little. Perhaps there was just a shade of the campaign orator in that last sentence.

"There's not a crowd to listen," said Eddie a little coldly.

"I beg your pardon," muttered the governor at once, aware of his mistake, and he flushed. "However, now you can understand!"

"I would hate to have a pardon from any cheap piker," declared Eddie Clewes. "I'm glad that I see where you stand, and now I'll tell you the facts. I didn't steal this stuff, Governor Harkness. I had half an idea that I *would* steal it. And then some things happened that changed my mind. One of the things was Exeter himself. He's the whitest man in the world. And there was something besides the colonel, at that!"

"His daughter, perhaps?" smiled the governor.

Eddie Clewes could not help coloring a little. He dropped his revolver into his pocket and, leaning back in his chair, he sighed a little.

The governor reached for his own discarded gun, closed a hand upon it, and then changed his mind.

"Go on!" said he.

"I want to go straight," said Eddie Clewes with a sudden huskiness. "And just as I had made up my mind to that, a crook took advantage of me, took away the keys that the colonel had trusted to me, and got the stuff from the safe. 'Dandy Dick' Pritchard. That was his name. I followed him. It was a hard trail. And when I got the stuff I started back with three of them on my heels. They almost got me. The fast express and the gamest cow pony in the world were just enough, combined, to get me away from them. And the three of them are still after me, and they always will be, until I kill them off, I suppose. However, I've brought back the stuff this far, and I intend to take it the rest of the way and put it into the hands of the colonel."

"If you're in danger, Clewes," put in the governor, "you had better deposit the jewels in this city. And when this case has been looked into a little — if there's the slightest proof that the truth is as you state it — you'll have your pardon, just as you wish. Is that all?"

"It's enough," said Eddie Clewes. "I'm starting south for Culloden Valley. God knows whether or not I'll get there, but I can't let anybody else hand this stuff to the colonel. I want to see his face when I bring back his jewels to him. That will pay me more than millions!"

CHAPTER THIRTY-EIGHT
A Chase in the Night

The governor dropped his broad, massive chin upon his fist. That hand had bulldogged many a yearling, and looked as much. It had grappled with political problems, since, and it had proved capable in both fields.

And his earnest, steady, eyes worked at the face of Eddie Clewes.

"Young man," said Governor Harkness finally, "I think that there is a chance that you may be able to do what you say."

"There is not a chance that I won't," said Eddie Clewes, "unless I'm tagged by a bullet in the meantime."

"You mean — reaching Colonel Exeter and returning the stolen things to him? But that's not my meaning. What will give you the acid test will be after the jewels are returned, and after you have received an official pardon, and after you have settled down in the quiet of Culloden Valley. I know that valley, Mr. Clewes. And I know that it's a very quiet little place. A very narrow little place. Why, many a cowpuncher used to going where only a cow pony can take him would find Culloden Valley too small for him. And you, Clewes, travel a wilder and a faster horse, and one that never tires. Am I right?"

"You mean the Iron Trail?" nodded Eddie Clewes. "Oh, I've had the fever in me, well enough, but I've done enough roaming to cool me off."

"You think so," said the governor, "and I hope so. But what I would like to warn you, young man, is that, after you have passed whatever perils lie between you and Colonel Exeter, and after you have received the pardon, even then your train will only be starting on a long, up-grade grind. I want you to think about that and to remember it."

"I'll never forget," said Eddie Clewes.

"In the meantime," said the governor, "the cards lie on the table. We can each see the other fellow's hand. There is a chance that all that you have been telling me is not true. That you stole the jewels and that you are now trying to buy your peace — and something more than your peace — by returning them! And for that reason, if you are caught before making such a return, I'll show you no more mercy than I would to a rattler in the nursery where my children sleep. But if you get the jewels safely back to Colonel Exeter, I am going to believe that you have told me the truth, give you the pardon, and feel that you are an honest man, whose past is worth forgetting. Now tell me, Clewes, what is there that I could do for you, not as a governor, but as a man who's interested in you?"

"There's one thing that I'd prize above all the rest," said Eddie Clewes without any hesitation. "And that's the mustang that carried me across the mountains ahead of McKenzie and the rest and brought me up beside the train. The owner of that pony will be making quite a considerable howl about losing him. Now, if you could manage to buy that horse for me, I'll pay you in hard cash for the money that you have to lay out on the deal. Can you manage that for me through one of your secretaries?"

"I can manage that by myself," said the governor, "and without a secretary's help, Clewes. And I think a good deal more of you for making such a request. Is that all?"

"That's all."

He stood up and started backing toward the door. Then, remembering what sort of a man he was leaving, he merely shrugged his shoulders and nodded: "Good-by, governor!" And he turned toward the door again.

"One moment," said Governor Harkness.

334

"You're in rags and tatters, man, and there's a heavy rain falling, now. It's cold, too, and you can hear the wind waking up and beginning to howl like a wolf. I have an old outfit that would hang pretty lose on you, but you'd better take it!"

"I'd compromise you, governor, if I were caught in your things," said Eddie Clewes. "And then to save you, I'd have to say that I'd *stolen* them from you. And, of course, in this State they'd hang a man that dared to steal from Governor Harkness. Besides — I stopped thinking about weather a long time ago!"

He went through the door and was out of the house in another moment, slipping like a shadow under the very nose of the unimaginative watchman, and fading away into the brightening morning. The rose of dawn was beginning. And though all the sky was sheeted with rain clouds except for a few little spots in the east, it seemed to Eddie Clewes that the great tomorrow was opening for him, now.

So he turned his thin, resolute face once more toward the Iron Trail, and as he walked, he heard the far-off scream of a train, signaling shrilly for a stop.

He stopped for a moment with lifted face, drinking in the sound and all that it suggested of an iron monster hurled down the shining

335

tracks with a banner of smoke fluttering above its head. And, as he paused, a chill sense of dread rushed over the heart of Eddie Clewes.

He did not pause even to turn his head over his shoulder but, with his catlike activity, he sprang to the side. And straight past him leaped the bulk of young Archie McKenzie — so sure of his prize that he had charged blindly to overwhelm the smaller man in that last instant.

Before he could turn to charge again, Eddie Clewes was twenty yards away.

What would he do now?

Well, what does a small hawk do when a great falcon drops at it out of the central sky? It takes to the brush, if it can only get down to it fast enough, and it dodges in the covert, where the broader-winged pursuer cannot follow with such agility.

So Eddie Clewes made his flight through the back yards of the capital city, whisking himself over slippery fences, ducking through narrow holes in hedges, and turning, twisting, dodging through every opening and covert that offered before him.

Twice, in his flight, a vast hand reached for him, and he dodged under the very shadow of it. And twice he sped away again, with the devilish, silent malice of Archie McKenzie turning his blood to ice.

There was no other man in the world quite

like this youth! All the rest of his enemies were as nothing. Archie McKenzie was all his dread!

He ducked from a side gateway down a narrow, wooden sidewalk toward the clattering sound of a milk wagon that passed in the street beyond, with all of its tall tins jingling and chattering one against the other.

And as Archie McKenzie followed, his great weight told against him. One of the crosspieces of the old boardwalk crunched beneath his foot, and he was flung heavily forward.

He was up in a second, but that second had put Mr. Clewes far away — so far away that he could afford a flying backward glance over his shoulder as he cut the corner into the main street, and that flying glance showed him the picture of McKenzie lurching to his feet, gun in hand. Ready to shoot now — yes, and shooting!

The morning was still dark enough to show the flash of the gun as it spurted forth flame, and a red-hot knife edge was drawn across the back of Mr. Clewes' neck. He felt blood trickling down his back, but he knew at the same time that it was not a severe wound. It merely gave him wings to bound into the street where the driver of the milk wagon was pulling in his span of ponies and yelling: "Now what is up with — "

337

Eddie Clewes, a compacted mass of wild-cats rather than a man, leaped into the seat, and the driver rolled out on the father side, more astonished than hurt, while Clewes gathered up the fallen reins and laid the whip on the backs of the team.

They carried him flying forward. But he stayed with them only for half a dozen blocks. Then he dismounted and left them cantering steadily away, while he took the straightest cut, with all his might, running toward the railroad.

There was still plenty of danger, but he hoped that even the keen wits of Archie McKenzie might be deluded by the noise of the milk wagon, which still was rattling briskly in the distance; and, while he was following that clew, Mr. Eddie Clewes would be safely in the railroad yard.

It was a perfect morning for such work. For, hardy a lot as they are, even the toughest shack does not enjoy the sooty, wet and slippery walking which he has to do on a rainy morning. And such a morning, in the dimness and the chill of the wind which cut through even heavy overcoats —

Eddie Clewes welcomed it all, for it would help him to screen his movements from all eyes, and, when he reached the station yard, what should he find there but what was, to him, as a broad-backed Percheron is to a circus performer — namely, a big, long, heavily loaded freight.

He looked upon it with a fond eye. After all, it was not fast, and then he wanted safety and surety, and not speed in his journey to the southland. To go slow and sure was the best of all, and the monstrous, puffing locomotive at the head of this train had fat round sides that seemed to promise to Eddie Clewes all that he could ask for.

He picked out his car with a luxurious eye. There was no question of taking chances, by trying to outwit shacks and journey in comfort. He simply slipped in under, and ensconced himself upon the rods.

There he lay, sprawled out, fitting himself to his place, and taking the keenest note of his surroundings, for, once under way, he might have need to know exactly what was around him.

But he knew these things by heart. This was his realm, and he was the king thereof. And presently, as though in obedience to a silent summons from him, he heard the quickened breathing of the distant locomotive. Then a shudder ran down the line of the cars, and they were rumbling slowly along on what he hoped might be the last of all his wild flights along the Iron Trail.

CHAPTER THIRTY-NINE
Three in a Box Car

That slow freight took him with perfect safety, if not with comfort, over the first section of his journey "home." But no one train could really land him where he wanted to go. By seven different lines he was forced to zigzag to the south and west toward Culloden Valley, turning corners and retracing a good many miles, so a rider with a relay of fast horses might almost have kept pace with him, he thought, if the rider had followed the air line, across country. However, he was contented to leave the saddle to others. The Iron Trail was the road for Eddie Clewes. He knew his strength, and his limitations.

He dragged himself from the rods at the next angling corner of his route. It was night, and he barely managed to slip out of danger as a group of men went hurrying up the line of cars, flashing a lantern under each one.

And as they went by, he saw by the swinging illumination of the lantern that the leader and director of the group was none other than his old companion, Cliff Matthews, the genial sheriff!

Eddie Clewes smiled to himself. Of all the dull-witted officers of the law it had been his pleasure to deal with, he felt that the honest sheriff deserved a place by himself. And yet he felt a sort of pity for Matthews, as well, feeling that the man might as well strive to follow the path of a comet through the sky as to attempt to guess out the wiles and the ways of Clewes along the Iron Trail.

He watched Matthews out of sight, and then he headed for the next stage of his journey.

That step was by freight, also. Not a loaded train, however, but a vast string of empties which were due to roar away to the south. And when they pulled out of the station, Eddie Clewes was aboard, stretched upon his back, and heedless of the jolting and the thundering as he fell into a sweet, deep sleep.

He had to leave that train at midnight in the middle of the desert and wait in the chill of the night beneath the stars for the coming of the westbound train on the road that crossed this line. And when that train came, it was a beautiful overland, nipping along at reckless speed, its headlight staggering a bit from side to side as it lunged along the Iron Trail.

It hardly slowed for the crossing, so it seemed, but it slowed enough for Eddie Clewes to hook aboard, and as blind baggage he rode out that section of his journey at a breathless and most satisfying speed.

He was almost glad to leave that rapid train and take to an empty freight which was being made up in the next yard, ready to drive south again, and bring him now fairly in line for Culloden Valley.

He selected in the procession a great, empty box car, a sixty-ton monster with enormous standing walls. A furniture van, he took it to be, or something intended for the transport of the like of light and bulky material. At any rate, he approved of it as a temporary home, and particularly when he found some scatterings of straw and old paper on the bottom of the car. This he kicked into a heap in one corner of the great van, and lay down upon it as a bed.

He was very, very tired. And before he reached Culloden Valley he was fairly well assured that a time would come when he should need all of his strength. So he threw out his arms, crosswise, and in another moment he was sound asleep.

The joltings and heaving of the great car across a very rough roadbed, rattled along by a fast engine, soon sifted him down through his pulpy bedding, so that the light straw worked up and finally covered him almost completely. And a very good thing it was, for night had come, and the wind was out of the north and freshly iced from the mountain-tops. So Eddie Clewes slept deep in his coverings, and blessed the warmth that secured his dreams.

It was a very maelstrom of noise through which he slumbered, with the loose planking in the bottom of the car heaving and rattling against its bolts, and the wall boards crushing from side to side, and the old and loosely fitted roof jogging up and down continually with an effect like the mythical car of Thor which rolls over the bridge of thunder.

But still, in spite of all these elements of confusion, the clever ear of Eddie Clewes was able to detect a strange sound, though much lighter than the rest — and this noise was the faint squeak of the wheels on which the door was run back at the side of the car.

Then, distinctly, he made out the noise of two men climbing down through the doorway — two energetic and wise travelers of the Iron Trail, or they would never have been able to negotiate such a complicated and difficult maneuver.

He lay perfectly still, hardly breathing, for a moment, until he remembered that the continued thunder of the car was sure to mask any sounds which he made, in moderation, just as the trick of the night was sure to conceal him from view. Unless they risked lighting a match.

And that was exactly what they did. For, the next moment, a match spurted blue flame that turned to yellow, and by the flickering light, two big men were seen there, close to the door which they had just shut, and turning their heads inquisitively from side to side.

They faced straight toward him, and he recognized the features of "Pinkie" Talbot and, at his side, Dandy Dick Pritchard! In the bitterness of his chagrin and his fear, he only wondered how it happened that the third and most terrible member of the company which pursued him was not here in this crisis.

They stepped closer. A match spurted again, and then the train slid with a rush and a humming out onto the comparative silence of a long trestle. And Eddie Clewes heard Pritchard say:

"He's not here, either."

"No, he's not here," replied Pinkie Talbot. "And he's not on the train, either. He's ducked off it long ago."

"What chance did he have to duck off it? Has it stopped or slowed up once?"

"What difference does that make to him? If

344

Clewes scented us, then he's off of this train, no matter how fast it has been going. What's speed to him? You forget what he did when the passenger — "

"Blast the express, and the horse that carried him to it, and principally, all of the time, blast him!"

"That's very well," responded Pinkie Talbot. "No doubt that you have a right to blast him, but I tell you that you're a fool to keep on searching for him. We've been through half of the cars in this train, already. There isn't a chance in a million that Clewes is aboard!"

"That one chance is worth working for," said Mr. Pritchard. "When you're working against Clewes, you've got to take advantage of every opening, or everything that looks like it *might* be an opening. I know, because I taught him."

"You taught him!" sneered Pinkie Talbot.

"Who says that I didn't?"

"I say that a barnyard chicken might be able to teach an old owl tricks, but you could never teach Clewes what he knows!"

"Oh, couldn't I? Couldn't I?" snarled Mr. Pritchard. "But what I say is — "

The trestle ended. The train struck the farther shore, there once more the rumbling and the rattling roared up around them with such a violence that the voices of the two in the car were no longer audible to Eddie Clewes.

He prepared his revolver for instant action, and then he waited. The train topped a rise and started gently down a long, gradual slope. Once more the voice of the two came to his ears, brokenly, and from a distance.

"I'm going to try the next car," said Pritchard.

"You're a fool, then," explained Talbot. "The thing to do is to take it easy, here."

"Take it easy, if you want. I'm going ahead."

"And tackle Clewes alone?" suggested Talbot.

This brought a volley of oath from Mr. Pritchard and an earnest declaration that he feared no Eddie Clewes, nor would he fear a dozen like that young man. His courage was absolutely dauntless.

"Aw," said Pinkie Talbot, "I know that you're not yellow, Dick. But be reasonable. You know that you don't want any part of Clewes' game, alone. And I'm tired of chasing after him through a train, chancing a broken neck every five minutes."

"You want to settle down and go to sleep," said Mr. Pritchard. "But if you had the sort of stuff that *I* have in the hands of that snake, you wouldn't be sitting so pretty."

"*If* I had the sort of stuff?" cried Talbot, his voice rising high. *If* I had it? And what have I got, then? What was the stuff that the dirty sneak took from me? You could buy the whole jewel case of Exeter with a single one of the sparklers that Clewes took away from me!"

"That's a lie!" declared Pritchard sternly. "But let it go. I ain't here to argue with you about that. What we both want is Clewes. After that, we'll have a chance to see the stuff on him — unless he's cached it away before this time!"

This suggestion brought a heavy groan from Mr. Talbot. "Have a heart, Dick," he said. "The thing for us to do is to settle down on that straw over in the corner and talk this deal over."

"Where's McKenzie? That's the main thing!" said Pritchard. "We need him, Pinkie!"

"Don't I know that we need him? But he's off on his own. You'll find that he'll show up wherever Clewes shows. Come over here and sit down!"

They started for the straw in the corner, and Eddie Clewes crawled out.

They passed him wonderfully close, and as they settled into the straw, he crawled down the farther wall of the car.

There was a sudden shout from Pritchard. "This straw is warm! There's been somebody here, Pinkie!"

CHAPTER FORTY
Death for Two

Eddie Clewes, crouching in the farthest corner of the big car, set his teeth and waited. He had tried the big sliding door of the car, as he went by, but he had found it fixed so firmly on its rusted slide that it would have taken a long and hard effort to push it back. And, in the meantime, the noise which he would have made, would be sure to bring the pair at him.

"Light a match. No, take a twist of this here straw, and light that, Pinkie!"

The train reached the bottom of the long, smooth descent, and struck a stretch of rough track. Once more the tremendous Niagara of noise swelled up and crashed about the ears of Eddie Clewes, shutting out the faint voices to which he had been listening.

Then a match spurted fire — flame rose, and there was Pinkie Talbot, standing with a lighted twist of straw held far in front of him, examining the car, and Dandy Dick crouched by the wall, a gun in either hand, and his face set with devilish determination.

Eddie Clewes knew that the time had come, and his revolver was trained straight on the bulky form of Pinkie Talbot. He needed only to pull the trigger, in order to send that dyed-in-the-wool criminal into another world.

And yet he could not fire!

He heard a scream from Pritchard:

"It's him! It's Clewes!"

And both the guns of Pritchard barked.

The bullets crunched through the wall of the car behind the head of Eddie Clewes. But the swaying, pitching floor was not meant to encourage accurate target play. The twist of straw was dropped and stamped on by the frightened Talbot. Still Clewes did not fire.

He waited until sparks of fire showed from the guns of his enemies on either side of the car. They were drilling the corner where they had first seen Clewes, but he had wriggled out to the opposite corner, and it seemed to him that it was best to move a little forward, to put himself where they would least expect him.

And, as he moved, the flashes of the guns showed him the set faces of the pair and must have given them instant glimpses of him. But those flashes wee nothing to aim by. They were mere tantalizing silhouettes of Eddie Clewes, as he glided here and there, never still for an instant.

They, secure in their weight of weapons, lay flat on their bellies, firing rapidly, cursing horribly as they shot. But Eddie Clewes was erect as a dancer.

Then, at last, he fired in turn, at a spot from which three successive times fire had spurted at him.

There was a loud yell in answer, a screech so shrill that it pierced for a moment through the overpowering uproar of the train of rattling empties. Either Pritchard or Talbot would be less interested in the fight, from that moment forth.

A bullet raked his shoulder, and then, as he sidestepped, four guns crashed at him at once, and he felt a long, stabbing pain go through his left side.

You have seen that Eddie Clewes was a careful and methodical young man, who rarely allowed his passions to interfere with his cool good sense. But when he felt this double wound and knew that he was being crowded into a corner and killed like a rat — with the feeling, indeed, that probably he had already received his death wound, Eddie Clewes went for the moment mad, and rushed forward, firing. Not a blind madness, but a craze that made his eye clearer and his hand steadier.

Four times in rapid succession he fired. He

had one bullet left, and only one, and now, with a gun belching at him hardly a stride away he fired his last bullet at that target, and strode back to the end of the car.

There was no more shooting.

He told himself that they knew he was hit, and they also knew that he had fired his sixth cartridge. Dandy Dick Pritchard would be clever enough to have counted the shots, and he would also be able to guess that Clewes would not carry extra ammunition, for he was no gunfighter.

So it was perfectly plain that the pair must be crawling up toward him, down the length of the car.

He held the Colt close to the muzzle of the hot barrel, and, resting his weight on one hand and a knee, like a crouched wild beast, he stared fiercely into the darkness and prepared to fight to the death.

Yet, still there was no gradual looming of men sneaking toward him; and all the while, he felt the soft and deadly ebbing of blood down his side.

Let the others do what they would, there was no reason why he should let himself bleed to death!

He took a firmer grip on the revolver.

Now or never he must end the thing, before his strength left him, and die fighting!

So he lurched to his feet and, charging forward, one hand stretched before him, he suddenly caught his foot and tumbled heavily upon a limp, loose body.

He leaped away from it with a sudden horror, because he knew that it was a dead man who lay there. And as he leaped, he rolled against a second form, and a faint groan answered the blow: "Hey, kid, you win! Gimme a light to die by will you?"

That was Dandy Dick's voice. And yonder, therefore, lay Talbot, dead!

It seemed to Clewes a miraculous ending to that adventure. He twisted a handful of straw into a hard stem and lighted it.

By that torch, he saw Talbot lying face downward. Dandy Dick was on his back, his head slumped awkwardly against the side of the car, whose shudderings were gradually working the thief's body out toward the center of the flooring.

And, through a swirl of powder smoke, he saw a face ghastly white, and eyes already partly filmed over by death watching him.

"It's all right, kid," said Pritchard. "I never should of took a hand against you. You was always out of my class, and I should of knowed it! But tell me, Eddie, where you learned to see in the dark, you cat!"

He coughed heavily, as the reeking air of

the battle stung his lungs, and bright-red bubbles of blood formed across his lips. His face turned livid, and his eyes strained outward from their sockets; never had death worked so visibly in laying his shadow upon a doomed man! The grim, inexorable shadow of the Great Reaper.

"What can I do to make you comfortable, Dandy?"

"I'm done, kid. But you might pull me over to the corner and put my head and shoulders on that soft straw. The jarring of these hard boards is terrible for me!"

Eddie Clewes did as he was requested.

"That's better — that's a lot better," said Dandy Dick when the work was done.

He added: "Now gimme a light so's I can see again what's coming at me."

Eddie Clewes made another twist of straw, and in the meantime the voice of Pritchard went on thickly:

"It's a queer thing, Eddie, the pictures that I'm seeing!"

"What pictures, Dandy?"

"You remember the pier head by the Fifty-ninth Street Bridge, where you and me waited that night for the launch?"

"I remember, Dandy."

"That night I thought that maybe I had better tap you on the sconce and take the loot all for myself. I guessed, that night, that I'd never have any more luck out of you. Well, I was a pretty true guesser. You never done another job for me, after that! And here you've paid me back for all of my training of you, at last!"

"Would I lie to a dying man, Dick?"

"I dunno. I suppose not."

"Then I'll tell you that your teaching will never do me any good, any more. Because I'm going straight, Dandy, and Exeter's stuff and what I took from Pinkie Talbot are both going back to the people that they were taken from."

"Are you meaning that, kid?"

"I mean that."

"Well, I'll believe you, then! Gimme that light, will you? Because I'm sliding away fast!"

So Eddie Clewes lighted the twist of straw, and the instant that the flame rose, bright and yellow, the hand of Pritchard darted out and caught up a revolver that lay on the floor. Too late, Clewes saw that movement and dropped the straw. Still it flared brightly from the floor, and gave Pritchard excellent light to swing the gun quickly onto the mark and pull the trigger, with the muzzle only six inches from the heart of his old pupil.

There was only a hollow click as the hammer rose and fell in answer to the trigger pressure. Pritchard had scooped up an empty gun.

"You'll win, kid," said Dandy Dick, "because you got the luck of the devil! Unless McKenzie can get you! And if it's possible for spirits to come back, I'll come up and give Archie a hand! So long, kid. I hate the heart of you!"

He opened his lips to speak again, but death twitched his mouth back into a dreadful grimace. His eyes glazed, and he died without so much as a groan.

As for Eddie Clewes, he held the hard-twisted wisp of straw patiently in his hand and let the light of it shine down into the eyes of his victim, and he remained there until his little torch burned out, forgetful of the slow running of the blood from his own side.

CHAPTER FORTY-ONE

Four Hours to Go

A strange feeling of being in the hands of an irresistible destiny possessed Eddie Clewes, from this moment forward. And as he made himself a bandage and knotted it hard about his wounded side, he told himself that, in spite of fatigue, weakness from loss of blood, the pain of the wound, and the many dangers that loomed between him and Culloden Valley, he would still win through. Not even Archie McKenzie could stop him!

How weak he was, he did not realize until he left that train at the next division line and turned southwest on the next local, riding blind baggage with much risk, and with his head beginning to sing with a fever.

There were black spots dancing before his eyes, when that day ended. The night came on cold and with a biting wind as he lounged through the station yard, trying to pick up information about the first train to Culloden Valley. And, at last, he ventured to ask a night watchman.

"I dunno, bo. Nothing before morning for you to beat your way on," sneered the other. "But if you want to get there bad, to Culloden Valley, why don't you hoof it? It ain't more than thirty miles!"

Thirty miles? Walk that far?

He thought of the stitch in his side, and he knew that he could never last out that journey. He thought, also, of the cold of the long night in the station yard, and he knew that, if he tried to wait there, he would be mad with delirium before the morning.

So he stumbled weakly out of the yard and into the outskirts of the little town, just as a great express came crashing and swirling down the tracks behind him. However, it had no interest for him, since it did not run on to Culloden Valley.

He dared not show himself, now, where any light could strike him. Not only were his clothes in rags, but he was daubed and sprinkled with blood from hair to heel, and he knew that there was something in his face which would frighten children and grown men, also!

So he skulked through the shadows of the little village and looked about him for another means of transportation to Culloden Valley. He felt much weakened and alone, now that he had given up the Iron Trail, which had brought him safely so far, and through such perils, but he also knew that within four or five hours, unless he had reached the house of Exeter, he would be helpless with the fever. He could not walk. He *must* ride. And yet he could not sit in the saddle.

He turned a corner and shrank back against the wall of the house, almost fainting. For yonder, passing across the yellow shaft of light that poured through a window, was a big rider on a great black horse — Archie McKenzie!

He told himself, as the monster passed by, that it could not be. For in no possible manner could McKenzie have guessed that he would appear in this town and at this time. It could not be, unless McKenzie, that night on the desert, had some vague premonition that Clewes would flee back toward Culloden Valley, and had driven straight across country, by the air line, to get to this last railroad junction. That would account for his presence, together with the presence of the great stallion.

The very knees of Clewes weakened and sagged beneath him, as the huge fellow rode past, and then he turned back, and went desperately up the next street.

A phaëton, drawn by a tall, lumbering animal that might serve a turn at the plow when not used as the carriage horse, drew up at a doorway not fifty yards in front of Clewes. He watched four people climb out of the heavy rig. He saw the big horse tethered, and the family go into the house. Then Eddie Clewes took possession.

After all, he did not want speed so much as surety, on this night, and here was a charger after his own heart! His fingers buckled weakly and refused to untie the strongly knotted rope. So he slashed it apart with his knife and then dragged himself into the driver's seat.

The effort sent the blood bounding in a great aching wave into his head. Sweat poured out on his forehead and beneath his armpits. He had to pause a moment before he lifted the reins, and a foolish feeling possessed him that, if he were discovered in the act of making this theft, he could be overmastered by the first country boy!

However, no one looked out from the front door or window of the house, and now Clewes turned the clumsy animal up the street and let it jog softly and slowly away.

A shouted question at the edge of the town directed him onto the right road, and as the honest horse started up its winding course, snorting cheerfully, and shaking its head at the grade, a cool wind blew into the face of

Eddie Clewes, and a fresher and a stronger hope welled up in him.

They went on at a slow pace, a very slow pace — but the colonel's house was a considerable distance on this side of Culloden, and the roads were good, so that at the most, he was not more than four hours away from his haven.

So thought Eddie Clewes, and, settling himself more comfortably against the back of the seat, he grinned partly with pleasure and partly with sheer agony of weakness and of pain.

There was no need to use whip or reins. The road stretched in a single, long, twisting ribbon across the hills. There were nothing but bridle paths, here and there, leading down to it, and therefore no chance for the horse to miss the way. And there was no use for the whip, because a stroke of it would make the big horse switch his tail impatiently up and down, but never mend his pace.

He had exactly calculated his gait, which was a long, shuffling stride, somewhere between a walk and a trot, which put away behind him about seven miles to the hour. And from this gait the horse never varied — perhaps wisely, because his bulk was not intended to make speed on the road, and this crawling pace it could maintain indefinitely.

In case of pursuit, there would be no question of making haste. And if it came to leaving the phaëton and taking to his heels through the woods or the underbrush, Eddie Clewes doubted his strength to go a hundred yards.

But the long miles went wearily, slowly, away behind him, one after the other, and the hours began to pass. And often it seemed to Eddie Clewes that, though his bleeding had been stopped, still his life was running out from him bit by bit, and the fever raged in him, alternately hot and cold.

A broad-faced moon came up like a fire through the eastern trees. It launched into the sky, and flooded the earth with black shadow and silver gilding. But it seemed to Eddie Clewes that the cold of that light sank to his very heart and stole away the last of his strength.

Somewhere behind him, now, he thought that he heard a regular, rhythmic sound, gradually approaching him, and, though he told himself that it was only the chucking of the wheels against the axles, still he mustered strength to turn in the seat, finally and look back. And there he saw, glistening in the moonlight, the great form of Archie McKenzie and the tall black stallion!

He looked upon them with a sort of detached interest, as though the coming of this man had nothing to do with him. For there was no escape. On either side of him, the forest had failed. He was surrounded by a sweeping fall of land, down the center of which he was driving, over a narrow ridge. Nothing could keep him, now, from the sweep of Archie McKenzie's vengeance.

And Eddie Clewes sat up in the phaëton and grasped at his revolver, though he knew that without cartridges it was of no use to him.

He swung the phaëton sidewise across the road, and there he waited while young Mc-Kenzie came with his long hair flying and the black stallion taking tremendous strides.

So the brother of dead Murdoch drew up his horse close before Eddie Clewes and called to him: "Are you ready, Clewes?"

The last vestige of the fever left the brain of Eddie Clewes. His body was weak as water and his hand shook with his feebleness, but his wits were as clear as glass, and with them he strove still to win a little delay. For one could never tell. Life is a precious treasure, and he who does not cling to so rich a thing deserves to lose it!

"Ready for what?" asked Eddie Clewes.

"You know what I mean," said the young man heavily. "You've got your gun in your lap, there. The moon is shining on it. D'you think that I'm blind, Clewes?"

"You expect me to fight?" asked Eddie Clewes.

"I expect it," said young Archie.

"Will you tell me what for?"

"Only a small thing," said Archie McKenzie, in a voice trembling with bitterness. "The murder of a brother — that ain't much. But even for that I'm gunna kill you here, Clewes, or you're gunna kill me!"

"Murdoch McKenzie is dead," said Eddie Clewes. "Is that a sign, man, that I murdered him?"

"Why," shouted Archie McKenzie, "ain't it a knowed thing? Ain't the whole world praised you for the killing of Delehanty and Murdoch?"

"I won't talk to you about what the whole world thinks it knows," said Eddie Clewes. "But suppose that they're right. And suppose that I *did* kill the two of them. Is that murder, Archie?"

"Murder?" asked Archie. "Aye, man! It's murder in my eyes!"

"Do you mean that I didn't kill them in fair fight?"

"Don't I mean that, though?"

"Why," said Clewes, "tell me your reasons for thinking that."

"Would a gent," asked Archie McKenzie,

"that has been able to kill Delehanty and Murdoch in a fair fight, have to run away from any single man, like the way that you've run away from me?"

There was such a convincing naïveté in this
answer that even Eddie Clewes could not re-
spond, for the moment. He looked down to
the fine head and to the glorious body of the
black stallion and then back to the young
rider.

"I'll tell you the fact, Archie," said he with
much gentleness, "there is nobody in the
world that I'd run away from — nobody that's
a crook and a thug. But you're not a crook,
Archie. You've gone straight, and you've
stayed straight. There's only one thing that's
tempted you to do a murder — and that's me.
Even with me, you wouldn't shoot from behind! But feeling that you are an honest man,
why should I turn back and kill you, Archie?
You've heard of what happened to Dandy
Dick and to Pinkie Talbot?"

"There was two that talked too much," said
Archie McKenzie. "I dunno what happened
to them. But I know that they talked too much!"

"They're dead," said Eddie Clewes.

"The two of them?" asked Archie McKenzie, a little impressed.

"The two of them," agreed Eddie Clewes.

"You're a slippery devil," said McKenzie. "I never figgered that, when I got up with you, I'd waste this much time at talk, instead of starting to work with guns on you. But still, I'd like to know what smart trick you used to kill Dandy Dick and Pinkie Talbot, because I've seen them doing target work, and I know that they was both good fighting men!"

"I used no trickery," said Eddie Clewes. "The two of them followed me until they caught up with me. And when they caught up with me, they found me in a box car. We fought it out, and I killed them both!"

Archie McKenzie was hugely impressed.

"It's the sort of a thing that I'd like to believe that any one man could do," said he. "Will you swear that it's true, man?"

"I'll swear that it's true."

"Exactly as you been telling me?"

"I swear on my honor that it happened exactly as I'm telling you."

And, for that matter, so it had. There was no need of telling Archie, unless he asked, that the fight had taken place in such thick darkness that chance took the place of skill in the delivery of wounds.

"Both dead," said Archie McKenzie, sitting a little straighter in his saddle. "Why, man, there was never anything that I ever wanted to do, any more than to fight you now. I thought that you were a sneaking rat that had managed to get rid of my brother and big Delehanty by a trick, but now maybe you *are* a first-rate fighting man — I wish you more power — and I'll beat you in spite of that!"

Far back over a dip of the road — a full mile away — a horseman swung up into view, and Eddie Clewes saw that, if he were to make any effort whatever, it must be made instantly. He had tried playing most of the few cards that were left to him. But now the last speech of the youngster placed another idea in his mind — that perhaps it was not sheer desire for revenge that had sent this youngster out on the long trail, but rather a sort of mistaken knight errantry, and a love of high adventure. He determined that he would try to outface him on this score.

"Aye," said Eddie Clewes, making himself sneer. "You wanted to fight it out with me, hand to hand?"

"I did want that, always."

"But with whatever help you could get?"

"What help did I ask for?"

"You had Pritchard and Talbot with you all the time."

"They trailed along with me, not me with

368

them. I never asked for their help!"

"So you say, now. But you seemed glad enough to let them help you plan to catch me. And now you've hung back until I'm done for, and all in, and hardly able to lift my hand. You pick a chance like that to jump at me, and murder me, and then you'll ride off and boast of what you've done to me!"

Archie McKenzie stared wildly.

"You lie!" he shouted at last. "You're faking and lying again. D'you think that you can fool me, though?"

"Look!" said Eddie Clewes, and he stretched forth his right hand. It was shaking and wabbling uneasily. And he himself laughed with a feverish recklessness that must have made his strained, starved face seem a devilish thing to young McKenzie. "There's what's left of me," said Eddie Clewes. "Or else you would never have dared to come up to me and face me in fair fight!"

"I tell you that you lie, and you lie again!" yelled McKenzie. "There ain't anything *but* lies in you, and there was never a time when I feared you or any other man!"

"You talk," insisted Eddie Clewes, "and all the time, your partner is hot-footing it to get up and help you fight me!"

"My partner?" asked Archie McKenzie, scowling.

"There!" said Eddie Clewes. And he pointed down the road toward the galloping horseman. "And between the pair of you there isn't enough manliness to meet me when I'm not shot to pieces and down and out, but you had to wait until my luck was out, and then you got up enough nerve to tackle me — the pair of you!"

"I'll turn him back," said Archie McKenzie, "and then I'll be back after you. I'll keep you with my own hands till you're well, and then I'll smash you to a thousand bits. You hear me?"

And in a fury of confusion and baffled anger, he whirled his horse about and drove it down the road to meet the advancing rider.

Eddie Clewes cast one glance of wonder after his departing enemy. But he had no time or strength to marvel at the fine straightforwardness of heart which he had found in young McKenzie. He turned the big horse, and whipped it vigorously down the road. They dipped out of sight before he could witness the encounter of the two riders.

And then he began to wait for the sound of the big stallion rushing up from the rear.

That sound did not come. Neither was there a crackling of guns behind him. But the weight of the moonlight seemed to press away all life, and leave the countryside buried in silence.

His own weakness swelled up in him like mounting waves of water. He had to keep his will fixed upon his work and his purpose with a relentless steadiness. Otherwise madness filled his brain.

And so time went past him, not moment by moment, but eternity by eternity, and each age a deeper agony than the last. Somewhere from behind him danger must surely be sweeping up. And still the dreadful miles stretched interminably before him, and his heart beat five times between the hoofbeats of the big horse.

But no, the miles were suddenly snatched away from before him. He had mounted a hill in the road, and now, before him, he saw the sudden brightness of a river beneath the moon, and the broad silver face of a lake set around with the dark forest.

Culloden River! Culloden Valley! And the village far off was Culloden town itself!

It swept the fever from body and brain. He sat erect. Down the reins went an electric force which even the stupid horse could feel, and it lengthened its stride to a semblance of a real trot.

So the old phaëton rattled down into the valley road, and to the entrance of the Exeter place, and then the gravel of the winding road crunched beneath pounding hoofs and grinding wheels.

He got down from the wagon. When he turned toward the house, it was wavering before him. The pillars of the veranda were as though he viewed them through cheap window glass — all full of crooks and knots. And when he reached the steps, he stumbled loosely forward and lay face down upon them.

His senses came back to him. For the bullet wound in his side was like the continual thrusting of a spur. Every beat of his pulse drove that spur deep into his vitals.

On hands and knees he crawled to the front door and reached for the bell. It was above his grasp!

He tried to rise erect from the knees — but the effort merely made him slump over on his side.

He called with all his might: "Colonel!"

There was no answer, not even an echo, and then he knew that, though he had tried to shout, there had been no sound that passed his trembling lips.

Now, down the valley road, he could hear the rapid pounding of the hoofs of a galloping horse. They were coming for him rapidly, now!

And he gathered all his might and, behold, he stood upon his feet and leaned his hand against the doorbell.

Inside the house, he heard the shrill, steady ring.

Suppose that they were not at home! He had not even thought of that, up to this moment.

Then a window opened above the veranda, and the clear, stern voice of the colonel was saying, "Who's there?"

He tried to answer, but his voice was still nothing in his dried throat.

"Once more — who's at that door?" called Colonel Exeter.

Eddie Clewes staggered weakly back from the entrance, and down the steps he half reeled, half fell. His stumbling fall was stopped against the side of the horse which he had left there, its patient head falling low after the long drive.

"It's nothing, Dolly," said the colonel. "Only a poor rascal, drunk."

Drunk!

And would they turn away and close the windows, again? He had not strength enough to mount those steps again and rouse them, he knew. And could they not hear the approaching hoofbeats which now were storming faster and faster down the valley road?

With all the might in his soul he strove to shriek at the two forms which now leaned above the veranda railing, watching him in disgust and contempt. But merely a bubbling noise came from his lips, and his head fell

373

weakly back against the shoulder of the horse.

The white moon shone full upon his face, and there was an instant scream from above him that went like a sword through the failing soul of Eddie Clewes:

"Dad, it's Ned come back — as I said he'd come back! It's Ned."

He strove with all his might to see. But he could not see. Blackness was blown across his eyes as by a storm. The moon itself was merely a pale hand reaching through a sea of darkness.

But he heard the colonel vainly protesting. Then a door crashed close at hand and the loudness of the sound went through him like a bullet and dropped him upon one hand and one knee. Dolly and the colonel; they were before him, laying hands upon him.

"Coming back like a beaten cur!" said the colonel's cruel voice. "Creeping back here to whine for help!"

A weak hysteria of laughter shook Eddie Clewes. From his pocket he drew the chamois bag which held the treasure. He bit his lip until his own blood moistened his mouth, and he said in a horrible, bubbling voice:

"It was Pritchard that stole it. I followed him. I brought it back. Dolly — "

"I told you! I told you!" sobbed Dolly Exeter.

The lean, strong arms of the colonel were gathering up this wreck of a man.

"I shall never forgive myself as long as I live," said the colonel. "I've robbed myself of the greatest treasure — faith!"

CHAPTER FORTY-THREE
Strong Medicine

It was Sheriff Cliff Matthews whose horse had galloped down the river road that night. But he was perfectly amenable to reason. He did not even ask for the privilege of seeing the prisoner.

"I can wait," said Sheriff Matthews. "I'm almost glad that I didn't catch up with him on the road. But I was stopped from that by a young gent that the world is going to hear of, one of these days. I mean, Archie McKenzie! It was Archie who worked out the trail of Eddie Clewes. He followed Clewes, and I followed Archie. And at the last minute, Clewes was smart enough to turn McKenzie back and send him to block *me* away. There is nobody else like Eddie Clewes. Not for brains, Colonel Exeter!"

"Eddie Clewes," said the colonel slowly, "will never go to jail. You can depend upon that. I'm waiting now for an answer to a wire I sent the governor that will, I believe, polish off this affair and enable you to pull up stakes and go home, Sheriff."

"Here's a kid from town now. Perhaps he has the answer."

The colonel read it, frowned, laughed, and then handed the yellow slip to Matthews.

Cliff Matthews spelled it out slowly, and never forgot what he read:

"If Clewes has reached you with the jewels intact, he is as free as any pardon of mine can make him, but if I were Colonel Exeter, I would arrange to keep this young man under my eye the rest of my life. He is probably worth it!"

That was the message from the governor. And Colonel Exeter carried the good news up to Dolly in the sick room.

As for Eddie Clewes himself, it was a full week before he was able to hear the tidings. And when he heard it, it drew him half the distance back to normal health at a stroke.

"And Archie McKenzie?" asked Eddie Clewes, as he sat wrapped in blankets on the balcony, looking over the orchard trees to the river. "What's become of Archie McKenzie, Dolly?"

"He came to the house and left a letter which he said you were to have as soon as you were strong enough to sit up."

"Let me have it at once, then!"

"I think that you'd better wait for a day or two. There might be a shock in it."

He insisted, and this was what he read, when he had torn open the letter:

EDDIE CLEWES: You have had your luck and got loose. But I ain't thru. I am waiting for the time when I shall hav a chans to get evun with you. I am riting this letter so az you can no that I am praktising with my gunz every day and I hope that you will be doing the saim.
Yours truly,
ARCHIBALD MCKENZIE.

There was a sudden, frightened little gasp.

"You shouldn't have read that over my shoulder, Dolly."

"I couldn't help it. We'll have the sheriff arrest — "

"Not a bit of it. I don't worry at all about Archie McKenzie, really. He thinks that he's bold and wicked. But sometimes people are a great deal better than they themselves guess. And Archie will never *force* me to fight. And as for shaming me, why, Dolly, I'm beneath feeling shame — or above it! There's one thing more important than Archie."

"Well?"

"That's the pony which the governor promised to find for me."

"It came yesterday. Look over into the pasture."

There in the pasture, with its head raised at that instant to watch the swoop of a passing hawk, Mr. Clewes saw the famous mustang which had saved his life on that day of days.

He dwelt long and earnestly upon the picture of the fine little creature.

"Not so fast as the Iron Trail," said Eddie Clewes, at last. "But kinder, Dolly. And kindness is the thing that counts!"

THE END